PLACER COUNTY
P9-CRL-262

Dead of the Day

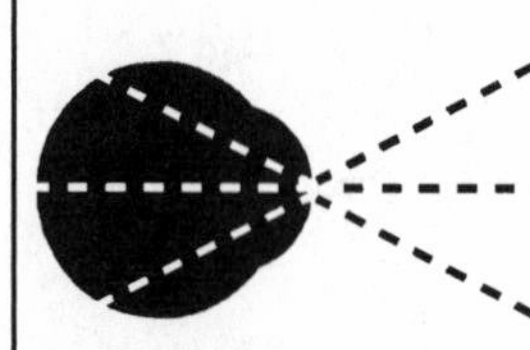

This Large Print Book carries the
Seal of Approval of N.A.V.H.

AN ANNIE SEYMOUR MYSTERY

DEAD OF THE DAY

KAREN E. OLSON

THORNDIKE PRESS
An imprint of Thomson Gale, a part of The Thomson Corporation

Detroit • New York • San Francisco • New Haven, Conn. • Waterville, Maine • London

Thorndike Press, an imprint of The Gale Group.

Thorndike Press® Large Print Mystery.

The text of this Large Print edition is unabridged.

Other aspects of the book may vary from the original edition.

Set in 16 pt. Plantin.

LIBRARY OF CONGRESS CATALOGING-IN-PUBLICATION DATA

Olson, Karen E.
Dead of the day : an Annie Seymour mystery / by Karen E. Olson.
p. cm. — (Thorndike Press large print mystery)
ISBN-13: 978-1-4104-0445-9 (alk. paper)
ISBN-10: 1-4104-0445-5 (alk. paper)
1. Seymour, Annie (Fictitious character)— Fiction. 2. Women journalists — Fiction. 3. Immigrants — Fiction. 4. Bee stings — Fiction. 5. Police chiefs — Fiction. 6. New Haven (Conn.) — Fiction. 7. Large type books. I. Title.
PS3615.L7525D43 2008
813'.6—dc22 2007043381

Published in 2008 by arrangement with NAL Signet,
a member of Penguin Group (USA) Inc.

Printed in the United States of America on permanent paper
10 9 8 7 6 5 4 3 2 1

To my mother

ACKNOWLEDGMENTS

Sometimes it takes a village to create a book, and I would be remiss in not recognizing mine: The First Offenders (Alison Gaylin, Lori Armstrong, and Jeff Shelby), my partners in crime; Maria Garriga, who lent more than just a name; Arturo Perez-Cabello, who gave me a glimpse into a world I knew existed but had never really seen; Reed Farrel Coleman for suggesting the title, and Helen Bennett Harvey for coining the term; Dr. Ann Wold, who taught me about stitches and wounds; George Mihalakos, who makes a helluva egg sandwich; Bonnie Winchester at the New Haven Police Department for an enlightening tour; Abram Katz for his droll sense of humor (do you have an idea for a column?); Liz Cipollina, who tells me when it sucks and when it's good; my writers group (Angelo Pompano, Chris Falcone, Chris Woodside, Cindy Warm, and Roberta Isleib); Melanie

Stengel for a kick-ass author photo; my parents, Ruth and Vern Olson, for letting me know I could be anything I wanted to be and it would be okay; my in-laws, Ernest and Edith Hoffman, who buy my books even when they can get them for free; and my aunt, Janet Dunfee, who encouraged an imaginative kid with a big dream. I also toast Eric Turton with a glass of red wine and a hunk of smelly cheese for keeping tabs on my career across The Pond. The University of Montana bee research Web site was invaluable, as was Doris B. Townshend's *Fair Haven: A Journey Through Time.* The Cobalt Rhythm Kings can be heard around New Haven. Very special thanks to Jack Scovil, as always. To Kristen Weber for her continued belief in my work and all of her exclamation marks! And to my wonderful, supportive husband, Chris, and daughter, Julia, who make me believe anything is possible.

Chapter 1

For a dead guy, Warren Black had a lot to say. I held the phone away from my ear a little bit; he was shouting about how we got it wrong.

No shit.

"Mr. Black," I managed to say when he took a breath. "Hold on a sec, okay?"

We don't have a HOLD button on our phones, so I cradled the receiver in my lap. "Marty?" I called across the aisle to the city editor. "I've got a guy on the phone who says he's Warren Black."

Marty Thompson peered over the top of his glasses. "But he was our dead of the day."

"Well, he says he's still alive."

Marty rustled some papers around on his desk, finally pulling a press release out from underneath the chaos. His mouth sagged open, then quickly shut again. "You'd better transfer him to me," he said, his voice so quiet I almost didn't hear him.

Not wanting to deal with Mr. Black's wrath any further, I quickly pushed the TRANSFER button and then Marty's extension before hanging up my phone. This was the second time in a month that our "dead of the day," as we called them, had not actually been dead.

Here at the *New Haven Herald,* we like to memorialize our neighbors who have passed on to life eternal with a little eulogy of our own. Family members and friends usually give us the stories of their lives so we can write up a quick ten inches. These aren't necessarily the pillars of our community — some are grandmothers, some are Elks, and one even turned out to be a child molester, but of course we didn't know that at the time it was written. His fan club, and I say that facetiously, notified us with a barrage of letters to the editor and about a hundred phone calls the next day.

I wasn't really sure what had happened with Warren Black, but it was likely that we'd put the wrong picture with the obituary. That's what happened the last time. If there were photos of two different people with the same name in the system, and the reporter writing up the story didn't know one from the other, we had a fifty-fifty shot it would be right.

Too bad we were on the wrong end of those odds today.

But I didn't have time to ruminate about *New Haven Herald* fuckups. I was trying to pull together my notes to write a feature about the city's new police chief. Tony Rodriguez had been on the job for two weeks now, and he was full of idealistic plans to reduce crime that couldn't possibly ever work, or at least would be stymied by the city's powers that be for political reasons. But he didn't seem to know that yet.

My assignment was to spit out everything he'd told me so the city could make up its own mind about him. It was not my favorite part of the job.

I glanced at the clock. I figured I had about two hours to get this thing done and sent over to the Sunday editor.

If I managed to pull this off, it would be happy hour, but I wasn't sure I had too much to be happy about on another Friday night alone.

It was my own damn fault. A few months ago, I was embarking on a relationship with someone who turned me on and challenged me all at the same time. We had three weeks together after Thanksgiving, three weeks during which I lost about ten pounds because of amazing sex and three weeks during which I actually felt myself softening around the edges. But that was probably from the sex, too.

Vinny DeLucia and I went to high school together, but he was a geek and I wasn't interested back then. Now he was a hotshot private detective with his own shingle, and doing occasional work for my mother's law firm. Our paths crossed several months ago while I was working on a story about a dead Yalie, and our relationship progressed from there. It seemed like things were going to work out with me and Vinny. Until Christmas.

Vinny didn't think we should spend Christmas together, at least not with his family, which was the only option since my mother's Jewish and my dad is in Vegas.

Vinny had just broken up with his longtime fiancée — for me, I might add. But his family wasn't too keen on that idea, and Rosie had been invited to spend the holidays with them, out of some sort of solidarity. I told Vinny he should boycott on principle, but he said he couldn't. It blew up bigger than a goddamn balloon, and there I was, telling him he was a fucking coward and walking out.

It was April now, and I hadn't seen Vinny

since. Not that I hadn't tried. He lives around the corner from me on Wooster Square, and I'd come incredibly close to being a stalker at times, but I still hadn't spotted him. It was almost as if he'd moved, but the Ford Explorer was there on occasion, parked in front of his building.

Yeah, I was being an idiot. All I had to do was call him, but I'd been too angry at first and then it just became a habit. With all the time that had passed, it would be embarrassing to call him now.

My notes swirled together in front of my eyes, out of focus enough that I wondered if I was going to need to get those drugstore glasses soon. Right, that would make me attractive to a man. I'd put those specs on and he'd know right away that the goods were getting a little old. And I wasn't even forty yet.

The scanner started to squawk behind me, and I leaned over and turned it up, causing Renee Chittenden, the social services reporter who sat two desks away, to frown at me. I shrugged. It was my fucking job.

A body had been found at Long Wharf. That wasn't too far away. I pushed my notes aside and grabbed my bag and jean jacket, making my way to Marty's desk.

"A body," I said, ready to leave.

"What about the profile?"

"I think a body supersedes the profile," I said, but when his mouth set into a grim line, added, "I'll stay late and finish the profile." I said it like it was putting me out, like I was willing to sacrifice my life for my job. Marty knew I was full of shit.

He nodded. "Take a photographer with you."

Wesley Bell was just coming around the corner of the photo lab. "Hey, Wesley, body at Long Wharf," I said, not stopping, knowing he'd grab his stuff and probably get there before I did. With his bow ties and penny loafers, he didn't look like a typical photojournalist, but his pictures were the best I'd ever seen. I wouldn't be surprised if Hagrid the Giant showed up one day with an invitation to Hogwarts and told him he was a goddamn wizard.

The road was blocked off, and I pulled into the Rusty Scupper restaurant parking lot. It was filling up with happy-hour traffic; I stuck my press card on the dashboard and hoped they wouldn't tow me.

The masts of the *Quinnipiack,* the old schooner, rose high above the pier that jutted out into the harbor perpendicular to the visitors information center. The tide was going out; there was a rank fishy smell hanging in the air. The yellow crime scene tape was flapping in the breeze, and I counted three police cars, their red lights spinning. I didn't count the cops, didn't pay attention to any of them except the detective in the tweed sport jacket, his blond hair a little mussed, his blue eyes taking in the scene.

"Hey, Tom," I said softly from behind him, the tape between us.

He turned around and nodded. "Hi, Annie."

I missed his quick smile, the twinkle in his eye that used to be for me. I wondered who got it now.

"Whatchagot?" I asked.

He took a deep breath. "Floater."

The fishy smell suddenly took on a whole new meaning. "Any ID?" I asked.

Tom shook his head. "He was naked. Hispanic."

He was telling me this only because he knew I'd find out eventually and it wasn't compromising anything. And a Hispanic man in New Haven wasn't exactly a rarity. Hell, I heard more Spanish around the *New Haven Herald* than I did English at times.

"Cause of death?" I asked.

"Not sure yet."

So it wasn't a gunshot wound or a stabbing. Probably the guy just drowned. Too bad. I wanted this to be bigger, so I would have a good excuse not to finish that stupid profile.

I took in the scene at the end of the pier, where the forensics guys were doing their thing. It was sort of like on TV, but the people weren't as good-looking. Except maybe Tom.

Tom and I broke up because of Vinny. He didn't know, or at least I didn't think he knew, that Vinny and I were history. And I certainly wasn't going to enlighten him.

"You okay?" Tom asked, and when I looked back at him, I could see genuine concern in his face.

I frowned. "Sure. I mean, why wouldn't I be?"

"You don't look great."

I'd had a cold that had hung on for weeks, and I'd finally shaken it. But I knew that wasn't what he saw. "I'm okay," I said gruffly. "Had a cold."

He was a detective and he could see the lie. But he played along. "Yeah, something was going around."

I spotted Wesley Bell over near the body, his face hidden by a gigantic lens, his camera recording everything.

"How did he get over there?" Tom muttered, starting to walk toward him.

I didn't have the heart to tell him about Wesley's powers.

Not wanting to go back, and abandoned by the only person in any position to tell me anything, I lingered for a few minutes, jotting down what I saw. It wasn't much. My eyes strayed across the harbor to the huge freighter docked on the other side, at the port. I'd been curious about what went on over there for a while now; no one covered the harbor anymore — not for years — because Marty said we didn't have enough reporters. But since 9/11 and reports about possible terrorists infiltrating the country's ports, my interest had been piqued. New Haven's port was the busiest in the state, with freighters bringing in fuel and scrap metal and some other shit. There was a jet fuel pipeline that ran from the harbor to the airport north of Hartford, which seemed like a pretty big deal to me but not to anyone else at the *Herald.*

I'd heard through the grapevine that there was some problem with scrap metal theft, but since I couldn't confirm it, Marty didn't want to know about it.

On a whim, I'd driven over there once but couldn't get past the fences.

"Interesting," I heard behind me.

Wesley Bell was tucking his camera into his bag.

"What's interesting?" I asked.

He looked up from the bag at me. "The dead guy. Wasn't in the water too long, from the looks of it."

Thank God. Wesley would have pictures of the body; none of them would be in the paper, but we'd all stare at them, our grisly senses of humor would spew forth, and there would be a lot of floater jokes tonight.

"See anything else?" I asked.

Wesley nodded. "Yeah. And I only noticed it because of my cousin." He paused. "He got stung last summer in the backyard. My wife put some baking soda on it and the swelling went down, but he said it hurt like a son of a bitch."

I frowned, trying to put two and two together.

Wesley was staring off at the floater on the pier. "Bee stings," he said. "On his stomach."

Chapter 2

Bee stings? I stared at Wesley. "How can you tell? How do you know it's from a bee?"

Wesley's eyebrows moved into his forehead and he shrugged. "Looks just like my cousin's sting last summer," he said again, swinging his camera strap over his shoulder and walking toward the street. "See you back at the paper."

I tried to remember that Wesley had powers mere mortals didn't have. But this still seemed far-fetched.

I sidled around the crime scene tape, tiptoeing along the pier between the tape and the edge. I couldn't see a damn thing between all those forensics guys and the coroner bent over the body.

"What do you think you're doing?"

Caught. I looked up into Tom's face and smiled. "My job?" I asked innocently.

I saw his mouth twitch, like he wanted to

smile back, but then he bit his lip to keep it at bay.

"Wesley said he saw something," I said. "Something on the body. Like bee stings."

A shadow crossed his face, and I began to think it wasn't so stupid to have asked.

"It'll be in the medical examiner's report if there's anything," Tom said. "You can't come any closer."

"Is there anything else you can tell me? Do you know how long he was in the water? Where did he come from?"

"I don't have any answers for you yet," Tom said, turning away.

Someone jostled me. A couple of cops managed to get in between me and Tom, and I turned around and made my way back down the pier. No one else would tell me anything, either. I knew that, so I wasn't even going to try. The specter of the police chief profile was still hanging over my head.

Shit. I didn't have a life, so why did I care that I was going to have to work late?

But instead of going back to my car, I walked in the opposite direction on the sidewalk along Long Wharf. My eyes found the lighthouse on the other side of the harbor and scanned the shoreline. Maybe the body floated across the water. Or maybe he fell in somewhere on this side and just washed up during low tide. I had no idea about currents in this water.

Vinny would. Vinny used to be a marine biologist and he spent a lot of time kayaking along the Connecticut shoreline. Since we'd gotten together in late November and broke up a mere month later, he hadn't gotten the chance to teach me how to kayak like we'd planned.

I wondered if he was out there now, while I was trying to figure out how this floater got into the water.

I took a deep breath and turned around, starting back for my car. I had to exorcise Vinny from my head. I doubted I could raise that relationship from the dead. It was over. I had to get over it.

I thought again about the bee stings. Weird. Especially this time of year. Those bees were supposed to still be in their hives, weren't they? I didn't remember seeing any bees until around Memorial Day, when they crashed the picnics. But as far as I knew, the bees could be out in the harbor on some little bee cruise.

Damn. I'd have to find a bee expert somewhere if I told Marty about it. I made a pact with myself that I wasn't going to say anything until I got something official from Tom or the coroner's office.

Dick Whitfield was climbing out of his car as I reached the parking lot.

"What are you doing here?" I asked.

"Marty sent me over, said you need to get back and finish that profile about the new chief." Dick had gotten more relaxed around me lately; he wasn't cowering with fear like he had just a few months ago. I blamed it on his girlfriend, TV reporter Cindy Purcell, who, with her large breasts and big hair, had managed to infuse a sort of cocky confidence that hadn't been there before. Bitch.

I hate change.

"Well, there's nothing more to report," I told him, happy to burst his bubble. "I've got it all." I tapped my notebook. "So you can go back and do whatever it was you were doing before Marty made you come out here."

Dick shifted uncomfortably.

"What?" I asked.

"It was me," he said softly.

"What was you?"

"I'm the one who got the wrong Warren Black picture for the dead of the day. There's another Warren Black. How the hell was I supposed to know?" His voice had gotten higher as he spoke, and now he sounded like some sort of odd bird.

"So Marty sent you out here to punish you?" I asked.

Dick shrugged. "I think he thought you'd yell at me and that was supposed to make me feel like shit."

I laughed. But when I saw him blinking too fast, like he was going to cry, my mirth disappeared. I actually felt sorry for the guy. Go figure.

"Listen, Dick," I said. "We've all fucked up. God knows you've fucked up before. Warren Black will have a funny story to tell his kids about how the paper screwed up and put his picture with a story about a dead guy. People like to see the paper make mistakes. It makes them feel superior."

"Really?"

He wasn't that green anymore; he should know this shit by now. I felt like Kevin Costner in *Bull Durham,* trying to explain things to Tim Robbins. "Yeah," I said. "Listen, I'm going back. Maybe you could get coffee or something for Marty. It'll put him in a better mood."

Dick's face lit up like a goddamn chandelier.

"And you could get me a latte while you're at it, no sugar," I added.

He didn't even bat an eye. "Okay, sure." And he bounced off toward his car, which I noticed was one of those hybrid Toyotas. As I went back to my own 1993 Honda Accord with rust around the edges, I wondered just how much Dick was getting paid these days.

It had been dark for three hours by the time I headed back to my apartment on Wooster Square. The floater story was a piece of cake; I didn't have enough for more than a few graphs. But the profile was eluding me — maybe I needed a vacation like Marty was always suggesting. I glanced down at the seat next to me, at the manila folders and notebooks that contained everything I needed for the story that I just couldn't make come alive. The Sunday editor wasn't happy, but I had promised I'd e-mail it by morning.

The windows were dark in my brownstone when I pulled up in front and parked. I live in the middle apartment. Walter something-or-other lives upstairs. A young married couple moved into the apartment below me a couple of months ago; I'm not much for socializing with neighbors, so I don't even know their names.

I sat in the car until Mick Jagger finished singing "Beast of Burden," then scooped up the folders, got out, and locked the doors before making my way up the sidewalk.

Something moved in the shadows. I caught my breath and I stopped, clutching my keys, wondering if they really could be useful as a weapon. My eyes searched the darkness. I took a step forward.

A figure moved into my path.

The dim glow from the streetlamp caught on his leather jacket and dark hair. There was something familiar about his shape, and instinctively I glanced over at Vinny's apartment house across the square.

He moved closer, and I found myself relaxing against my will.

But when he stepped into the light, I saw it wasn't Vinny, even though he looked remarkably like him.

"Annie?" His voice was deeper than Vinny's, and as he came a little closer I saw that he was shorter. Who the hell was this guy?

"What can I do for you?" I asked loudly in my best curt reporter voice, the one I save for people like Warren Black.

He held out his hand. "Rocco DeLucia."

Shit. Vinny's brother. I let out the breath I'd been holding. "You scared the crap out of me."

"Sorry." He smiled then, and the resemblance to his older brother was even more pronounced. Damn. Two brothers who looked like a young, thin Frank Sinatra.

"What do you want?" I asked, more sharply than I intended because he'd thrown me for a loop.

But it didn't seem to bother him. "You don't remember me, do you?"

I had not met Vinny's brother. Rocco was a best-selling crime novelist, and he'd been in Europe on a book tour during the weeks Vinny and I'd been rolling in the hay. "We've never met," I said matter-of-factly.

He nodded. "Yes, we have. I worked at the paper for a week a few years ago, doing research for a book. I wrote a story about a carjacking. They offered me a job. I met you then."

I tried to remember. We'd had a best-selling author working at the paper? Of course, I could be very self-absorbed most of the time so I might not have paid any attention, but if he'd covered a carjacking then he may have been in my territory.

"When was that?" I asked.

"About five years ago."

That explained it. It was before my time as police reporter. I was covering courts then. "I really don't remember," I said when I realized he was waiting for me to suddenly recognize him.

He shrugged. "Oh," he mumbled.

"So you're here now, why?"

He cocked his head in a very Vinny way. "Maybe we should go inside."

To my apartment? Jesus, why did these DeLucia boys think they could get so familiar with me so quickly? "Why don't you tell me here?" I suggested.

"I want to talk to you about Vinny."

I guess I knew that, but I wasn't sure I wanted to talk about Vinny with his brother. He saw me debating this with myself.

"Really, Annie, I think you'll be interested in what I have to say. If you don't want to go upstairs, we could go over to Libby's and get a coffee."

I appreciated that he switched gears on that, but I had my police chief files with me and I didn't want to bring them or leave them in my car. "No, no, that's okay. Sure, you can come up." But I was still a little uncertain.

He followed me up the stairs and held the door open for me on the landing and then at my apartment.

I dropped my stuff on the kitchen counter. "Want a beer?" I asked.

"Sure."

He was looking at my books when I tapped him on the shoulder and handed him the bottle. "Thanks," he said absently, probably noticing that while I liked Michael Connelly and Laura Lippman — both former journalists — his own books were not among my collection.

I took a long drink, not sorry that he hadn't started talking yet. I watched him move through my living room, checking out my space: the relatively new IKEA sofa, a hand-me-down teak coffee table from my mom, a Japanese ink drawing of cherry blossoms, the pile of newspapers in the corner that reached mid-thigh because I hadn't gotten around to throwing them out yet.

He finally turned and looked me straight in the eye.

"What the hell is going on with you two?" he demanded.

I snorted. "You might want to ask Vinny that."

"I did, and he won't say a damn thing about it. Hell, Rosie's gotten her hopes up, and I don't want to see her hurt again."

So that was what this was all about. Rosie. I peered a little more closely at Rocco's face. He had the hots for his brother's former fiancée. That would make things handy, if in fact Vinny and I were able to get back together. But that was a big "if."

"He might have thought about that when he decided to pretend that he'd never broken up with her at all."

Rocco frowned. "What?"

I sighed. "Christmas. She was going to spend Christmas with your family. So I couldn't. It pissed me off."

Something akin to amusement crossed Rocco's face and that pissed me off, too, but I kept my mouth shut as I watched him visibly struggle with what he was going to say next. He was wise to take his time; it made me respect him.

"So that's it?" he finally asked. "That's all it was about?"

I shrugged and took another swig of my beer. "Okay, so I can be a little stubborn. But he could've apologized."

"You've got a stalemate."

"One big fucking stalemate," I said.

He laughed at that, a big, vigorous laugh that was his own, something he didn't share with Vinny. And I liked him. Not in the way I liked his brother, of course, but in the way someone who hasn't got a brother might when she suddenly finds herself with one.

I knew in that instant that I wasn't going to have to grovel to get Vinny back. Rocco was going to help me. So I smiled.

I was about to ask him if he wanted to go get a pizza or something — I was starving — when the phone rang.

"Excuse me," I said, grabbing the phone off the kitchen counter. "Hello?" I asked, turning away from Rocco even though the apartment was small and he couldn't help but hear everything I said.

"Annie?"

Marty was looking for that goddamn profile.

"Marty, I'm working on it," I lied. "You really will have it in the morning."

"No, Annie, that's not what I'm calling about." I could hear the tension in his voice. "Do you have your scanner on?"

My scanner was in the backseat of my car. "No. What's up?" But even as I was asking, I could hear the cacophony of sirens somewhere in the distance.

"You have to get over to the Yale Rep right away. Someone gunned down the police chief on the steps as he was going in to see tonight's performance."

Chapter 3

I had to park three blocks away from the Yale Repertory Theatre because of the pandemonium. Red and blue lights flashed against the black sky. I'd never seen so many cops in one place. I shifted my bag up over my shoulder and hugged my jacket closer. It was mid-April, but it was still damn chilly, especially when the sun went down. I weaved around the throngs of people who'd gathered to see what was going on. Without seeing him, I knew Rocco was here somewhere, too.

I'd put the phone down and told him I had an emergency at work, asked if we could continue the discussion some other time. But I should've known that I couldn't fool a DeLucia; his eyes grew wide and he knew something was going down. Hell, he could hear the sirens, too.

He played along, said okay, and pretended to walk down the block when I pulled out of my parking space. As I stopped at the light at the corner, I glanced in the rearview mirror and saw him get into a shiny white BMW and follow me. As long as he kept out of my way, I didn't much care. Vinny had told me his brother was always angling for a plot for his next book, and even though I hadn't told him about the police chief, Rocco knew whatever was going on was big enough for him to tag along.

My eyes scanned the crowd ahead of me, wondering where Tom was. I passed Claire's restaurant, Basta, the meat place next to her vegetarian one. The scent of garlic and onions that wafted out onto the sidewalk was tantalizing, but I forced myself to ignore it.

What the hell was wrong with me? I was too easily distracted; I hadn't felt that immediate adrenaline rush when Marty called. Had Rocco's visit thrown me for a real loop? Or, God forbid, maybe I really was as burned out as everyone kept telling me.

Maybe it was just that I was feeling guilty. Really guilty. Because my first thought had been that I didn't have to do that stupid profile after all.

I should've been concerned about the guy. Getting gunned down on a Friday night on Chapel Street in front of the Yale Rep was unfathomable. Chapel Street was lined with cute little shops, mouthwatering restaurants, two great art museums. This was Yale territory, where the tourists came, where it was supposed to be safe. The Yale Rep puts on a lot of plays that are "experimental," written by students and performed by people who go on to Big Things, like Meryl Streep, Sam Waterston, and Jodie Foster. I go sometimes, if we get free tickets through the paper. Otherwise, it's just not my world.

My world consists of those other neighborhoods in New Haven, where shootings are just a matter of course, routine for the patrol cops, a three-inch police-blotter brief for me.

Through the crowd I spotted Tom, his head bobbing up and down as he moved from the Yale Rep steps down into the street, but then he disappeared. Cops were trying to push the curious onlookers back, to cordon the area off with the familiar bright yellow crime scene tape. I made my way to the edge of the line, just to have a uniform cop slam me in the stomach with a roll of tape.

"Goddammit!" I said involuntarily, the wind knocked out of me.

The cop's eyes grew wide. "Sorry, I didn't mean that, but you've got to stay back." I could see the deer-in-the-headlights look, like he wondered if I was going to press charges against him. He was young, someone I hadn't seen before, but there were a few new recruits these days I hadn't had the opportunity to run across yet.

I pulled out my ID and waved it in front of him. "Annie Seymour, with the *Herald,*" I said.

The surprised look turned into a frown. "I can't talk to you," he said, moving quickly out of my way.

I was tempted to go under the tape. Tom and Sam O'Neill, the assistant police chief, were about fifty feet away, and a makeshift tent had been set up next to an ambulance. Probably Rodriguez. I wondered how badly he was hurt. Maybe he was dead. Whatever it was, I abandoned my idea of going under the tape because if I did that no one would ever talk to me again.

I tried to get Tom's attention by waving my arm like an idiot, but if he saw me he didn't indicate it.

"Maybe you should just shout," came a suggestion to my right.

Rocco was standing next to me.

"Why did you follow me?" I demanded.

A smile played at the corners of his mouth. "It seemed important. What happened?"

It dawned on me then that even though there was a large crowd, it was probable that few, if any, of these bystanders knew what exactly was going on. I mean, Marty had told me because he heard it on the scanner. Regular people don't listen to police scanners unless they're real geeks.

"Someone got hurt," I said, feigning ignorance, but I could see Rocco wasn't buying it. "You know," I added, "you don't really need to come to crime scenes to write about them. I mean, you write fiction, right? You can do whatever you want, make shit up."

He was nodding. "You're right, but I like authenticity. I don't mind chasing a few ambulances to get a really good description for my books."

It had been worth a shot to try to get rid of him, but I should've known better. It took more than that to get rid of a DeLucia, although I was pretty sure I had it down to an art form.

Somehow among the chatter surrounding me I heard a cell phone ring and realized it was my own. I dug into my purse and turned away from Rocco as much as I could to hear Marty asking, "What the hell's going on over there? What do you have?"

"Not much," I admitted, my voice carrying over the din. "Just a shitload of people and cops and some sort of tent near the ambulance. I can't get very close."

"Where's Tom Behr?"

Marty still thought I had some clout with Tom, God bless him. I didn't have the heart to tell him that those days were long over. I glanced over at the tent again, but Tom was gone. But I did see someone familiar catty-corner to where I was standing.

"What the fuck's Dick doing out here?" I asked Marty.

"You can't do this alone, Annie. This is big. Deal with it and get me something soon to start working with. Wesley's out there, too, shooting." Maybe not the best choice of words, but that's what we call it, so that's what we say, even at times like this.

"Okay," I said, punching END on my phone. I turned to see Rocco staring at me. "What?"

"What is it?" he asked again.

I sighed, leaned toward him, and said softly, "The new police chief got shot."

He frowned. "What?"

"The police chief got shot," I said more loudly. A lot more, apparently, from the hush that came over the people standing near us.

"What'd she say?" someone asked.

"The police chief got shot."

"It's the police chief."

It was like that fucking telephone game, but everyone was getting it right. Just my luck.

"What the hell are you doing?" Tom's voice resonated in my ears, and I turned to see him glowering at me.

I shrugged. "My job?" I tried.

He lifted up the tape and pulled on my arm, so I had no choice but to follow him. We stepped up onto the sidewalk and then down the steps to Scoozi, an Italian restaurant next to the theatre that sat below street level. I've never eaten there, but hear it is good.

The street sounds grew dimmer the lower we went, until it was merely background noise.

"Are you trying to cause some sort of riot?" Tom demanded, his blue eyes almost violet with anger.

"No. I got a call from Marty. He asked what was going on. I had to speak loudly." I could glower with the best of them, and I did my best to keep up.

Tom ran a hand through his blond hair, his face contorted with exasperation. "Jesus, Annie, this is fucked up."

"What happened?" I asked after a few

seconds when it was clear he had calmed down a little.

He shook his head. "I didn't tell you this." He paused, and I nodded for effect. I wasn't sure why he was telling me a damn thing, but I certainly wasn't going to stop him.

"It was a dark Honda, souped-up. Sam said it skidded to a stop just before the light, sat there a second or so. He didn't think anything of it; the light was red. Next thing he knew, he heard two shots and Tony was on the ground." Tom took a deep breath. "Car took off. We found it on Route Thirty-four, Sherman Avenue intersection, abandoned." His eyes were darting around, looking up the stairs, knowing he had to go back. "You know, with a drive-by, you can't take aim. Anybody can get hit, or no one will get hit. It's a fucking crapshoot."

What he was saying sent shivers up my spine. This car had stopped. The shooter had taken aim. Tony Rodriguez had been a target.

"Is he dead?" I asked softly.

Tom's eyes came back to me, and I wondered if he was going to lie. "No," he said firmly. "He's hanging on."

It wasn't a lie. His eyes didn't flicker; he didn't look away.

"But it's bad?"

He nodded. "Yeah, it's bad."

But then I had another thought. "Anyone else hurt?"

Tom shook his head wearily. "No, thank God. His wife is in shock, but she wasn't hit." He paused. "Sam was with them, had a date. It was a goddamn double date."

Gossip indicated Sam O'Neill and his wife had separated, and Tom had just confirmed that.

I watched him as he went back up the steps and out of sight. But then I saw him. Wesley, with his paisley bow tie and his camera swinging around his neck. I knew what we needed, and it wasn't here anymore.

"Wesley," I shouted as I came up the steps.

He turned, recognizing me and nodding. "Hi, Annie."

"They've got a Honda over at Sherman and Thirty-four. It's the car they shot from. Do you have enough from here?"

He grinned. "I'll get right over there."

I lost myself in the crowd, not even hearing the noise anymore. Tom wanted this in the paper; he wanted us to print it so maybe a witness would come forward. That's why he told me. That's why he told me where the car was. We'd print a picture and someone might recognize it.

"Is he dead?"

Dick Whitfield had snuck up on me, and I jumped back. "Shit, Dick, don't do that," I chided, but I don't think he heard me. We watched as the ambulance was loaded up. It was taking off now, its sirens screaming away from us.

"Is he dead?" Dick asked again when the noise dulled slightly.

I shook my head. "Tom says no. I sent Wesley over to shoot a car they think was abandoned by whoever did this."

"Why the hell would someone shoot him?" Dick mused out loud.

I ran over my interview with Rodriguez in my head, wondering the same thing. He'd seemed so benign, so out of his element, which is probably why I had such a hard time writing up the story. He had been promoted from within, but he'd had no commendations, no big busts under his belt. Hell, Tom had more experience than this guy.

But Rodriguez did have something that Tom didn't have. He had the right genetic makeup. It was an election year, and the mayor was covering all his bases. The Hispanic population was growing by leaps and bounds, and Rodriguez's family was a nice mix of Puerto Rican and Mexican, making him the dish of the day.

His eyes were warm and his smile quick. He said all the right things, like it was a fucking script, which was another reason why I couldn't write the story. His answers were too pat, too correct. There had been something missing.

His goals for the department were ambitious. He planned to reorganize all the shifts, make a sort of rotation for the officers so they wouldn't do the same job for more than six months. That wasn't going to go over well; it had already started to leak out and the ranks were getting pissy about it.

Rodriguez wanted to mandate that all department employees take Spanish language classes, too, which was another plan that would go awry if he ever got a chance to implement it. While on paper it was a good idea, who was going to pay for it? The mayor would probably stand by it, but, as I said, it was an election year and promises had to be made in order to get reelected.

The only thing I thought would make points was Rodriguez's proposal for the harbor. He wanted to beef up security down there; he'd been deeply affected by 9/11, with the loss of a close friend in one of the Trade Center towers. He didn't want to take any chances here, he told me, and I had to agree with him on that one.

I stepped back, away from Dick and onto someone's toes. "Sorry," I mumbled, turning about ninety degrees, but unable to go farther because the crowd had moved up into my way. I saw a pair of jeans and a leather jacket. Rocco again. I wrenched my head around a little more and took another step as I said, "Listen, maybe you should just leave me alone now."

But it wasn't Rocco.

It was Vinny.

CHAPTER 4

"Long time no see," Vinny said, but instead of looking pissed off, like I thought he would, his eyes were twinkling even though he wasn't smiling.

I was too surprised to say anything for a second. I'd imagined all sorts of speeches I'd make when I finally saw Vinny again, and all of them seeped out of my head as I tried to keep myself from grinning. If he could keep himself in control, then hell, I could, too.

"Fancy meeting you here," I said.

He nodded. "How have you been?" he asked, like we weren't at a crime scene, like we were the only two people there.

My cell phone rang.

Without taking my eyes off him, I pulled it out of my bag, punched it on, and held it up to my ear. "Yeah?" I asked.

"What's going on?" Marty's voice was frantic, and it pulled me back into the moment.

I turned around, away from Vinny. "Wesley's gone off to shoot a car they found near Sherman. I don't know where Dick went." I couldn't keep the contempt out of my voice.

"Jesus, Annie, don't get territorial on me now. Just get the fucking story. What happened?"

"He was shot, but he's not dead. I'm going over to the hospital now."

"Call me when you get something." He hung up.

I stuffed the phone back in my bag and turned back to Vinny.

But he wasn't there.

I strained my neck and pushed my way through the throngs, looking for him. Christ, had I imagined him? No, I wasn't that bad off.

I went back down Chapel, away from the theatre and toward my car. I had to get to the hospital. I had to get the job done; then I could deal with Vinny and the jumble of emotions I was feeling right now.

It wasn't far to the hospital, but it took forever with traffic being detoured from the crime scene, one-way streets, and stoplights. As I pulled up near the emergency room, I hoped Rodriguez wasn't dead. I might not be sure about his future as police chief, but he certainly didn't deserve to be dead.

The lights of police cars — I counted six — almost blinded me. I double-parked next to a cruiser, slipping my city parking pass onto the dashboard.

I couldn't get near the entrance because a cop, Ronald Berger, stopped me before I could even cross the street, his face grim.

"You can't park there."

"I just need a few minutes," I said.

He shook his head. "Sorry, Annie, but you're wasting your time."

"Is he all right?"

Ronald shook his head. "We don't know. No one's telling us shit, either."

"He must have had some enemies," I said, hoping to prompt him into telling me something anyway.

He shrugged. "We all do. For God's sake, Annie, you know that."

"They're looking at that Honda over at Sherman," I said. "Drive-bys are usually drugs. Rodriguez was undercover for a while, right?"

Ronald stared at me. "Where the hell do you get your information?"

"I interviewed him. I'm doing a profile." Or was. "He told me about the undercover stuff, but said he hadn't done that too long."

"Well, that's all you're going to get," he said. "You've got to get out of here."

I wasn't going to get shit out of him. I was lucky Tom had told me what he did. I turned around and was about to get into my car when I saw Wesley approach from somewhere to my left.

"That was unbelievable," he said, his camera swinging from his shoulder.

"What?"

"The car, the cops all over it. They towed it away minutes after I got there, but I got some good shots." Wesley tapped the top of his camera.

I smiled. "Great job."

"So what's going on?" He tilted his head toward the emergency room entrance. "They won't let me get any closer."

"You and me both," I said, telling him the little that I knew. "And we'd better get back or Marty's going to have a coronary."

Wesley nodded and went back in the direction he'd come from. I let my thoughts stray back to Vinny as I unlocked my car door. What the hell was that all about? How could he just ask how I was like that and disappear? I wanted to be angry with him, keep that going, but I wasn't sure I had the energy.

I leaned over to my glove box and pulled

out the Rolling Stones' *Exile on Main St.* When I slipped it in, Mick sounded a little far away — the tape was fading, I'd played it so much. One of these days I'd get a new car, one with a CD player in it. Problem was, this car just wouldn't die. Two hundred thirty thousand miles on it and it just kept going.

I turned up the volume and lost myself in the music as I made my way back to the paper.

"What's going on?" Marty demanded before I even had a chance to take off my jacket.

I tossed it on the desk beside me and plopped into my chair, booting up my computer for the second time in twelve hours. "He's in the hospital, not dead, according to the cops. Wesley's got some good shots, apparently." That was an understatement. "Tom said no one else was hurt. Rodriguez's wife is in shock."

"Write it up."

I nodded, then looked around me. "Where's Dick?"

"He's still out there. He'll call in with updates if he gets them."

"If" being the operative word here. Okay, Dick had gotten better in the last several months. We'd managed to get along and I wasn't even cursing at him as much anymore. But I knew he still wanted my job, and if I wasn't on my toes, he could very well get it. Bill Bennett, the publisher, liked Dick, and God knows Bennett and I had a tenuous relationship, despite the fact that he and my mother were, at this very moment, somewhere in the Caribbean basking in the sun and drinking tropical cocktails by the pool.

So far they hadn't moved in together, but I knew it was only a matter of time. She rarely asked about my father anymore, although he continued to ask after her when he called from Vegas.

My fingers flew on the keyboard, and I got the story done in about twenty minutes. Dick still hadn't shown up. Marty didn't seem too happy about that, and he nodded as he read my piece.

"Okay, go back out there and see what the hell's going on and where Dick is." His voice was tight; he was pissed at Dick for not checking in, and it made me smile.

I grabbed my jacket and bag without saying a word and went back out into the night.

The people were still there. The cops were still there. It was funny — since I'd already filed the story, I felt a sense of closure about the situation, but here I was again, in the middle of it. Tom was talking to Sam O'Neill over near the entrance to the theatre, and I watched their body language. Tom's shoulders were stiff, his arms crossed over his chest. He didn't like what O'Neill, who was gesturing wildly, was saying to him. But I couldn't hear what they were saying, the tape keeping me too far away.

"Where'd you disappear to?"

I turned to see Rocco standing behind me. "Had to go file the story." I paused. "Where's Vinny?"

Rocco shook his head. "Dunno."

"He was here earlier."

"Yeah, saw him. But not for a while. Not since I last saw you."

All sorts of thoughts started crashing around in my head. Vinny had been known to follow me around in the past, but it was usually because he thought I needed some sort of protection. There would be no reason for that this time, so there was no reason I should think he'd fallen back into old habits. "Why would he be here anyway?" I asked.

Rocco chuckled and waved his hand, indicating the people who were still milling about. "Why is anyone here?"

Christ, another smart aleck. "Okay, okay.

Anyway, I have work to do. Did you want anything?"

"Maybe we can hook up tomorrow on that other matter," Rocco said.

I shrugged, like I didn't care. "Yeah, sure. Give me a call." I turned back toward the crime scene, hoping he didn't see my face flush.

But I didn't have too much time to think about it. Tom was on his cell phone, and his face distracted me. His mouth was set in a tight line. He took the phone away from his ear, punched it, put it on his belt clip, and looked at Sam O'Neill.

While I couldn't see Tom's face, I could clearly see the assistant chief's in the glare of the spotlight that the cops had set up in the street.

I read his lips, and it's not hard to make out "fuck," even though I certainly wasn't an expert in lipreading.

I was willing to bet that Rodriguez was dead. And I needed it on the record. Which meant I had a decision to make. Before I could think about it, I forced myself to go under the tape and walked over to Tom and Sam.

"You're not allowed over here," Sam said sternly, but I wasn't paying attention.

Sprays of blood splattered the steps of the

Yale Rep, and I stopped, unwilling to go further. I looked up, and Tom was glaring at me.

"Get out of here," he hissed.

"Is he dead?" I asked.

Tom's eyes narrowed. "Get out of here."

"Is he dead?" I asked, more loudly this time, glancing at Sam O'Neill, who was nodding without realizing it. "Can I get that on the record?" I asked him.

Tom bounded down the steps, grabbed my arm, and pulled me across the sidewalk, back to the tape. I felt his breath on my neck and heard the word "Yes" whispered in my ear.

He let go of me and held the tape up so I could scoot underneath it. I wasn't sure whether he was saying "yes" that the chief was dead or "yes" that it was on the record, but before I could ask, he had turned away.

I headed back to my car, weaving in between the TV vans that crowded the narrow street. It was time for the eleven o'clock news — just their luck. Cindy Purcell, Dick's main squeeze, was holding a microphone in front of a camera, her blond hair teased high, her bright pink jacket squeezing her breasts a little too tightly. If she didn't watch out, they'd come tumbling out à la Janet Jackson, causing some poor old coot watching the news to get a real treat.

I didn't see Rocco or Vinny as I walked down the sidewalk toward Temple Street. A few stragglers had decided the show was over, and I overheard them saying they were heading for Caffe Bottega, where the Cobalt Rhythm Kings were playing. Maybe I should stop in for a beer — the blues would match my mood — but I knew I had to get back to the paper and top off the story.

For a second, though, I wondered if I shouldn't just call it in and go for that drink, but the thought of a drink alone was pretty pathetic. It dawned on me, too, that I hadn't seen Dick out there. I hadn't seen him in a long time.

He wasn't in the newsroom, either.

"Where's Dick?" I asked Marty.

"Beats me. You didn't see him?"

I shook my head and told him what Tom had said.

"But all it was was a 'yes'?" Marty asked, frowning. "What the hell did that mean?"

"He was confirming that Rodriguez had died," I said more confidently than I felt. Had he? I wasn't completely sure. Maybe I really did need to get it from someone else.

And Marty agreed with me.

"You need it officially," he was saying.

I went back to my desk and picked up my

phone. I hesitated a minute, then dialed a number that was still in the recesses of my brain.

"Hello?"

Tom knew it was me. His voice was curt; he was pretending it wasn't me. He was probably still standing on those steps with Sam O'Neill, amidst Rodriguez's blood.

"You said 'yes' in my ear. I need to know for sure. Is he dead?"

"Yes."

"Can I say you told me?"

"No." His words were clipped, and the call ended.

Police sources. That's what the story said. Police sources confirmed that Police Chief Tony Rodriguez was dead from gunshot wounds after a drive-by shooting in front of the Yale Rep as he headed in for the night's performance with his wife and his best friend, the assistant chief.

Marty nodded as he read it, his lips moving with the words. When he was done, he looked at me and smiled. "Good job," he said.

Wesley's pictures were perfect, and we still had a head shot from the interview I did with Rodriguez for the profile. It was going to take up the entire front page.

Dick still hadn't shown up. He hadn't

called. Marty tried his cell phone, but the voice mail picked up right away, indicating that the phone was turned off.

I was actually starting to worry about him. But I would never admit that.

"Can you go out there again and look for him?" Marty asked.

I also would not admit that I hoped I would run into Vinny again in my search for Dick, but that was running through my mind as I circled the Green for the third time that night in search of a parking spot.

I finally found one on Temple, not too far from Chapel, and didn't bother with the parking pass since it was now close to midnight.

The Green was quiet, dark. The moon lit up the silhouettes of the trees. Someone was crossing Chapel Street, coming toward me, and I clutched my keys tightly. This part of the city was fairly safe, but at this hour anywhere was ripe for a crime and I didn't want to be a victim.

The figure hurried past me, probably just as concerned about me as I was about him. I moved up the sidewalk quickly, turning to my right onto Chapel.

At College Street, two cop cars blocked traffic from going any farther on Chapel, their lights flashing blue and red against the buildings. I scurried past them on the sidewalk and as I reached the High Street intersection saw the crime scene tape hanging limply near the ground, its ends still fastened loosely around two parking signs on either side of the street. The TV vans were gone, their few minutes on the air over. They'd probably gone to camp out at the hospital to get some sort of official word on Rodriguez. And where there had been a crowd several people deep only an hour ago, they had now dispersed and there were maybe ten people still on their side of the tape. Two cops were chatting nearby, standing sentry and making sure no one, like me, tried to get past them. I strained my eyes and saw Tom and Sam, no longer on the theatre steps but farther away, leaning against the side of another cop car blocking the intersection at York. A couple of forensics guys were still at work.

I glanced around at the other people milling about, but none of them was Dick. Where the fuck had he gone? I didn't see Rocco or Vinny, either. This looked like a futile trip, and I started walking back toward my car. The desire for a drink at Caffe Bottega was much stronger now; as I walked briskly, I saw the door open two blocks away and the faint sound of music streamed into the night air.

I picked up my pace. One drink wasn't going to hurt. And maybe Dick was there. That was it. Maybe Dick had gone to Caffe Bottega to listen to the music, maybe to get a drink himself, after working a crime scene.

Even as I thought it, I knew how stupid an idea that was. Dick wouldn't not check in. He'd be following me around or going to the newsroom to try to get the story done before I got back.

I stopped in front of Ann Taylor, the headless mannequins in the window towering over me. I was going to have to go ask Tom if he'd seen Dick. Because even though Dick was a moron, he'd somehow grown on me and I really was worried now. When I found him, I'd let him have it, but right now I had no choice.

I headed back up Chapel, promising myself that drink once I found Dick, as sort of a congratulation to myself for doing the right thing, even though it was getting late and I might not make it before last call.

I had just crossed College when the gunfire pierced the black silence.

Chapter 5

I sprinted up the sidewalk, sirens echoing, moving farther away the closer I got. I glimpsed the taillights of two cop cars as they sped down Chapel, leaving behind bits of yellow crime scene tape in the street. A few people clustered under the overhang at the Yale Center for British Art.

"What happened?" I asked between breaths. I was way out of shape, but it wasn't like I ever tried not to be.

A tall, lanky black kid, maybe around twenty or so, took a drag off a cigarette, a plume of smoke wafting out of his mouth and nose, and said simply, "Shooting."

"I heard that," I said, trying not to sound impatient. "But who? Who was shooting?"

He shook his head. "Heard a car. It was really loud, like it needed a new muffler. Ran right through that yellow tape past the cops over there on York Street. Heard the shots as it reached Chapel. Didn't stop. Just kept going."

"Who was he shooting at?"

"No one in particular, it seemed."

This whole thing was surreal: the police chief, the location, everything.

As I was sifting through it, my eye caught movement to my right and I stiffened, stepping toward the kid who'd just spoken to me. A short woman wearing a backpack stopped in front of us.

"What's going on?" She was looking right at me.

"Didn't you see anything?" I asked. "It happened up that way. A shooting."

She pushed her hand through a mane of hair and glanced over her shoulder at the street. "No. Didn't see anything." There was a lilt to her voice, a slight accent. I wanted to guess Hispanic, but it was dark and the shadows didn't let me see her face too clearly. She could've been Asian, too. I'm not too good at picking out accents.

I looked around at the other six people who were talking softly among themselves.

"Did anyone see anything?" I asked loudly.

They looked up, seemingly startled at the sound of my voice. Each said "no," then resumed talking.

"Are you sure?" I asked, not about to be ignored.

But they did just that. The black kid chuckled as he took another drag off his cigarette. "No one ever sees anything," he said.

He was right.

"I'm a reporter, with the *Herald,*" I told him. "Can I quote you on what you saw?"

He took the cigarette out of his mouth and threw it to the ground, grinding it into the pavement with the heel of his shoe. Finally, "Do you need my name?"

I smiled. "That would be nice."

He was silent for a few seconds, then, "I'd rather not."

I couldn't blame him. But I needed something. "I could just use your first name."

He shifted uncomfortably, then, "Just my first name?"

I nodded.

"Okay," he said slowly. "It's Dwayne."

"Thanks," I said, pulling my notebook out of my purse and writing it down, along with what he'd seen. "You said he came down York and just started shooting?"

Dwayne nodded. "There were two cops on the steps of the Rep. They hit the sidewalk."

Tom and Sam O'Neill. I caught my breath. "And then what?"

"The cops took off after the car," came a

soft voice behind me. It was the woman with the backpack. I felt a rush of relief when I realized Tom hadn't been hurt.

Dwayne and I stared at her.

"I thought you said you didn't see anything," I said, a little harshly.

She didn't seem to notice. "I saw the cop cars. The sirens were loud. They all got into the cars and took off."

"And your name is?"

She hesitated, then, "Marisol."

"Can I have your last name?"

She paused again. Shit. Another squirrelly witness.

"Are you a Yale student?" I asked. Maybe I could get in the back door on this one.

She laughed. "Oh, no. You think so because of my backpack?"

It was a logical question, I thought. Here we were, in the midst of Yale, and she's wearing a backpack that could contain textbooks.

"I saw the lights and wondered what was going on," Marisol continued, answering my next question without me having to ask it. "I was over at Toad's, but my cousin called me, said to meet her at Starbucks."

I saw the Rolling Stones at Toad's many moons ago, as well as Springsteen and Billy Joel, back when people admitted to wanting to see Billy Joel. Usually, though, the bands were less well known, sort of like the Cobalt Rhythm Kings.

"Starbucks closed an hour ago," Dwayne said thoughtfully, pulling another cigarette out of his breast pocket and raising his eyebrows at me as if to say, "She's lying."

But before I could call her on it, my phone started to chirp inside my bag. I scrambled to pull it out and stepped away from Dwayne and Marisol as I answered.

"What the hell's going on over there, Annie?" Marty's voice was about an octave higher than usual with the night's stress.

I filled him in on the shooting as quickly as I could, telling him I was talking to witnesses.

"What about Dick?"

I'd forgotten all about Dick. "I haven't seen him. He's not back yet?"

"Jesus." I could hear the worry in Marty's voice. "Where could he be?"

I glanced over at Dwayne and Marisol, who were chatting about something. "What do you want me to do? Keep looking for him?"

"Hell, I don't know where to tell you to start."

"Maybe he's still over where they found that car on Sherman," I said, although Wesley had said the car was already gone, evidence in the shooting. "I'll take a trip over there."

"Okay," Marty said. I could hear his doubts in that one word.

"Listen, let me wrap this up here and I'll call you right back." I put the phone back in my bag and pulled out a couple of business cards, handing them to Dwayne and Marisol. "If you can remember anything else, could you call me?" I asked.

Marisol stared at the card for a second, then stuck it in the back pocket of her jeans. It would probably go through the wash and she wouldn't even remember what it was. Dwayne put the card in his shirt pocket.

I started back toward my car and called Marty. "Let me give you the quotes from the witnesses." I recited what they'd said, and I could hear Marty's fingers tapping on his keyboard, taking down every word.

He didn't like it that I only got their first names, but he seemed to be distracted enough by Dick's disappearance that he wasn't going to give me a hard time about it.

"Where the hell could Dick be?" he asked.

I sighed. "You know, Marty, he'll show up. He's probably chasing some ambulance or something." As I said it, I stopped walking and stared straight ahead at the dark sidewalk. Dick had said something several months ago about having a source at the hospital. If he was there, that could explain why he didn't answer his cell phone. You can't have them on at the hospital. I told Marty my theory.

"You know, you're right," he said. "I'll be here for a little while longer anyway. It's getting too late to make any more changes to the story, but I can wait to see if he calls. You can go home. You did great."

"What time tomorrow?"

"Sleep in a little. You must be beat. I'll be here at noon."

"I'll see you then." I threw the phone back in my bag and continued down the sidewalk. It was after one a.m. now, too late to check out Caffe Bottega. Everyone would be drunk, and it would be ugly. Marty was right; I was beat and needed to go home.

The sun was shining through my mini-blinds, blinding me when I opened my eyes. I squinted at the clock. Nine a.m. I thought about pulling the covers over my head and going back to sleep, but even though I'd been exhausted when I crawled into bed, I was wide awake now and knew it was time to get up.

I padded into the kitchen and put some water on to boil. I'd bought a French press, feeling very European, and discovered it made better coffee than my old coffee-maker. It didn't even take much longer.

I stuck a bagel in the toaster before going downstairs to get the paper on the stoop.

I was halfway back up the stairs when I finally shook it open to see how it all ended up. A headline reading POLICE CHIEF GUNNED DOWN screamed across the top of the page, at least 100-point type. My byline underneath, the story about Rodriguez's shooting, death, and then the other shooting later on.

But then I saw it. Dick's byline. A sidebar. And it wasn't what I'd expected.

"Suspect Shot by Police."

What the fuck?

I ignored the whistling of my teapot and sat on the couch, smoothing out the paper as if doing so would smooth out my bruised ego. While I was talking to Dwayne and Marisol, Dick obviously had been with the cops as they went after that second shooter. How the hell had that happened?

I couldn't stand the sound of the kettle anymore, so I wandered over to the stove and poured some water onto the coffee in the press. As I waited the requisite four minutes before pressing, I scanned my own story again, turning the page to read the jump.

Dick had been at the hospital, as I suspected. He had a tagline saying he contributed to the story, and I found his contribution. Three paragraphs of color about the scene at Yale–New Haven Hospital, the grim faces, the silences, the confirmation of Rodriguez's death.

I finished making the coffee and poured myself a cup before calling Marty at home.

"How the hell did he do this?" I demanded.

"Annie?" His voice was gruff. I'd woken him up.

"How did Dick get this shit?"

I heard a chuckle. "Now don't go off half-cocked, Annie. You would've had the same thing if you were in his position."

"Which was what?"

"He was at the hospital, and one of the cops offered to take him back to his car downtown. While they were en route, they heard the call about the other shooter, and they responded."

Holy shit. He was right there with them. In the goddamn police cruiser. This is what pissed me off about Dick Whitfield. He was a boob, but he had the best fucking luck of any reporter I'd ever met. It was a good thing he couldn't write a coherent sentence or he really would put the rest of us out of business.

"I need to get some more sleep, Annie," Marty was saying. "I'll see you in a couple of hours."

The dial tone rang through my head. I put the receiver back in its cradle and took a drink of coffee, but I couldn't even taste it. This thing with Dick could be bad for me. His stock would go up even higher.

As I put on a pair of jeans and a long-sleeved T-shirt — it was Saturday and there was no dress code — I pondered my next move.

I blamed the phone for interrupting my train of thought, which was going nowhere, as usual, but no one had to know that.

"Hello?" I asked as I picked up the receiver.

"Hello, Anne." My mother's voice was softer than usual, probably from all those cocktails and massive doses of sunshine down in the Caribbean.

"Hi, Mom," I said absently, not wanting to think about someone else's vacation. "What's up?"

"I have a favor to ask, dear."

Shit.

"Could you stop by the house?"

"I thought you had someone doing that," I said. It wouldn't take too much time to swing by, but I was going to be busy today and didn't want to be bothered. "And anyway, aren't you coming home tomorrow?"

"Please just stop in for a few minutes, okay? Ira said he was sending me a fax and I need to make sure it got there. I can't reach Lourdes to see if she can check."

Ira Hoffman was head of my mother's law firm. Lourdes was her cleaning woman. I'd teased my mother when she'd hired Lourdes a couple of months ago, especially since she'd made a point for years about never letting anyone else scrub her bathtubs. But since she and Bill Bennett had hooked up last fall, she was doing a lot of things that were out of character. Like letting him talk her into the Caribbean, when my mother's previous vacations were all in Paris or Rome or Madrid. I never knew her to sit on a beach and do nothing. But Bill Bennett asks her, and where is she? Baking on a beach, basting herself with sunscreen.

I couldn't say no. I wanted to, but I knew if I did, she'd manage to pile on the guilt so I'd regret it for years. But it still bothered me. "You'll be back tomorrow, so why did he fax it to the house? Can't you just see it at the office?"

I heard her take a deep breath. "I don't think I have to explain this to you, but since you're insisting on giving me a hard time, Ira and his wife are going on vacation today, and it's something I want to work on tomorrow when I get home. My office is being painted this weekend and I would rather not be overcome by fumes while trying to work there."

I'd pushed it too far. "Sure, okay, I'll stop by before work."

"Work? It's a Saturday."

"Yeah, well, we've had some excitement here." Understatement of the year. "New police chief got shot down in front of the Yale Rep last night, died in the hospital."

"The police chief?"

"Yeah. No clue who did it, at least no one's saying right now."

She was quiet a minute, then, "If the fax is there, can you put it on the desk in my basket? If for some reason it hasn't come through, call me." She rattled off a phone number, and because I have a million pens and pencils scattered around my apartment, I was able to take it down next to Dick's sidebar about the shooting. "Thank you for this, and if I don't talk to you, I'll call you tomorrow when we get in."

I said good-bye and hung up, grabbing my jean jacket off the couch as I went out. I could make it over to Westville and back to the paper in about half an hour, if I was quick about it.

But I couldn't make my getaway that quick, because when I stepped outside, Rocco DeLucia was leaning against the railing.

"I'm on my way out," I said, trying to sidle past him.

"Wondering what's going on today," he said, following me down the steps and to my car.

I paused. Damn — if he didn't look like Vinny. "Listen, Rocco, I have to get going, okay?" I unlocked the car door.

"Do you mind if I tag along? I'm researching another book. This one's with a reporter, and I'd really appreciate it." He smiled Vinny's smile, but it didn't have the same effect.

I shook my head. "No, I don't think so." I climbed into the Accord and started it. He hadn't walked away, but I eased away from the curb and drove down Chapel Street, watching him in the rearview mirror.

The Rolling Stones tape was sticking out of the tape deck like a plastic tongue, and I pushed it in, trying to forget about Rocco DeLucia, but it reminded me that Vinny had been there last night and I still wondered why. I hadn't bought Rocco's explanation that "everyone" turned out for a crime like that. And anyway, where had Vinny gone? If he was as curious as Rocco made him sound, then he should've stuck around.

As I crossed over Temple and then College, I slowed down a little past the Yale Art Gallery on the right and all the little shops, Starbucks, and the British art center on the left. As I got closer to the Yale Rep, I could see the little bits of yellow tape littering the street and sidewalks. But today it was business as usual; people were bustling, Yalies lingering in knots, car horns honking as someone took a little too long at the light at York.

I managed to make all the lights and got to my mother's in record time. The house loomed tall in front of me, and I pulled into the driveway, staring up at the window of my old bedroom. I hoped Bill Bennett wasn't going to make my mother sell this house and move in with him.

I rummaged in my purse for the cheat sheet so I could disengage my mother's security system without having the entire New Haven police force turn out. I unlocked the side door that led to a mudroom and quickly punched in the numbers on the keypad, standing still for a few seconds just to be on the safe side. The little button was blinking, which meant I was okay, and I pushed open the door to the kitchen.

A week's worth of mail sat on the kitchen table, and I leafed through it, but there was nothing interesting there. A Talbot's catalog, cable bill, phone bill, and a flyer for a new pizza place a few blocks away on Whalley.

I made my way to my mother's den and found Ira Hoffman's fax sitting in the little slot where it should be. At least I didn't have to call her back.

As I picked it up, I looked at it — she had to know I would — but all it was was a list of names. Hispanic names, I saw when I studied them more closely. She did pro bono work sometimes with Legal Aid, but since this came from Ira Hoffman, maybe it was something else. I'd ask her about it tomorrow, even though I knew she probably wouldn't tell me anything.

I slipped the fax into the empty metal basket and figured, while I was here, I might as well make sure everything was in order. All the houseplants had been watered recently; the dirt was moist. Lourdes had obviously been here; the house was spotless.

I wiped my dirt-coated finger on my jeans and started back out, but something wasn't right.

I turned to face the kitchen. The pantry door was ajar. If my mother came home and saw that, she'd have a fit. In four strides, I reached the door and tried to push it shut. But it was stuck. I pulled the door open and looked inside to see what was jamming it.

Lourdes was crouched on the floor, stuffed between a bag of potatoes and a six-pack of Perrier.

Chapter 6

I stooped down and gave her a nudge on the shoulder. She rocked back a little, then settled again in her original position.

Goddammit. I didn't need this today. She didn't look dead, but her eyes were closed and the skin around her jaw was slack.

Then I thought about the odds. The odds that I'd come in contact with three dead bodies within twenty-four hours. I felt like Bloody Mary.

A soft moan interrupted my thoughts. She stared up at me, surprise imprinted on her pupils. Thank God she was alive, but hell, what had happened to her?

"Are you okay, Lourdes? Can you get up?" I asked softly, holding out my hand to her.

Lourdes tentatively took it. I yanked her arm, and she managed to pull herself up and out of the pantry.

"I'm sorry," she whispered.

I frowned. "For what? What happened?"

Lourdes shook her head. "I thought you were a burglar." She had that soft Hispanic lilt in her voice, but she'd been in the country for several years and her English was very good.

I'd been accused of many things in my lifetime, but this was a first. "I didn't see a car out front," I said. I had another thought. "The alarm was set when I got here, so I didn't think anyone was here."

"I like to keep the house secure when I'm here," she whispered. "Just in case."

A little paranoid, maybe? But I didn't say anything.

"My cousin brought me," she continued, still whispering. "He's going to pick me up in" — she looked up at the clock — "ten minutes."

"If you want, I can stay until he shows up," I offered.

She shook her head again. "No, no. I don't want to put you out."

But I wanted to be put out. Something didn't feel right, and it wasn't just Lourdes' chilly fingers on my forearm. "I'm going to stay," I insisted.

Lourdes straightened herself up and smoothed out the front of her button-down white shirt. I was more than a head taller than she was, and I looked down on her sleek black hair pulled into a long braid that snaked down her back. My mother had told me she was Cuban and most definitely legal. I trusted my mother had checked that out, her being a thorough attorney and all. Another Westville lawyer had lost out on becoming the country's first woman attorney general because she'd neglected to pay her nanny Social Security wages. No way would my mother allow herself to follow in those footsteps.

"If you think someone's breaking in," I admonished, "you might want to call nine-one-one." I indicated the phone that still sat in its cradle on the counter next to the pantry. "You could've just brought it in there with you."

But Lourdes' eyes were skirting around me and out the window, where I turned to see a green Honda Civic pulling up against the curb. The driver's face was obscured by the shadow of a big maple tree with fledgling leaves, and a short honk indicated he wasn't going to wait long.

"He's early," I said, but she wasn't listening.

Lourdes almost knocked me down as she squeezed past me. "Thank you, but I'm fine," she said, her voice stronger now as she threw open the door and rushed to the waiting car.

I watched from the window as she climbed inside. But the car sat there, idling, and I could see the driver's face was angry as his mouth moved. I could only see the back of Lourdes' head.

Worried that it could get uglier, I stepped outside, pulling the door shut behind me and walking to my car in the driveway but not taking my eyes off the Civic. I took my cell phone out of my purse, just in case.

The driver saw me then. He got out of the car. A bandanna was wrapped around his head and a scar ran down the length of his cheek. He wasn't very tall, but he was solid, like a Rottweiler, and his hands were knotted into tight fists that I was sure could do some serious damage. This was not a guy to fuck with, and my fingers moved against my phone, flipping the cover up.

He took a step toward me, but before he could go further, a white BMW slid up behind the Civic and Rocco DeLucia threw his door open and got out, standing in the street, daring the guy to move.

For a long second we all stared at each other, then, finally, Rocco said, "Time to go, isn't it?"

The driver scowled but got back in the Civic and peeled off, leaving a stream of exhaust behind him. Rocco beckoned. "We don't have much time," he said loudly, opening the passenger door to his BMW.

I had no idea what he was up to, but hell, why not? I sprinted to the car, slid onto the black leather seat, and closed the door at the same time Rocco floored it and we careened in the same direction as the Civic. I had managed to pull on my seat belt when I saw the Civic up ahead.

"There it is," I said, like I should be surprised the Beemer could move faster than the old shitcan I owned. Hell, the Civic we were following was newer than my Accord. I thought of Dick Whitfield's Prius and wondered what sort of financial choices I should be making these days. I wasn't getting any younger, and driving a fourteen-year-old car with over two hundred thousand miles on it indicated that I wasn't progressing the way I'd thought I would when I started out in my twenties.

But instead of dwelling on what could be pretty depressing, I eyed the Civic and asked, "What're we doing?"

"I don't like the look of him," Rocco said softly.

No shit. Who would?

"Do you know him?" Rocco asked.

I shrugged. "Lourdes says he's her

cousin."

"Who's Lourdes?"

"My mother's cleaning lady."

"That's your mother's house?"

"Yeah."

He was quiet for a second. "Do you think she's telling the truth? Lourdes, I mean, about him being her cousin."

I wasn't sure. Her reaction certainly didn't indicate there was any real familial love going around. "What are we going to do when they stop?"

Rocco grinned. "Who the hell knows? All I know is, Arnie would follow them after that."

"Arnie?"

He blushed a little. Really. "Arnie Fawkes. He's the cop in my books."

"Do you usually think he's a real person?" I began to wonder about his state of mind.

"He *is* real," Rocco said, taking one of his hands off the steering wheel and tapping his head with his forefinger. "He's up here. All the time."

Oh, Christ. Vinny never told me his brother was schizo. But then again, Rocco's books were on bestseller lists with regularity. I'd even read one after Vinny told me about his brother, and it was pretty damn good, although a little overwritten, in my own opinion.

And here I was, in the guy's Beemer following my mother's cleaning lady and a guy who looked like Marlon Brando at the end of *Apocalypse Now.*

What was wrong with this picture?

We followed the Civic through Westville center, down Whalley Avenue, past the jail, all the used car lots, and the Stop & Shop. We managed to make all the lights down Elm, past the city Green and City Hall. When we crossed State Street and drove up Grand Avenue, I knew where we were going. Fair Haven.

Grand Avenue is peppered with storefronts and restaurants, one of my favorites being El Charro, a great Mexican place. I wondered if we'd have time to get lunch once we were finished with this pseudo–private eye shit.

This neighborhood had a long history of immigrants settling there after the old New England Yankees decided life might be better in Fair Haven Heights, on the other side of the Quinnipiac River. The Italians and the Irish infiltrated the area in the nineteenth century, and now, at last count and continuing the immigrant tradition, there were between five and seven thousand illegal Latinos living here. It had been cheaper to live here than in other parts of the city back then, and it certainly was less expensive now.

The neighborhood hadn't completely shed its Italian roots, however. A little farther down Grand was Geppi's restaurant, and Rocco's Pastry Shop — no relation to my companion — on Ferry Street was another reminder of who had been here first.

As we passed it, C-Town grocery store was looking a bit gray and tired. A knot of young black men sauntered along the sidewalk, a couple of Latino women pushed strollers, and two girls wearing low-rise jeans and jackets that were cropped short enough to show off their bellies giggled as they pointed toward an old man stumbling out of a market that could've been south of the border because, if the signs were any indication, "Hablo Español" was all you'd get.

We turned left at the light down Blatchley Avenue, and Rocco slowed as we saw the Civic pull into the driveway of a three-family house that needed that *Extreme Makeover: Home Edition* in a really bad way. It stuck out among its more tidy neighbors on either side.

The Beemer hugged the curb, and we sat idling, watching as Lourdes and her cousin climbed out of the car.

The front door opened, and a young woman stepped out on the stoop. The guy shoved past her and inside, but Lourdes lingered on the bottom step.

Rocco's hand was on the shifter between us and put the car in first. As he eased back out into the street and slowly made his way toward the house, both Lourdes and the young woman looked at us. Lourdes frowned and moved in our path. Rocco stopped, rolling down his window.

Lourdes leaned in, looking at him and then at me. "What are you doing here?" she demanded, obviously more confident in her neighborhood than in my mother's.

"We wanted to make sure you were okay," I said.

The young woman's face peered at us from the stoop, and it took a second before I recognized her.

It was what's her name. Marisol. The girl from last night, from the shooting.

A flicker of recognition crossed her face, too, but then she concentrated on Rocco. "What are you doing here?" she scolded, and in just a couple of strides she pulled Lourdes away from the car. "It's not safe for you here," she hissed back at us. "Go away."

And with that, she and Lourdes scrambled

up the stairs and inside.

We didn't talk until we were about four blocks away, the windows rolled back up and the doors locked, even though the crime rate had dropped slightly in recent months. I'd heard that it was because the cops were finally making a dent, but it was hurting business. Not a lot of crime meant there was less money to spend. It was ironic, really.

The gangs here were mainly black or Afro-Caribbean, and they picked on the Hispanics who weren't here legally because they were less likely to report a crime. In our interview, Rodriguez had said one of his plans as police chief was to have even more of a presence in Fair Haven, to try to reduce crime even further. The mayor supported him — hell, he couldn't not support reducing crime — but there were rumors that he wasn't as enthusiastic as he should be. It could have a lot to do with the fact that he just might not give a shit because most of the people in this neighborhood couldn't vote anyway.

I thought about Marisol. Was she one of the so-called "undocumented workers?" Maybe that's why she didn't want to give me her last name last night.

"Seemed like she knew you," I said finally.

Rocco's face was scrunched up like he was thinking about something. "Yeah," he said absently.

"Do you know her?"

He shrugged. "Beats me."

That was odd. Because it really did seem like she knew him. And the way he was tapping his fingers on the steering wheel made me wonder if he was lying to me.

"I'll take you back to your car," he said.

"Sure." I thought a second. "Why did you follow me this morning?"

He gave me a cocky grin. "You led me to a crime scene last night. I thought maybe you would again today."

He was a nut. In the little time I'd known Vinny, I knew the crazy gene had not passed on to him.

"Are you really that desperate for a book plot?" I asked, noticing for the first time the new-car smell and the smooth leather that was emanating heat beneath my ass. Heated seats, for Chrissakes. He might have been crazy, but he had to be loaded with a car like this. That book thing must be pretty lucrative.

"I told you, my new book has a reporter in it. A woman reporter." He paused as I swallowed that information. "I hoped maybe you could help me with it."

I snorted. "All you had to do was ask, not follow me around."

He mulled that over before asking, "What about you and Vinny? What's going on with that?"

The change of subject threw me for a second. "Nothing. We had this conversation already."

"He's just as stubborn as you."

"Tell me something I don't know," I grumbled. We weren't getting back to Westville fast enough.

"Want some help?"

"Why should I want your help?"

He glanced at me and chuckled. "Jesus, you two are made for each other. I can't believe you live a block from each other and neither of you will give in."

I refused to talk to him after that. It was none of his fucking business, even if he was Vinny's brother. Obviously, Vinny felt the same way I did.

I was glad I was an only child.

When we finally reached my mother's I was more than aware of the rust that was beginning to develop on my old Honda. Next to this sleek Beemer, my car was merely another reminder that I wasn't in Rocco DeLucia's tax bracket.

As I climbed out into the crisp April air, I heard him say something.

"What?" I asked, leaning in toward him.

He looked startled for a moment, then said a quick, "See you around." I jumped away from the car as he sped away.

Chapter 7

The newsroom was dark and deserted. It was only eleven a.m.; no one would be in this early on a Saturday. I flipped the switches, and the lights flashed brightly against the dull brown of the carpet, reflecting off the dark computer screens. We were scheduled to get new computers, but so far they were still sitting in boxes somewhere in the recesses of the building. We were taking bets on when they'd actually end up on our desks. My money was on October, only a little less than six months away and long enough for them to become obsolete if, in fact, they were now state of the art. Dick Whitfield, I'd learned, was more optimistic than I was — no surprise there — and thought we'd be working on them in a month.

It just proved how naive he could be.

The system we were working on now took more than a year to get up and running, and we'd had it for seven years. Seven years in which technology had moved beyond our capability. Word had it that we still wouldn't have sound cards, even with the new system. I wondered if the powers that be thought if we had sound that suddenly the newsroom — one big room without dividers so we were all out in the open — would become as noisy as a casino.

Not that we weren't entertained every day anyway by someone's new tune on his or her cell phone.

I booted up my computer and, as I waited, I regretted not picking up some more coffee on my way in. I could've used the caffeine rush before seeing Dick and hearing all about his "adventure" with the cops that landed him on Page One next to yours truly.

"You're here early, Annie." The voice startled me, and I swiveled around in my chair to see Marty walking through the newsroom toward his desk, just a few feet from my own. He'd read my mind. He was carrying one of those big boxes of coffee from Dunkin' Donuts, a bag full of cups, and a box of Munchkins, which he dropped on the communal food desk. "Help yourself."

I poured a cup of coffee and rooted around in the Munchkin box for a couple of chocolate frosteds, pushing the jelly-filled ones out of the way. I'd read somewhere about how they get that jelly into the doughnuts, and I didn't want to go there.

As I sipped my coffee and chewed the Munchkins, I could feel Marty's eyes resting on the back of my head.

"What?" I asked, turning toward him.

"We have to find out why the hell someone would gun Rodriguez down like that. Do you have anything in your notes that might indicate he pissed someone off?" He pushed his glasses up farther on his nose as he stared down at me. Marty is about six foot four, and usually I see him hunched over at his desk. Standing, he was very intimidating. Especially since I'd been combing my notes for just what he'd asked and hadn't found a damn thing.

I shook my head. "No. He was benign."

Marty snorted. "There was something. Find it."

"No shit, Marty."

"Have you touched base with the cops this morning?"

"Not yet."

He sighed. "I know you're burned out, Annie, but you really have to get motivated on this one. When it's over, you can take a week off."

I felt a bubble of anger rising; then it receded. He was right. I was burned out and tired. What the hell was wrong with me? One of the biggest stories of my career was sitting in my lap. I resolved to give a shit. "Okay," I said, retreating to my desk and picking up the phone.

Tom's "Hey, Annie" was tight in tone, but I ignored it.

"Just wondering if you've got anything on Rodriguez's shooter. Is it the same guy who shot at you?"

"Can't say anything, Annie. You have to understand that." He was telling me this was too sensitive even to give me something off the record.

"The guy who got shot. Is he alive?" I asked.

"Yeah, but barely. Dick got a break, didn't he?"

I didn't want to talk about Dick.

"Listen, Annie, I gotta go." And I heard the dial tone.

I was getting nowhere fast. As I got up to get another Munchkin, my phone rang, and I sat back down.

"Newsroom," I announced.

"I'm looking for Annie Seymour." The voice was soft, lilting.

"May I ask who's calling?" I hate identifying myself to anyone who might be a nut.

"Just tell her it's the girl she met last night."

Marisol. Whom I'd just seen as I sat in Rocco DeLucia's luxury sedan. "This is Annie, Marisol. What can I do for you?"

"I need to talk to you."

I wondered if it had anything to do with Rocco, but decided I'd let her tell me. "Sure. When?"

"Half an hour. IKEA. The restaurant." She hung up.

IKEA is still a relatively new phenomenon to New Haven. Before IKEA, there had been a plan to build a huge mall next to the highway that the city claimed would've created scads of jobs and boosted the city's economy. But the traffic nightmares that would've resulted from the plan were enough to stick a stake in the proposal's heart. Thus, IKEA was the saving grace, the Store That Would Save New Haven.

So what if IKEA customers didn't even know how to find downtown New Haven? They built it and they came in droves, coming off the exit ramps with empty trunks and flatbeds and getting back on the highway heavy with their new build-it-themselves furniture.

The store is cavernous, and I decided to get a plate of meatballs while I waited for Marisol. I dunked them in lingonberries and mashed potatoes, washing them down with some sort of orange Swedish soda.

I saw her just as I was finishing my lunch. Her dark, curly hair was pulled back in a ponytail, accentuating her high cheekbones, smooth skin, and smoky eyes. She was a goddamn knockout. She wore a peasant skirt and a T-shirt with a fuchsia hoodie that did nothing to conceal a voluptuous figure. She stepped around a woman with a stroller and sat down across from me.

"Hungry?" I asked, indicating my plate.

She shook her head. "Thanks for meeting me."

I waited as her eyes took in the people around us.

"What were you doing with him?"

I raised an eyebrow and took a bite of roll. "Who?"

"I saw you in the car with him."

"Who, Rocco?"

Marisol leaned toward me. "He told me he wouldn't tell anyone about me, and he brings you to my house. Why?"

So Rocco did know her. "Why don't you ask him?"

She took a deep breath and pursed her

lips for a second before speaking. "I don't know how to reach him. I recognized you from last night and I still had your card. So I thought I could find out from you."

I shook my head. "Listen, Marisol, Lourdes is my mother's cleaning lady. She got picked up by a really scary-looking guy and we decided to follow them, to make sure she was going to be okay. It's just a coincidence that we all ended up at your house." I paused. "How do you know Lourdes, anyway?"

"She's my cousin," she said. "Your mother's cleaning lady?"

"Yeah. I was worried about her." I thought a second. "Is your last name Gomez, too?"

She bit her lip and nodded, then leaned back, her eyes skipping around the restaurant.

"Who's the guy who picked her up?"

"My brother."

I didn't see the family resemblance.

"Do you all live there, you and your brother and Lourdes?"

She nodded, but I could tell she didn't want to tell me about her home life.

"Did your friend tell you about yesterday?" Marisol asked.

I had no clue what she was talking about, but it never hurt to pretend. "Why don't you tell me your version?" I asked.

She moved her chair closer to me then, her face inches from mine. Her brown eyes flickered, and I could see fear in them. What the hell was going on?

"You wrote about it," she whispered.

"Everyone in the state wrote about it," I said. "It's not every day the police chief is shot and killed."

But she was shaking her head. "No, no. Not that. The body, the one that washed up at Long Wharf."

"What about it?"

"It had to be the one I saw."

She was being far too cryptic. "Saw where?"

Marisol took a deep breath. When she spoke, her voice was barely above a whisper. "I saw someone dump the body in the water."

Chapter 8

"Does Rocco know about this?" I asked.

Marisol nodded.

Rocco was holding out on me, and it pissed me off.

"He was there, too, but he didn't see it. Only me." She paused.

"Where were you exactly?" I asked.

Marisol shrugged. "I was at the park, you know, Criscuolo Park, on the river."

My heart was beating faster, wanting to tell her to hurry up, but I knew from experience that if I did that, she'd get spooked. She had to tell me in her own time what happened out there.

"It was a man, a man dumped the body in the water. Across the river, but you know, it's not too far across at that point."

"Which side?" I asked.

She frowned.

"Quinnipiac or Mill River?" The park stuck out into the water where both rivers converged into the harbor.

"Quinnipiac."

The port was over on that side. I wondered again about currents, how the body had gotten all the way to Long Wharf. But she was interrupting my thoughts.

"He saw me then."

I frowned. "Who saw you? Rocco?"

"Your friend? No, it was the man who dumped the body. I started to run, and ran right into your friend on James Street. He asked me what was wrong. I told him. At first I didn't think he believed me, but we got in his car and he took me home. He said I should call the police." She was curling a lock of hair around her finger so tightly I thought she'd cut off circulation.

"Did you?"

She shrugged. "Why would they believe me?"

"Because a body was fished out of the harbor yesterday. You're a witness. You need to tell the police."

She shook her head. "No, I can't."

I stared at her. "Are you here legally, Marisol?"

She frowned. "That's what he asked me, too."

"Who?"

"Your friend."

"Why did you tell him what you saw?"

Marisol sighed. "I was afraid. I thought maybe he would call the police for me, tell them so I wouldn't have to be involved. He wasn't from the neighborhood."

Made sense. Everyone here seemed to know everyone else, not to mention that a lot of them were related to each other in some way or another. And if she wasn't legal — she hadn't answered my question — the last thing she'd do would be to go to the cops herself.

I found myself getting pissed at Rocco. Even though he claimed he was following me so he could research his next book, he obviously had a big fucking story already. What did he need me for? Or did he have something even bigger in mind?

"Why did you tell him it wasn't safe at your house?" I asked.

"Too many people might wonder how we knew each other." She gave me a small smile. "And I didn't want Hector to start asking questions. He gets upset."

"Your brother?"

She bit her lip and shrugged.

I wouldn't want to piss him off, either. She twisted another curl. This girl was wound tighter than a fucking clock.

"You should call the police, tell them what

you saw, regardless of your situation," I advised. "I have a friend who's a detective. He would make sure no one would know who gave them the information." I pulled my notebook out of my purse and wrote Tom's cell number on a sheet, ripped it out, and handed it to her.

She shrank from it like I was offering her a goddamn poisoned apple.

"It's okay." I tried to sound reassuring. "Tell him I told you to call."

Marisol reluctantly took the paper and clutched it. "But what if he doesn't believe me?"

"He will," I said, then thought about something else. "You didn't by chance see any bees down there, did you?"

"Bees?" Her tone was incredulous, like mine would be if someone had asked me that.

"Forget about it," I said. "Were you close enough so you could identify the man who dumped the body?"

"I don't know," she mumbled, her eyes moving past my face now, and I would be willing to bet she could pick him out in a lineup.

I wondered what was up with Rocco. I hadn't had time to follow up on the floater, so I didn't know if he'd called the cops himself with this information after talking to Marisol. And if he hadn't, I wanted to know why not, because it would've been the civic-duty thing to do. I was going to have to track him down and grill him about this.

She was asking me a question.

"The guy who's in the hospital? The one who shot at those police? Do you know anything about how he is?"

The change of subject jarred me out of my thoughts about Rocco.

I shook my head. "I don't know his name, which is a problem. No one can get information about a patient at the hospital without a name, and the cops haven't told me anything."

There was something about her expression that made me ask my next question.

"You wouldn't know who he is, would you?"

She chewed on her lip for a second and shrugged. "I didn't know last night, when you saw me. Really, I didn't."

I felt my heart start to pound. Now this was more like it. This is how I should react when faced with the prospect of getting information that no one else had. "I don't care about that," I said, although I did and wanted to get back to it after she told me what she knew. "What's his name?"

"He's around the neighborhood," she stalled. I wanted to grab her by the shoulders and shake her, but instead kept my hands folded in front of me and waited. "His name's Roberto. Roberto Ortiz."

"Did you call the hospital and ask about him?" I asked.

She shook her head. "They wouldn't tell me anything except he's in critical condition."

They probably wouldn't tell me anything more, either, but I could ask Tom directly now, and he might be so surprised I had a name that he would tell me without thinking about it. At least I hoped so.

"So why were you there last night? You're sure you didn't know what your friend was up to?" I asked, hoping to get even more out of her.

But something happened — she'd seen something or someone — that made her push back her chair and stand up so quickly I hardly had a chance to react. I stood up, too, but it was like a time delay as I watched the fear cross her face. She turned and fled across the restaurant, down the stairs, and out of sight.

I glanced around but didn't see anyone acting suspiciously or going toward her. So I figured it was up to me to find out what the hell had scared her so much.

I turned in pursuit and was immediately blocked by two women dressed in identical purple sweat suits pushing a carriage piled high with pillows, a rather large wool rug draped over the side.

I caught my foot in the rug and sprawled across the floor as they stared at me.

"Oh, did you trip?" one of them asked.

"No, I always like to fall on my face in the middle of a Swedish furniture store," I growled, hauling my ass up, pissed, knowing I wouldn't be able to catch up with Marisol now.

They didn't even ask if I was okay as they meandered away.

I looked around again, but all I saw was the back of the purple sweat suits and a line of people waiting to pick up a meatball lunch. No one looked out of place; no one looked threatening.

I pulled my bag up higher onto my shoulder and winced a little as I realized I'd twisted my arm in the fall. Great. I went down the stairs and forced myself not to think about the cinnamon buns at the snack bar. Why was I so hungry?

I stopped on the sidewalk outside, staring at the Pirelli building — an odd-looking piece of concrete that was deemed too architecturally historic for anyone to tear down, even though it would improve the landscape immensely if it wasn't there anymore.

I hated to do it, but I needed Dick's help. He had a source at the hospital, and my source was on maternity leave. This was one of the most unpleasant things I'd ever have to do.

Dick was in the newsroom, a big shit-eating grin on his face, basking in the glory that only a front-page exclusive story can bring. Kevin Prisley, our city hall reporter, was chewing on a pencil as Dick's arms flailed about, telling his tale. All he needed was a goddamn bullhorn and everyone in the building could hear him.

I grabbed one of his arms and pulled him toward the cafeteria, apologizing to Kevin, who seemed relieved to have been released from the prison that was Dick's story.

"What are you doing?" Dick demanded, wrenching his arm from my hand. But I didn't stop until we were alone in the hallway, and I noticed he continued to follow me. I had that sort of hold over him.

Either that or he thought I was going to buy him lunch. Fat chance.

I swung around suddenly and stared him

down. "Roberto Ortiz," I said flatly.

His eyebrows crinkled into a frown. "Who?"

He didn't know the guy's name. I had him on that one. "The guy the cops shot last night. That's his name. We need to find out how he's doing. An address would be great. Do you think you can handle it?"

I'd thrown down the gauntlet, and the frown disappeared. "Ortiz?"

I nodded.

The grin was back, along with the cockiness. Shit. But if I wanted the information, I was going to have to put up with it.

"Don't worry, Annie, I'm on top of it."

That was exactly what I was worried about, but I couldn't let him see that. "Let me know as soon as you get it." I turned to walk away, but I felt his eyes on my back. I glanced behind me. "What?"

"What are you doing?"

"Me?"

"Yeah, what angle are you working on?"

He knew better than that. "Just find out about Ortiz, okay?"

I left him in the hall as I made my way back to the newsroom.

I needed to talk to Rocco about Marisol, but I wasn't sure how to find him. He could show up on my doorstep, but I had no clue where his doorstep even was. I vaguely remembered Vinny telling me something about Ninth Square, but there were too many new apartments and condos to start knocking on doors.

Yeah, I could break down and call Vinny, but after a four-month silence he might get a little suspicious if I started inquiring about his brother's place of residence.

A Yahoo! white pages search turned up nothing, not that I thought Rocco would be listed anyway.

I could drive around and look for a white Beemer. There weren't too many of those in my neighborhood.

I was grabbing at straws.

But then I had another thought. Maybe Rocco DeLucia had a Web site with an e-mail contact. A lot of writers have those. I punched his name into Google, and wouldn't you know. There it was. A black-and-white picture of Rocco in a leather jacket, the collar turned up in a James Dean sort of way, the Brooklyn Bridge his back-drop. Six book covers surrounded him, the most recent one larger and touted as a *New York Times* best seller. It had just come out, and I was tempted to procrastinate a little and read the first chapter. But Marty was wandering the newsroom and it wouldn't be easy to explain that if he snuck up on me. I found the "contact" page and sent a quick e-mail, putting my name in the subject line and giving Rocco my cell number, and asked if he could call as soon as possible.

I logged off the Internet and stared at the phone on my desk, willing it to ring.

After a few seconds, I knew I had to have another game plan. I wasn't quite sure just what that would be, so I shoved my notebook and a couple of mechanical pencils into my bag. As I stood up to go nowhere in particular, the shrill ring of my phone scared the crap out of me.

I sat back down. Rocco couldn't have gotten his e-mail so quickly, and I had given him my cell number, not my work one.

"Newsroom," I said when I picked up the receiver.

"Annie?" Tom's voice was higher than normal. Something was wrong.

"What is it, Tom?"

"You'd better get over here to your mother's. There's been a break-in."

Chapter 9

I tried to remember if I'd set the alarm when I left my mother's house. But with Lourdes in the pantry and then her creepy cousin in the Honda, I must have forgotten. This was my fault, and I just hoped there was nothing really valuable missing.

Who was I kidding? My mother had valuable shit all over her house, and any thief would be an idiot not to take it.

One cop car, Tom's Chevy Impala, and a private security agency car were sitting outside my mother's house when I arrived. I pulled into the driveway. Tom was waiting for me on the front stoop.

"How bad is it?" I asked when I approached him. "Did they clean her out?"

Tom patted the step next to him, like he wanted me to sit down, so I did. He looked at me for a couple of seconds without saying anything, then, "It doesn't look like anything's missing at all."

I frowned. "What?"

"Okay, I'll start from the beginning. A call came in. A neighbor saw a brown car out front, a guy going into the house. Alarm didn't go off."

I was right. I did forget.

"Smashed the window in the door, just turned the knob and got in," Tom continued. "TV's still there, stereo's still there, silver's still there, looks like jewelry intact. Nothing out of place, no signs of ransacking." He paused. "Does your mother have a safe or anything?"

I shook my head. "She keeps all her papers in her office and copies in a safe-deposit box. She never liked keeping anything here."

Tom stood up, and I took that as my cue we were going in. I followed him through the open side door into the kitchen, taking note of the broken glass and being careful not to step on too much of it.

"Don't touch anything, just in case," Tom warned, like I would be stupid and start putting my fingers all over everything. I know better than that; I watch *CSI*.

He led me through the kitchen and watched as I went into the den. Nothing was out of place, like he'd said. The fancy iMac G5 computer that my mother had just bought sat smugly on the desk.

"Nothing missing here," I said, and now it was my turn to take the lead. I went into every room, up the stairs, and into my mother's bedroom where I looked through her jewelry box. She didn't have much, but the few gold and silver pieces she did own were there. I closed the box, noting the TV in this room was still there as well as the one downstairs.

Tom had gone into another room, and I reluctantly followed him.

He stood in my old bedroom, the one my mother felt obligated to keep as it was when I was in high school. The rest of the house had been updated, but every time I went into my old room, it was like walking into a time warp. Why she never did anything with this room was beyond me — I didn't care about that stuff anymore — but she felt oddly sentimental about a time in my life that had been the worst time of my life.

It explained a lot about our relationship.

The poster of Jim Morrison and the Doors elicited a chuckle.

"Don't say a fucking thing," I hissed.

Tom bit his lip, trying not to laugh, as his eyes scanned the room, falling next on my bookshelves that housed *In Cold Blood, Helter Skelter,* and — God help me — *Love Story* and *Jonathan Livingston Seagull.*

A pile of record albums was stacked in a milk crate, and Tom glanced at the one on top. *John Denver's Greatest Hits.* He raised his eyebrows at me.

"Shit, Tom, I got that when I was twelve."

"So your mother has been away how long?" I was grateful he changed the subject, but he didn't leave the room. I was feeling some pretty bad karma in here, and I wanted to get out before my ghost of teenage past decided to come back and offer me a bong hit.

I took a step backward, toward the door. "They've been gone a week. They're back tomorrow."

"They?"

"She's with Bill Bennett." I sighed, wishing it weren't so but not able to do anything about it. "She called me this morning, asked me to come by and check for a fax. It was here. I saw her cleaning lady, and then the cleaning lady got in a car with a creepy guy and took off." I didn't want to tell him that Rocco was here, too, and we'd followed Lourdes. That might make it a little too complicated, and it didn't seem altogether relevant. I took another step toward the hall.

"You were here this morning? And your mother's cleaning lady?"

"Yeah, but obviously someone broke the

window after we left." I paused. "Did anyone call my mother?"

"I told the security guy to wait for you to get here," Tom said. "She might not panic so much if you break the news to her."

I took a deep breath. "I'd better call her then." I used that as my excuse to step out of my childhood room. Tom followed me back downstairs.

I went into the den to call her. Tom went into the kitchen to talk to the security guard, tell him everything was okay and he could leave.

As I dialed my mother's cell number, I realized that wasn't the number she'd given me this morning. And when the call didn't go through, I knew her cell must not be working in Aruba. I looked around on her desk to see if she'd left any numbers there, but didn't see any.

The kitchen. She'd always left her contact numbers for me on the refrigerator, so I started toward the door.

But my brain caught hold of something and made me stop and turn.

The fax that I'd checked for earlier was gone.

Chapter 10

I tried to remember what had been on that fax. A bunch of names, that's all. None of them were memorable, except that they were all Hispanic. And I distinctly recalled leaving it in the metal basket. No one else had been here since then — except for the person who broke in and took nothing.

Maybe.

I got on my hands and knees to look under the desk, just in case it had fallen. But there was nothing on the floor. My knees creaked as I pulled myself back up — for Chrissakes, I wasn't that old yet, was I — and wondered why someone would break a window, risk setting off an alarm, to get a fax. The original was in Ira Hoffman's office; why not just go after that?

"Tom," I called out into the hallway. "Come here."

His face was flushed when he rushed in. "What's wrong?" he asked, worry lines creasing his forehead.

I told him about the fax.

He snorted. "You called me in here over a fax?"

I shrugged. "It's the only thing that's missing."

He looked at me like I had three heads. Okay, so maybe it did sound a little crazy, but all I had to do was call my mother and ask her. Tom followed me into the kitchen, where the phone number of the resort was stuck to the refrigerator with a magnet. My mother was a creature of habit.

When I got her on the phone, my mother's voice was relaxed, and she almost drawled her words. What the hell were they giving her in those little umbrella drinks, anyway?

"Hey, Mom, it's me."

"Didn't the fax arrive?" A twinge of anxiety tainted her vacation mode.

I quickly told her about the break-in. "Tom called me right away," I said without giving her a chance to say anything. "Everything looks like it's here. But the fax, well, it was here earlier, and now it's gone."

"I'll call Ira." If she'd been taken over by a pod person earlier, she'd shaken it off now. This was the voice I knew, the one that won lawsuits and put criminals behind bars. It also verified my suspicion that the fax was what the burglar had been after. "I want you to do something you might not want to do," she said then. "But it's important that you do it. Immediately." She paused. I waited. "Call Vinny. Vinny has to know." And before I could ask her anything, she hung up.

I stared at the phone in my hand.

"What'd she say?" Tom's voice rang in my ear.

I put the receiver back in its cradle. "She's going to call Ira Hoffman." I didn't know why I didn't tell him she wanted me to call Vinny, but something told me not to. "This fax was what they were after. She thinks that, too."

Tom ran a hand through his blond hair. "Okay. If that's it, then I'm going to get going. I sent the security guard back. But you might want to get that window fixed up so no one else can get in."

I nodded. "Sure."

I walked him out the kitchen door. "Thanks for coming," I said. "You didn't have to."

"I heard the address on the radio when the security company called it in. Figured I might as well check it out myself. I wasn't too far away."

Tom's apartment was on Fountain Street,

just a few blocks from my mother's.

"Thanks again," I said as he climbed into his Impala.

But he didn't drive off right away. He sat there, looking at me for a few seconds before asking, "You okay?"

All I could think about was how I had to get rid of him and call Vinny. Call Vinny. After four months, I had a direct order from my mother to do what I'd wanted to do for most of that time but didn't have the balls to after the scene I'd caused.

I thought quickly. "What about you? What's going on with Rodriguez? Do you have any idea who might have killed him?"

The change of subject threw him. He shook his head, and I could see him trying to come up with something to say, but he finally just gave up. "I can't talk about it. You know that." He started the engine and backed out of the driveway. I waved like fucking Donna Reed before walking back into the house, clutching my phone so tightly I was sure it would become embedded in my palm.

For some reason, I found myself climbing the stairs and standing in my old bedroom again. I glared at Jim Morrison, who looked at me with a sort of reproach, like it was my fault I'd grown up and left him behind.

I turned my back on the poster, staring out the window, listening to Vinny's cell phone ring.

"So to what do I owe this pleasure?" Vinny must have seen my number on his phone. But he didn't sound pissed; his voice was playful, and it brought back a memory that I shoved out of the way. I had to stay focused.

"My mother asked me to call."

"That's what all the girls say." He was teasing me, flirting with me, and I felt myself getting warm all over.

"No, really," I said, struggling to remember this was business. "Her house got broken into."

"Did you call the police?" I could hear the sudden tenseness in his voice, the concern.

"Tom was here, but he left. I'm here. My mother said to call you. The fax is missing, the one Ira Hoffman sent earlier. She seemed to think you needed to know that, and you must know what I'm talking about, right?"

Silence for a second, then, "Yeah, Annie, I know what you're talking about."

"What was it, Vinny? Looked like just a bunch of names."

"You saw it?" His indignation came

through loud and clear.

"My mother asked me to make sure it got here. What's it all about?"

"It's been nice chatting. We have to do this again sometime. See ya." And the phone went dead. I pulled it away from my ear and stared at it, like it would somehow miraculously bring Vinny back. But I would need Madame Shara, the psychic who rented an office above his on Trumbull Street, for that. I was a mere mortal.

I went back down the stairs and into the kitchen. The glass was scattered all over the floor. Who the hell was I going to find to fix that window? I had to get back to work, but Tom was right. I couldn't leave it like that.

I knew only one person who might be able to help me. Who might be inclined to help me. I flipped my phone open again and dialed a familiar number.

"Hey, Dad, it's me," I said when I heard his big "Hello." He was in Vegas, but I knew he could still pull some strings in New Haven if he needed to. He knew everyone, everyone knew him, and someone usually owed him a favor.

"Hi, sweetheart, how's it going?"

I told him about the break-in.

"You're there now? And they only took a fax?"

"Yes to both questions. But I need to get the window fixed up so no one else can get in, and you know how handy I am with a hammer." I was referring to the time when I accidentally broke my big toe while trying to build a tree house with him.

He chuckled. "I'll take care of it. Let me make a call, and I'll call you back."

I still didn't like that my father could "take care of" things, but desperate times call for desperate measures.

Not even two minutes later, my phone rang.

"Louie and his boys will be there in half an hour. You can let them in, but you can leave them alone if you want. They won't do anything but fix the window."

I knew that. That was the world my father knew and I'd come to know just a few months earlier. Louie and "his boys" would get paid well for their work, and my mother probably would never even be able to tell the window had been broken.

I said good-bye to my father and went into my mother's den to wait. I figured Marty probably was wondering where I was, so I punched his number into my phone.

"What's up?" he asked.

"I should be there in half an hour, forty-five minutes," I said after explaining the situation as vaguely as I could. "I talked to Tom, but he won't tell me shit about Rodriguez. I'll give it another shot later."

His silence told me he was disappointed. "Maybe you need to talk to Sam O'Neill on this one. He's acting chief now, and he was there. He could give you an eyewitness account."

"Okay, I'll make some calls while I'm here," I said.

It was easier said than done. I struck out trying to get Sam on the phone and was mulling my next step when I saw the pickup truck pull up outside. Louie and his boys — all two of them — proceeded to clomp up the steps in their work boots and get down to business without much more than a nod hello.

I didn't want to stick around. They were measuring the door and I could hear mumbling about "Home Depot" and "new door." I told them if they had to replace the lock, they should leave the new key in the bird feeder in the backyard and I'd come to get it later. I got a couple of nods, an "okay," and I left them to their work.

CHAPTER 11

There was too much going on. First, the missing fax, which was being attended to by Vinny, whom I'd seen at the shooting the night before, along with his brother, Rocco, who knew Marisol Gomez, who had seen a body dumped into the harbor — most likely the same body I'd seen later that had some sort of bee stings on it — and she also knew the guy who shot at Tom and Sam. And then there was the dead police chief.

I felt like I was playing *Six Degrees of Kevin Bacon.* Except I was missing Kevin Bacon.

I knew I had to go back to the paper and follow up on the Rodriguez shooting, but now my head was wrapped around my mother's break-in and the stolen fax. What the hell was so important on that fax? I wondered if a quick stop at Vinny's office might not be in order.

Granted, he could be at home — it was

Saturday, after all — but as much as my mother was a creature of habit, so was Vinny, and all his investigative stuff was in his office. So even if he'd been home when I called about the fax, he probably went to his office after we talked.

I pulled in front of the brownstone on Trumbull Street, noting Vinny's Explorer in the lot in the back as I passed the driveway.

I peered out at the door, hoping that Madame Shara, who will read anyone's palm for a price, wasn't lurking somewhere. She'd managed to pull me up to her "office" a few months ago and scared the shit out of me. I still wasn't sure if her predictions had come true.

The coast was clear. At least I thought it was. So I got out of my car and ambled up the stairs.

I had to ring his bell, and through the muted glass I saw the door to his office open. He stopped when he saw me, but it was only a second of hesitation. I was watching for it, otherwise I probably wouldn't have seen it.

"I should've figured you'd drop by," he drawled as he held the door open for me.

He let me lead the way back to his office, which was as immaculate as usual. Vinny was a fucking neat freak. I was always half tempted to cart in some dust bunnies just to feel at home.

He stepped around me and behind his desk, where he dropped into his chair, leaned forward, and folded his hands in front of him. "I can't tell you about the fax. So you wasted a trip."

I sat on the leather couch across from him and tried not to remember a particular night when I had found myself in this exact spot after an evening of sidecars and music. And the way Vinny was smiling, I could see he was remembering, too.

But I wasn't here for that. At least not right now. "Come on, Vinny, my mother got burgled, for Chrissakes. What the hell's going on?"

The smile disappeared, replaced by real concern. "And the sooner you forget anything you saw on that fax, the safer it'll be for you, too."

I frowned. "Jesus, Vinny. Is my mother in danger?"

He shook his head quickly. "Oh, no, don't worry about her. I've got it covered." And as he said it, I knew he was going to watch out for her. Like he'd watched out for me on a few occasions. But it only increased my worry and curiosity.

I decided to change the subject. "What's

your brother up to?"

He was genuinely confused. "What do you mean?"

"He's been following me around."

Vinny chuckled. "Oh, that. He's got some ridiculous plot for his next book that has to do with a reporter. He's just doing his research."

"I don't think that's all."

"Why not?"

I wasn't sure just how much to say. Should I tell him about Rocco and Marisol Gomez?

Vinny saw my hesitation. "Spit it out, Annie."

I told him how Rocco had followed me to my mother's and then our trip into Fair Haven. But I only got as far as mentioning Marisol before Vinny slid back his chair and stood, his hand up, indicating I should stop.

"That doesn't mean anything," he said, but I could see something was going on in that head of his. It sure as hell meant something. "I wouldn't worry about it. Like I said, Rocco's working on a book and he always gets a little weird."

Vinny's hand was under my arm, lifting me up off the couch and moving me toward the door. "I've got some work to do, and I think you probably do, too."

He stopped then, his face inches away. I

could feel his breath on my cheek, his fingers moving between mine in a more intimate way. And he kissed me. Really kissed me, like he used to. Like nothing had ever happened between us.

But as I moved into him — reflex, really — he pulled away. "I'll call you later," he said, his voice gruff as he dismissed me, turning back to his desk.

I stood for a second, watching him, before I stepped into the hallway and back out into the day.

Dick Whitfield was at his desk, his fingers moving across his keyboard. Damn. While I was preoccupied with my mother's fax and Vinny's lips, Dick was going to continue to ride this train to its inevitable destination: more status in the newsroom for him, less for me.

I threw my bag on my desk and noticed the red light blinking on my phone. A voice mail.

"Miss Seymour, if you really want to find out who shot Rodriguez, you should talk to your boyfriend. He knows what really happened, even if he says he can't tell you."

The voice was muffled, deep, and I couldn't tell if it was a man or a woman. But obviously it was someone who knew about me and Tom, and knew that Tom could give me some answers.

I saved the message and hung up.

"So where are we?" Marty's voice startled me, and I stiffened.

"Jesus, Marty, don't sneak up on me," I said, stalling, because I really didn't know where we were or what we had.

"Dick's back from the hospital. The guy the cops shot is in intensive care in a coma."

Go figure. Dick really did have a source at the hospital.

"What have you been able to find out?"

Marty's eyes bore into mine, and I felt like a loser. I hadn't found out shit.

"Maybe you need to go talk to Rodriguez's wife."

This was the dreaded "call the dead boy's mother" request, the one every reporter hated but the one every editor had to make. He was right, but it sucked, and how the hell was I going to get in to talk to her since all the TV people were probably camped out on her doorstep, waiting for her to emerge?

"Just go see her," Marty said. "Didn't you talk to her when you interviewed Rodriguez?"

I had, but he'd been alive then. She hadn't seen him gunned down in front of her. That changed things, but Marty didn't seem to think it was a problem, since he was heading back to his desk, confident in his assignment, confident that I could get her story.

I had my doubts.

Tony Rodriguez and his wife lived in a tidy condominium that backed up to the river in Fair Haven Heights on Quinnipiac Avenue. They didn't have any children, and I hadn't felt it was anyone's business why not so I hadn't asked. His wife, Lin, was Chinese and a scientist at Yale. She did something with bugs and genetics, but it was all over my head. I'd set a wastebasket on fire during my baby chemistry class in college — that pretty much summed up my science background.

The couple met at Woolsey Hall at a concert seven years ago and married only months later. I'd been struck by how comfortable they were together, but you never know what goes on behind closed doors.

And as I stood in the parking lot in front of their building, debating how I was going to present myself, I could see their door was most definitely closed.

Only one TV van graced the parking lot. Channel 9. Dick Whitfield's girlfriend, Cindy Purcell, was leaning against the side of the van, chatting with the camera guy as I approached. They both looked up at the same time.

"She won't come out." Cindy pouted, her bright red lips making her look like a deranged Marilyn Monroe.

"Have you said 'please'?" I asked rather nastily. I went past them, noticing the smirk on the cameraman's face.

I rang the bell and heard footsteps, but the door stayed shut. I thought I saw a shadow cross the peephole. "I'm Annie Seymour with the *Herald,*" I said loudly. "Mrs. Rodriguez knows me; we spoke last week."

The curtain fluttered in the window next to the door. I waited for a minute or so, and just as I was going to call it quits, I heard the sound of the door unlocking. It opened a crack and two eyes stared out at me.

"You're alone?" whispered a voice.

"Yeah," I said, glancing back at Cindy and her cameraman. They were watching me, but not attempting to come closer. I would've, and I knew then why Cindy Purcell was still in the station's New Haven newsroom and not at the main one in Hartford.

The door opened a little more and I squeezed inside, allowing the woman who let me in to lock it behind us before I looked around.

While this condo had been bright with sunshine a few days ago, now it was dark, as all the curtains were drawn and only a dim light was on in what I remembered as the kitchen. I turned to the Asian woman who'd let me in.

"I'm Annie Seymour," I repeated. "With the *Herald.* I spoke with the Rodriguezes for a story this past week. I'm so sorry about what's happened."

The woman nodded. "I'm Lin's sister, Mei. She will talk to you."

Mei led me into the kitchen, where Lin Rodriguez sat slumped over a cup of tea at a small table. She looked up and tried a smile, but it didn't work.

"I'm so sorry, Mrs. Rodriguez," I said again, sitting across from her.

Her sleek dark hair was pulled back from her face, which was white with her sorrow. "Thank you," she said softly. "My husband spoke kindly of you."

He did? Well, he hadn't been on the job too long.

"Would you mind terribly if I asked you some questions?" I asked, pulling my notebook out of my bag.

Mei took a step toward us, but Lin held

her hand up. "I'll answer her questions. I have to do what I can." She turned back to me. "What do you want to know?"

"Did you see the man who did this?"

She took a deep breath. "It was a car. I never saw a face, or even a gun. It was a dark car, loud music. It was so fast."

"You were there to see the play?"

She did smile then. "We have season tickets. Tony loves the theatre." Her eyes filled with tears, but she blinked a couple of times to keep them at bay. "We always go on opening night. Whoever did this may have known that."

Maybe, maybe not. So far, this wasn't really helping much.

"You don't know of anyone who might want to hurt your husband?" I asked.

The hesitation was slight, but it was there, and I saw her eyes flicker toward her sister, then back to me. "No. Of course not."

I glanced at Mei, but her face was unreadable.

"Are you sure?" I asked Lin. "Anything might help."

She shook her head; this time there was no hesitation. "I'm afraid I know nothing. My husband was a police officer. They have many enemies, but none I know of." She sighed. "That's all I can say. Thank you for coming."

I was being dismissed. I stood up and allowed Mei to walk me to the front door. But before she could open it, I turned to her and whispered, "What's going on? Who is she afraid of?"

I could see Mei struggling with herself, wondering if she should say anything. Finally, "Tony had been getting phone calls."

"What kind of phone calls?" I glanced back at the light in the kitchen, but something else caught my eye. Behind Mei was one of the most interesting paintings I'd ever seen, a sort of mosaic modern interpretation of a beehive that was filled with gold and yellow and streaks of black that turned the beehive into a bee. "Wow," I whispered without realizing I was speaking out loud.

Mei sighed. "Tony bought that for her a few months ago when she started the project."

"What project?"

"She's working with bees now. She's been a bit secretive, but she usually is when she starts a project."

Bees? My thoughts jumped back a day to the body the cops had fished out of the harbor. I had to find out if it was always bee season. Seemed like Lin would be the best one to ask, but this wasn't the time.

I shook myself back to the matter at hand and remembered what I'd asked a few seconds ago. "What were the phone calls about?"

Mei shrugged. "I'm not sure. Lin is very secretive about it, like with her projects. She said it had nothing to do with his job, it was personal. But whatever it was, it was upsetting to her." She paused. "It was a few months ago, so I'm not even sure it's relevant."

So why the hell did she mention it? If the calls were really that irrelevant, why bring them up? But before I could push the issue, she opened the door and I stepped back outside, hearing the click of the lock behind me as I walked toward Cindy.

"How'd you get in there?" she demanded as I got closer. I saw she'd put on more lipstick and that her skirt showed off muscular calves. Jesus, Dick had actually gotten himself a hottie. She was dumb as a brick, but she was hot.

"My natural charm," I said lightly, grinning as I went past, the cameraman chuckling.

CHAPTER 12

Sam O'Neill was my next stop. A phone call wasn't going to do it, obviously, since I'd struck out earlier. So I pointed my Honda in the direction of the police station. Thinking about what Mei had told me, I wondered if Sam knew about the mysterious phone calls since Rodriguez had said he and Sam were tight.

I found a parking spot on the street across from the station. It was a miracle, really, since the train station was just a block down and there were still no meters on this side. Commuters usually jammed these spots, unwilling to pay for the garage, which was always full anyway.

The police station is one of those big blocks of concrete that passed for architecture back in the 1960s and 1970s. The old New Haven Coliseum was another one, but they tore that down after the minor league hockey team's contract was up and not renewed. I'd been sorry to see that building go, despite its ugliness; I'd spent a lot of time there at concerts when I was in high school and college. It was a part of my personal history. I didn't want to think about how long ago it'd been.

I was reminded, though, when the cop at the desk looked up at me. He was young, really young, maybe just out of high school. Or middle school. Everyone was looking younger these days. Except me.

"Annie Seymour here to see Sam O'Neill," I said, although just as I said it, I wondered if I shouldn't say "Assistant Chief Sam O'Neill." Oh, hell, I'd never stood on formalities before. Why start now?

The young cop picked up the phone and dialed. I pretended not to listen, but heard him say, "Annie Seymour . . . she's right here . . . she wants to talk to you . . ." He hung up the phone. "He doesn't want to talk to you," he said flatly.

I frowned. "Call him back and tell him I have information about Rodriguez."

The young cop pursed his lips, not unlike the way Cindy Purcell had outside Rodriguez's condo. But to his credit, he didn't argue, picked the phone back up, and when O'Neill answered, told him just what I said. When he hung up this time, he nodded.

"He'll be right here."

I hated it when I wasn't allowed into the inner sanctum, but this would have to do.

The lobby was dingy, the fluorescent lights casting a sort of unearthly glow. I didn't want to sit in any of the plastic chairs lined up along the wall. Who the hell knew what sort of germs were residing there. So I busied myself with reading the names of the officers who had fallen in the line of duty and studying their pictures. The most recent listed was in 1970. Did that mean no cops had died in the line of duty since then? I made a mental note to try to find out.

It must have been ten minutes later when the glass door swung open and Sam O'Neill came out. He looked only slightly better than Lin Rodriguez. His reddish-brown locks were slicked back, and even his freckles were pale against his white Irish face, which looked only whiter under his dark eyebrows.

"Hey, Sam," I said. "Somewhere we can go?"

"Let's take a walk."

I followed him out the door, down the stairs, and onto the sidewalk. He started walking toward the train station at a pretty good clip.

"So what's your information?" he asked

as I struggled to keep up.

"Rodriguez had been getting phone calls at home. His wife was concerned about them," I said, hoping that by being cryptic he could fill in the blanks and I could get more information.

Sam stopped suddenly and looked at me. "She told you about that?"

I nodded, crossing my fingers in my pocket.

"We're looking into it, but I'm not sure it's as big a deal as Lin is making it sound. Hell, we've all broken up with people who couldn't handle it. Anyway, she stopped calling a few months ago."

That coincided with what Mei had told me, but those irrelevant calls seemed to be getting a lot of attention, even though they'd ended a while back.

"But they've been married, what, seven years?" I asked, following his train of thought but not sure where it had been or where it was going. I was just going along for the ride. "This woman is from his past?"

Sam's eyes narrowed as he searched my face. "Just how much about this do you know?"

He was onto me. "Probably not as much as you do," I admitted.

"Did Lin tell you she thinks this woman

is responsible? Because Lin is distraught, and we've already considered that, but there's nothing to it." Sam suddenly turned and started walking back to the station. He was quiet a few seconds, then, "I don't want you going to Behr about this. He's got his hands full and he doesn't need you pushing him for answers, either. I don't like it that he talks to you at all, and that's going to change if I stay in this job."

Shit.

"If you have questions, you have to go through official channels, talk to me, and I'll decide what you get and what you don't get." We were at the bottom of the steps now. "Do you hear me?"

"Loud and fucking clear," I said, not happy at all with this turn of events. I probably should've just called Tom about Rodriguez since Sam seemed to have a real bee in his bonnet over me for some reason, and my anonymous caller had said Tom knew something. I probably shouldn't have cursed, either, but it just came out.

But to my surprise, he laughed. "Christ, Annie, don't get pissed. We're all on edge here, and I can't let you start printing shit that could fuck up the investigation."

I watched him as he went up the steps and disappeared into the building. As I went back to my car, I realized I hadn't asked him anything about the shooting itself. Marty wouldn't be happy about that — if I told him.

My conversation with Sam only made me more curious about Rodriguez's former girlfriend. My stomach rumbled, interrupting my thoughts, and I checked the clock on the dashboard. It was four o'clock, no wonder. I hadn't had anything to eat since my early lunch before meeting with Marisol.

But I knew I couldn't stop to eat now. I had to get back to the paper to write up my interview with Lin Rodriguez for the Sunday paper. I didn't really have much of a follow-up — I'd lost a lot of time with my mother's break-in — but I'd do the best I could with what I had.

Dick Whitfield, however, was typing furiously with two fingers as I tossed my bag on my desk.

"What've you got?" I asked through clenched teeth. From the look of determined concentration on his face, I could see Dick had something and I dreaded finding out what it was.

He looked up at me with a wide smile. Suddenly I wasn't so hungry anymore.

"That guy, Roberto Ortiz? He works in the mailroom."

I frowned. "What mailroom?"

"Our mailroom. The one down the hall." Dick cocked his head in the general direction of the *New Haven Herald* mailroom, where about twenty people stuffed advertising inserts into the newspaper every night.

"No shit?"

"He's worked here for about a year." He paused. "And his sister works here, too."

Goddammit. How the hell did Dick get this? But he was talking, interrupting my thoughts.

". . . met her at the hospital while I was over there earlier," he was saying, answering my unspoken question. "She told me their life story." He leaned toward me, whispering now. "I don't think they're legal."

They probably weren't, but that posed a bigger question. Would the powers that be want us to print a story about a *Herald* employee who might not be legal who went around shooting cops? It was probably a good thing that Bill Bennett was still on that tropical island with my mother. But it would have to go through Marty, and then the executive editor, Charlie Simmons, who had just been brought in from corporate. We'd been operating without an executive editor since last summer, when Wallace Morris had keeled over and died after eating a tuna sandwich from the cafeteria. While there was no proof that the sandwich had actually killed him, it was true that Wallace was about a hundred years old and had been at the *Herald* since Nixon's resignation. When the paper was bought out by the big corporation that now owned it, the CEO decided not to rock the boat and kept Wallace on. But he had very little power and decisions were made higher up.

Even though we all questioned Wallace's existence, we were struck with fear when faced with the thought of a new editor, one who would perhaps have more say in our day-to-day operations and who would stringently tout the company line.

Charlie Simmons was still an unknown quantity, a big man with red cheeks, a bulbous nose, and a swath of black hair that poufed up and made him look sort of like an Elvis impersonator. To his credit, he listened to Marty and the other editors, although we knew there would be a day when he would stop listening and start making the rules.

Looking at Dick and thinking about Roberto Ortiz working in the mailroom made me realize that this could be that day.

"You might want to leave out that last part. About them not being legal," I advised.

"Who's not legal?" Marty had come up behind me, a Dunkin' Donuts coffee in one hand, his glasses in the other.

I shook my head violently at Dick, but in his dense way he must have thought I had Tourette's or something because he blurted out, "Roberto Ortiz and his sister; they work in the mailroom here."

A flush crept up Marty's neck and into his face. "They're not legal?"

"Now, we don't know that for sure," I butted in. "Dick just assumes that."

"And they work here?" Marty ignored me and looked at Dick for an answer. "If you don't know it for fact, we won't print it."

"But she said she was waiting for her green card; she didn't have it yet," Dick argued.

I sat down and pretended to look at a press release. Dick was digging a hole for himself but didn't seem to realize it. Now if it was my scoop, I'd probably fight for it, too, but I'd try to find another way to get it in the story without coming out and openly saying the *New Haven Herald* was hiring illegal aliens or, as the politically correct like to say, undocumented workers.

That is, if I wanted to keep my job.

Jesus, I sounded like someone who plays by the rules. What the fuck was going on?

Marty herded Dick toward Charlie Simmons' office. I turned on my computer and, as I waited for it to boot up, movement caught my eye over near Kevin Prisley's desk. Another mouse. They'd had babies and were everywhere.

Hoping that the mice stayed out of my way, I started writing up the story about Lin Rodriguez, every once in a while glancing over at Charlie's office. I wanted to be a fly on the wall, but at the same time was glad I wasn't involved.

Roberto Ortiz and his sister kept invading my thoughts, even while I was writing. I glanced toward the hallway that led to the mailroom. It was like a goddamn moth to the light. She was probably out there now, putting the inserts together.

I peeked over at Charlie's office. The door was still closed. Who would be the wiser if I went out there to talk to her?

Okay, so maybe I'd get something new, maybe not. But it would put more of a face on the story for me. Or so I told myself as I sauntered down the hall, hoping no one would ask me where I was going since there was nothing in that direction except the mailroom, and who the hell would want to go there?

It was noisier than a fucking bulldozer. The machines were running, and I looked up to see a large zipperlike contraption carrying shiny, colorful Wal-Mart inserts between its teeth. That yellow smiley face taunted me as it passed overhead. I had a smiley face necklace when I was thirteen.

Why was everything reminding me of my teenage years?

A group of young women were sorting papers in what looked like an assembly line. I walked up to a guy who was leaning against the wall; he was the supervisor. He was a head taller than me, bald, with some sort of Chinese character tattooed above his left ear. He wore a plaid flannel shirt and jeans. The paper was more relaxed with dress code out here. He'd been at the paper for a long time, probably as long as me, and I usually ran across him in the cafeteria.

But I didn't know his name. I held out my hand. "Annie Seymour."

He looked at my outstretched hand. After a second, he took it and nodded. "Garrett Poore. This is my Poore-house," he said, laughing, like it was funny.

I pulled my hand away when I realized he wasn't going to let go. I couldn't put my finger on it, but there was something smarmy about this guy.

"I'm looking for" — I realized I didn't know her first name — "Miss Ortiz," I said loudly.

He frowned, like I was some sort of alien invading his world. "Ortiz!" he shouted after a second, and I followed his eyes across the room to a young woman in the costume of the day: a pair of jeans and a blue apron. Her hair was pulled up and knotted at the back of her neck, and as she approached, I could see sadness in her eyes.

I held out my hand. "I'm Annie Seymour. We're working on a story about your brother. You talked to my colleague earlier, Dick Whitfield?"

She nodded, took my hand limply, then dropped it, glancing at her boss with a worried expression.

I looked back at Garrett Poore. "Can I talk to Miss Ortiz for a few minutes? It won't be long," I said quickly.

He narrowed his eyes at me, studying my face. "Okay," he finally said. "You know, Roberto is a good worker. I don't know what happened to make him do what he did."

I made a note to give that quote to Dick, in case the Boy Wonder hadn't gotten out here yet.

"I'm sorry, I didn't get your first name," I said as I led Roberto's sister out into the hall, out of the noise.

"Rosario."

"I know Dick talked to you about Roberto, but I just want to follow up." I was so full of shit, but she didn't know that. "Has he been acting strangely lately? Any sort of clue that he would do something like this?"

"He started hanging around Hector too much," she said, her voice so low I had to move closer to hear her.

"Who's Hector?" But as I said it, I remembered. Marisol had said her brother's name was Hector. How many Hectors could there be?

Something crossed her face, but I couldn't tell if it was fear or annoyance that I wouldn't know the answer. "Hector helped us when we first came here, got us a place to stay. He helps everyone who comes."

"Comes from where?" I prompted.

She shrugged. "Traxcala."

"Where's that?"

Now she did look annoyed, but I didn't care. I just wanted an answer.

"Mexico."

The lightbulb went off in my head. I knew that most of the Mexican immigrants were coming from this state in central Mexico, as well as Puebla, a neighboring state. They tended to go places where they had a support system, and obviously this Hector was the Ortizes'.

"You don't look like you like Hector much," I said flatly.

Rosario shook her head. "He asks for too much money."

"For what?"

"He say expenses, but I know it all goes to Lucille."

This was getting complicated. "Who's Lucille?"

Rosario's eyes widened, and I could tell she thought she'd said too much. Which set off my alarm bells.

"She nobody. Don't worry about it." Rosario tried to step past me, back into the mailroom, but I put my hand on her upper arm, stopping her.

"I won't tell anyone. Really. I won't put it in the paper. I just want to know how all this works, you know, with you coming here. How did you get here? How did you get out of Mexico?"

But she shook her head violently and threw my hand off, scurrying back into her safety zone. I stared after her a few seconds, wondering about Hector and Lucille and what they were up to. I wondered if it had anything to do with Rodriguez, but couldn't see a clear connection except that Roberto Ortiz had shot at cops on a city street for no apparent reason and now lay in a coma.

Garrett Poore was giving me a dirty look. I shot him one back as I left.

Dick was at his desk when I wandered into the newsroom.

"Where've you been?" he asked.

Since I hadn't gotten anything from Rosario, I just shook my head. "Bathroom. I'm allowed to go, right?" I asked snidely.

Without any warning, he gave me the finger. I stared at him as he quickly pulled his hand back down to his keyboard, a red band of flush crawling up his face. I chuckled. "Jesus, Dick, if you're going to give someone the finger, you should just do it and not get embarrassed afterward."

He really needed to get more of a backbone and realize that I wasn't pissed but happy that he was finally standing up for himself. But I shouldn't have to spell it out for him like that. He still had a long fucking way to go.

Chapter 13

I was starving by the time I climbed the stairs to my apartment an hour and a half later, unlocking my door and letting myself inside.

I opened the fridge and stared at its contents: three sticks of butter, half a container of orange juice, some leftover Chinese food — but I couldn't remember just when I'd had the Chinese, so it was probably a science experiment by now. Opening the cardboard top, an unpleasant odor hit my nose, confirming my suspicions.

I had to go get something to eat. I grabbed my bag off the floor where I'd dropped it and made my way back down the stairs, trying to figure out if I wanted to go across town for Indian or just down the block for a pizza. I was so busy running the options through my head that I didn't see him until he stepped out of the shadows just as I reached my car.

I dropped my bag, a notebook skidding across the sidewalk. He leaned over and picked it up, handing it to me. "Did I startle you?" he asked, without a trace of a smile.

I took the notebook. "Shit, Tom, what are you doing here?"

He cocked his head at me. "Why are you going to Sam O'Neill about Rodriguez? Why didn't you just talk to me?"

I was going to come back with a smartass retort, but his expression made me pause. Something was up here, and I had to find out what it was without alienating him.

I shrugged. "Thought I could get something official."

Tom shook his head. "Annie, everyone's on edge. You're not going to get shit."

"Right, tell me something I don't know." I couldn't keep the belligerence out of my voice.

He sighed. "You have to tell me what Lin Rodriguez told you. Sam's all hot and bothered about it."

"He told me I couldn't talk to you anymore."

"He doesn't know I'm here." Tom's eyes held mine. "You have to tell me what you know. It could be important."

"He didn't think so."

Tom didn't say anything, indicating that

he had a different opinion.

I nodded. "Okay. But it wasn't Lin, it was her sister Mei. She said there had been some phone calls. Sam slipped up and said it was an old girlfriend, but he downplayed it." I paused. "What about you? Do you think this old girlfriend could've had something to do with this?" My anonymous caller had said he knew more than he was saying. I wanted to see what he would tell me.

"We have to look at everything. I'm not sure —" He was cut off by my stomach. Dammit. He chuckled. "Hungry?"

"Shut up."

"Want to get something to eat?"

"You're not supposed to be talking to me."

"A pie at Sally's?"

I thought about the best pizza in the city — anywhere, actually. But it was a Saturday and just after six p.m., and there was bound to be a line a mile long waiting to get in.

"We won't get in," I argued, but only halfheartedly.

Tom grinned and pulled his jacket back to show off his gold badge. "Want a bet?"

My stomach growled again. "What the fuck, sure," I said. If anything could get us past the crowd, it was that badge. Flo, the owner, had a soft spot for cops.

We started walking. "So what's your

theory about this? Between you and me," I said.

"Off the record?" He smiled at me, surprised.

I needed something, and I'd try to get whatever he said confirmed by someone else later. "Yeah," I promised. And he knew I wasn't shitting him; I would honor the deal because I'd honored it before and that's why he talked to me, even now.

"Rodriguez's father was Puerto Rican, so his family was legal. The mayor wanted him to crack down on all those illegals in Fair Haven, wants us to start checking the day workers for green cards. He wants to come down hard. You know, it's an election year."

I nodded. I'd seen the day workers hanging out in their spot on State Street early in the morning, waiting to get picked up by the contractors and landscapers who hired them for cash for a day. I was torn about the situation; hell, they were illegal, but they were being exploited, too, since the people who hired them didn't have to pay them the going wage, and who would do the shit work for next to nothing if they were gone?

"I got the impression Tony wanted to leave it to the feds, but the mayor wouldn't take no for an answer," Tom said.

We'd gotten to Sally's and the line was

only about twenty people deep, but Tom pushed his way through the door, ahead of everyone. Flo greeted us with a big grin and led us to a table that had just been vacated. The people at the front of the line scowled as we cut ahead, but they knew better than to make a fuss. Flo would never let them back in again if they did.

We slid into the booth and immediately ordered a large white clam pie and two beers.

"So do you think the mayor's request about the day workers has something to do with Rodriguez's death?" I asked softly, not wanting anyone to overhear us, but not too worried since the people at the other tables were more concerned with their own conversations and pizzas.

Tom let out a deep breath and leaned back. "I'm not sure. We're looking at everything. That kid in the hospital? We think he's illegal." He paused. "You know he works at the *Herald?*"

I nodded, not wanting to tell him my own suspicions about Roberto Ortiz. "If he was the one who shot Rodriguez, why come back later and try to shoot you?" I asked instead.

"Good question." And the way he stopped talking, I guessed he wasn't going to even attempt to speculate.

We were quiet for a few seconds. I was trying to figure out how I was going to get back to Rodriguez's old girlfriend when Tom surprised me.

"So were you ever going to tell me that you and Vinny broke up?"

I felt myself blush. "How did you find out?"

"Shit, Annie, I've known since Christmas."

And from the look on his face, I could tell that he'd been waiting that long.

"Aren't you seeing someone now?" I asked, although I didn't know if he was.

He shook his head and smiled. "You're a tough act to follow."

I wasn't quite sure about that, but before I could answer, the pizza showed up. Even though it was steaming hot, I pulled a slice off the cookie sheet and shoved it in my mouth, immediately regretting it. The roof of my mouth shriveled into a burned mess and I reached for my bottle, chugging the beer like I hadn't done since college. When I finally looked up at Tom through teary eyes, he was laughing.

"Annie, I didn't think I'd have that effect on you."

How could I tell him that I was still waiting for Vinny? Especially since he was looking so damn good, his blue eyes twinkling, his biceps bulging as he shrugged out of his jacket. He took it off right then because he knew it would get to me. Asshole. But a fine-looking asshole.

It had been four months since I'd had my eggs poached, four long months. I thought about Vinny and our kiss that afternoon. After the drought, it looked like a fucking flood was on the way.

As I pondered this, my cell phone interrupted. I pulled it out of my bag, more than aware of Tom's eyes on me as he continued to devour the pizza. Me, well, it wasn't pizza I was hungry for now.

"Hello?" I asked as I flipped the phone open.

"Annie? Where the hell are you?"

It was Marty. "I'm at Sally's having a pie." I stared at the portrait of Frank Sinatra on the wall, reminding me of Vinny and throwing me back into turmoil.

But I didn't have much time to think, since Marty's next words shook everything out of place.

"Get a to-go box. They just took Lin Rodriguez to the hospital."

Chapter 14

I followed Tom to Yale–New Haven Hospital, but we agreed that we'd make it look like we hadn't seen each other just a few minutes before, that Tom hadn't kissed me in front of my brownstone as I got into my car, and that he hadn't said he was sorry our evening had to end this way.

He didn't see me glance reflexively over at Vinny's building afterward, hoping he hadn't seen it. But the Explorer was nowhere to be seen.

Not wanting to deal with trying to find parking near the hospital — it was even worse over here than on the other side of the 34 connector — I parked in the Air Rights Garage and walked through the pedestrian tunnel that looks remarkably like a hamster tube. I was going to walk around to the emergency room entrance, but something stopped me.

Dick Whitfield hovered on the sidewalk at

Cedar Street, like he was waiting for me. He frowned when he saw me. "Where did you come from?"

"Marty called me. He knew I'd been over to see her earlier. What happened?"

Dick put his finger to his lips conspiratorially. "My source says she took an overdose."

I took a deep breath. "Fuck."

Dick nodded. "Yeah."

"Her sister find her?" I asked.

Dick looked surprised.

"Dick, I'm not completely in the dark, you know," I said harshly. "I met her sister this afternoon."

But he wasn't paying attention. His eyes moved behind me, and I turned to see Cindy Purcell about twenty feet away, a cameraman setting up his shot next to her. She was wearing a bright blue business suit with just a peek of lacy camisole above her breasts. Jesus, Dick was practically drooling.

"Earth to Dick," I said sternly, shaking him out of his stupor. "You have to stay focused."

It was a lost cause, especially since Cindy had spotted us. She ignored the camera guy and came over to us.

She licked her lips as she smiled at Dick. "Hi there," she drawled.

I was going to vomit if I stood here much

longer, and the camera guy was shaking his head in disgust. I grabbed Dick's sleeve and started pulling him away.

"Gee, Cindy, nice to see you, but Dick and I have some work to do," I said.

Dick shook off my hand but followed me anyway.

"I hope you're not telling her shit," I hissed when we were out of earshot.

He pouted. "Of course not, Annie. What sort of journalist do you think I am?"

Well, that was the million-dollar question now, wasn't it? Since I didn't quite know how to answer it, I ignored it. "Let's just say that she knows what she's got and she's not afraid to use it. She could get you in, say, a compromising position and you wouldn't have a fucking clue what you were saying."

I still wasn't sure what Cindy Purcell saw in Dick Whitfield, but maybe he was good in bed. Oh, Christ, I really was going to vomit now.

He laughed. "Okay, I get it, don't get pissed. I haven't told her anything."

Not yet, maybe. I'd seen the look in her eyes, and no doubt she knew about his hospital source.

"Let's see what we can get and go back to the paper and wrap this up," I said. "It's been a long day."

I wasn't really that callous about Lin Rodriguez's suicide attempt, but fatigue had hit me and it was all I could do to keep my eyes open. Dick and I split up — he purportedly to find his source for an update, while I went to the emergency room and talked to the cops.

Half an hour later, it was no dice. Dick had come around to the ER only to find that neither of us had anything except that she'd OD'd. Didn't even know on what.

We went outside into the crisp night air.

"I'm in the garage," I said. "Where are you?"

Dick pointed down the street. "Over there. Listen, Annie, why don't you go home and get some sleep? You look beat. I can write this up."

I didn't want him to do it. But I was exhausted. I pulled out my cell phone and dialed Marty.

"Hey, Marty, I'm over at the hospital."

"Whatchagot?" he asked.

"Not much. Could probably just top off the story I did earlier." I quickly told him everything we had, and I could hear him typing as I dictated a new lead paragraph: "Lin Rodriguez, widow of Police Chief Tony Rodriguez, was hospitalized Saturday night after an apparent overdose, police sources said."

"Then you can go into my interview with her," I instructed Marty.

"This is good. Thanks. Dick still there?"

I glanced at the Boy Wonder. "Yeah."

"Tell him to go home. You go home, too. If you want, you can make some calls tomorrow, but unless you get anything new, don't bother coming in. You've put in too many hours this week." Marty paused. "Dick, too. Tell him the same thing. And I'll see you Monday."

I closed my phone and stared at it a second. The one thing Charlie Simmons had done was to mandate that no one could put in more than 37.5 hours each week. The company wouldn't pay overtime. I'd worked more hours than that at times in the past and never asked for overtime, but we'd heard there had been a labor dispute over just this very issue at one of the chain's other papers that prompted this new rule. One of the problems was that it meant stories got left hanging for too long and the papers in Bridgeport and Hartford ended up beating us in our own backyard.

I told Dick what Marty had said, and when he started to protest, I shook my head.

"I don't want to hear it. Marty doesn't want to hear it. Just go home and wait for Little Miss TV Reporter to finish up."

I didn't even wait to hear his whining.

I woke up to rain slamming against the window. April showers and all that shit. It was dark enough so that when I looked at the clock and saw it was nine a.m., I was surprised. I had fallen asleep almost immediately when I went to bed.

As I showered and then pulled on a pair of jeans and a long-sleeved T-shirt, it dawned on me that I didn't have to work today if I didn't want to. But there were still so many questions left hanging that I knew I'd end up doing something on the story even if Marty didn't want me in the newsroom.

The slim pickings in my refrigerator stared out at me again. The pizza was hours ago, and I wanted eggs for breakfast. I glanced out the window and saw the rain hadn't let up, was maybe coming down even harder now. I regretted not going shopping. Because I was going to have to go out.

My umbrella was in the car, so I had to find something waterproof to wear between here and there. The bright yellow rain slicker was stuck in the back of my closet. It was there for a reason: I could be seen for miles in that thing, and sometimes I just liked being invisible.

Well, today I would be a goddamn beacon, the hell with it. I wrapped the slicker around myself and went down the stairs and out into the rain.

Water dripped into my eyes from the curls that hadn't been secured under the hood. It was also damn chilly, and I cranked the heat on in the car, waiting for it to kick in.

Now, where to go for breakfast? Without even really thinking about it, I headed toward Whitney Avenue, where I knew I could get a bacon, egg, and cheese on a hard roll. No one else made a better breakfast sandwich than George over at Clark's Dairy. He knew just how I liked it, with crispy bacon and a runny egg.

I managed to find a parking space across the street, said screw the umbrella, and made sure I was all covered up in the slicker as I bounded toward the door.

I slid into a plastic booth, but before I could order George spotted me. "Your usual?"

I didn't come here that often, but George and I had struck up a sort of peripheral friendship and he always remembered what I liked.

"Yeah," I said as he poured me a cup of coffee.

I was leafing through a copy of the *Herald* that had been left on the table when I heard the door open and turned to see Vinny come in. His office on Trumbull was just a block up, so I wasn't really surprised to see him, even though it was Sunday, but I *was* surprised to see Rocco walk in behind him. I slumped down in my seat, uncertain whether to advertise my presence. I wanted to see both of them, but for very different reasons.

Before I could make a decision on what to do, however, George made it for me.

"Here's your breakfast, Annie," he announced in a booming voice, causing every head in the place to swivel in my direction.

I mumbled a "thanks" just as Vinny and Rocco slid into the booth across from me, shaking out their own slickers. Vinny eyed my plate as George hovered.

"I'll have the same," he said, and Rocco nodded. "Me, too," he said.

George grinned knowingly, like there was some sort of weird ménage à trois going on with egg sandwiches, and moved back toward the grill. I scowled at my new breakfast companions.

"Who said you could sit there?" I said,

trying to sound pissed off, but Vinny was smiling at me with a twinkle in his eye. It reminded me that I'd kissed two men yesterday, and I felt like a heel for leading Tom on the way I had. I forced myself to concentrate on my sandwich, but it felt like I was chewing sawdust and my stomach churned. I wasn't hungry anymore, but if I stopped eating it would seem too unnatural, so I took a quick drink of coffee.

"Glad we ran into you," Rocco said in a conspiratorial whisper. "We've got something for you."

Vinny scowled at him, but I couldn't tell whether Rocco was telling secrets out of school or Vinny was just pissed that Rocco was telling me first. I hadn't seen the two of them together before, so I wasn't familiar with their sibling dynamics.

"The police chief didn't have a lot of friends in the department," Rocco continued.

I shrugged. "None of the guys ever like the chief. That's a given."

"No, really, Annie. I've got some friends on the force and they said the chief was into something with the feds, but they didn't know what."

I took another bite of my sandwich casually, like I wasn't curious. After I swallowed,

I took another sip of coffee and asked, "The feds? Who exactly?"

Rocco shook his head and leaned forward. "I don't know. That's all anyone would say, except that the chief had a meeting with someone from Homeland Security a few weeks ago."

I chuckled. "Rocco, he was beefing up security down at the harbor. He told me that in my interview last week. Of course he'd have a meeting like that."

Rocco's face fell like a deflated balloon. I'd stuck a pin in it, all right.

"I told you it wasn't a big deal," Vinny scolded, speaking for the first time.

George appeared out of nowhere and put plates down in front of Rocco and Vinny. He gave me a sidelong glance, winked, and went back to the kitchen. I'd have to stay out of here for a while; I didn't want to face his inevitable questions. Vinny and I had come here a few times for breakfast during our three-week affair. George had a long memory.

"No, no," Rocco insisted after taking a bite out of his sandwich. "It was more than that, I know."

Vinny and I exchanged a look that told me we were both on the same page on this one. Rocco was looking for a plot for his book.

"You're going to have to make shit up," I said. "There's no story there." I paused. "Not that it wouldn't make for a good crime novel. It really would. Sort of like Tom Clancy, maybe."

I wanted to ask him about Marisol Gomez; he hadn't indicated whether he'd gotten my e-mail, so he probably hadn't. But I couldn't say anything with Vinny here, since Vinny had put his own pin in my idea that there was something going on with Rocco and Marisol.

"So who exactly do you know at the police department?" I asked. "Why would anyone tell you anything?"

Rocco chuckled. "Annie, I've seen parts of the police station that you've never seen. As a novelist, I have a lot more access than reporters do."

What the fuck was that all about? I made a mental note to talk to Tom about it.

We finished our sandwiches in silence. I stole a few glances at Vinny and caught him looking at me more than once.

George had left the check on the table, but when I reached for it, Vinny snatched it up quickly. "I've got it," he said, pulling some bills out of his wallet. Rocco didn't even argue; I thought that was pretty piss-poor, since obviously Rocco was the rich and famous one here.

We found ourselves on the sidewalk, huddled under the overhang, trying not to get too wet and awkwardly looking at each other. I pointed across the street. "My car's over there," I said.

"I'm going to my office," Vinny said. He looked at his brother. "Coming, bro?"

Rocco shook his head. "I'll see you later."

Vinny looked from Rocco to me and back to Rocco. He nodded. "Okay, sure." He took a step toward me, cupped my cheek in his hand, and gave me a quick kiss on the lips. For a second I felt his tongue, but then it was gone, and he was gone, walking away from me.

I took a deep breath and noticed Rocco was staring. "Are you guys back together?" he asked. "Why am I the last to know this?"

I shrugged. "Shit, Rocco, beats me, I don't think so, we haven't even talked about it." My run-on sentence was about all I could spit out, so I started toward my car, Rocco on my heels.

"Did you get my e-mail?" I asked as we stood next to the Honda.

Rocco nodded. "Yeah. I was going to call you later."

"So what's up with you and Marisol?" I looked at him, ignoring the rain. "She said she told you she saw someone dumping a body into the river."

His expression changed slightly, but I couldn't read it. "What did she tell you exactly?"

"She said you gave her a ride home and told her to call the cops. Which she didn't." I paused. "What's going on, Rocco? Did you tell Vinny?"

Rocco bit his lip, his eyes narrowing as he studied my face. I don't know what he was looking for, but finally he said, "No, and I don't want you to say anything, okay?"

That didn't seem like a promise that would be too hard to keep so I nodded. "Sure. But did you call the cops? To tell them what she saw?"

He shook his head. "No."

"You know, you should have —" I started, but he interrupted me.

"It's complicated," he said, stepping around the car and onto the sidewalk as I unlocked the door. "I'll see you later," he added, turning and jogging down the block, making a quick escape.

Chapter 15

There was some weird shit going on with Rocco and Marisol, and I wanted to know what it was. With all the stuff about the police chief and his wife, I had pushed that dead Hispanic man to the back of my mind, but now he was forcing his way to the front. I wondered again about the bee stings, but knew the medical examiner's office wasn't going to have anything for me until tomorrow, at least.

But the bee reminded me of Lin Rodriguez's project. I wondered what she might be involved in. Her sister said she'd been secretive. Why? What could be so secret about bee research? Maybe I could find someone to tell me.

That meant I had to infiltrate the Yale community in some way. The public relations guy hated the press; he never told us shit.

I thought about our science reporter, a

quiet guy who wrote myriad stories about the weather, but in a very clever way. He had lots of sources in the science world, especially at the local universities. Maybe he knew something about this. But to get in touch with him, I'd have to go to the paper and get his phone number.

The newsroom was dark at this time of the morning; I actually had to turn the lights on. I could hear the rain crashing into the roof, and I just hoped that this storm's leak would be somewhere other than over my desk.

As I dialed the number, I spotted a dark spot on the ceiling tile over Marty's desk. Not good.

"Hello?" The voice on the other end of the line startled me even though I'd been expecting it. But the leak had distracted me.

Now I'd never really talked to David Welden before; we traveled in very different circles. So I had to identify myself twice before he put two and two together.

"What do you want?" he asked. "You know, it's Sunday morning."

No shit, Sherlock. But I forced myself to stay pleasant. "Quick question, Dave —"

"David."

"What?"

"My name is David."

"Okay, sure, fine. Anyway, you heard about Lin Rodriguez?"

"Just saw it now, in the paper. Too bad."

"Did you know about this bee project she's working on?"

I didn't miss the second of hesitation. "Did that have anything to do with this?" he asked.

"Do you know about it?"

"I can't talk about it."

"What?"

"I can't talk about it. Sorry."

"That's bullshit, Dave, David, whatever. We're colleagues."

"You don't even know my name," he said flatly.

Okay, he had a point there. But it wasn't going to deter me. "Touché. But it might have something to do with her suicide attempt." I had no clue whether it did or not, but that got David's attention.

"They're not ready to announce it yet. I promised to sit on it until next week."

"Announce what?"

"I really can't say." His monotone was pissing me off. I hated talking to people on the phone; I couldn't see his expressions.

"A hint?" I was this close to begging, since he did know something.

"You know, Annie, that if I tell you and

you let it out of the bag early, they'll make me write it now. And I promised I wouldn't. It's not a big deal, really. It's not breaking news or anything."

I thought fast. "Okay, David, how's this? I won't tell Marty or Charlie, but I'll keep it to myself. I really don't need it for a story, just background."

"So you really don't think it had to do with her suicide attempt? I mean, I don't see how it could've, really. She was doing something amazing, something that will get her national attention if it works. And I want to be the first one to write about it."

"I promise I'll keep a lid on it, David. Really."

More hesitation, then, "Okay. But you better not be screwing with me."

"I'm not." And I wasn't. What the hell could it have to do with anything? I was just curious.

But David's next words hit me in the gut like a brick.

"She's working with Homeland Security on training bees to sniff out bombs at the harbor."

CHAPTER 16

Despite David Welden's protestations, this was big fucking news. Bees sniffing out bombs? Can't get much better than that. But I'd promised I wouldn't step on his toes, so I couldn't say anything. I had to keep reminding myself that this was his story, not mine.

But the more I thought about it, the more I wondered if his story hadn't intersected with mine at some point, especially since Rocco's comment this morning about Tony Rodriguez working with Homeland Security on something. It must be his wife's project. What the hell else could it be?

My hands were tied. My only hope was to get someone to tell me about it, but I couldn't even ask about it or David would know I'd broken my promise.

I was between a goddamn rock and a hard place.

"So how do they do it?" I asked David.

"How can they train bees to sniff out bombs?"

A long, drawn-out sigh indicated I was an idiot. "They use sugar water as a reward to condition them," David said. "One bee can train the entire hive to forget about looking for flowers and look for TNT or anthrax instead." He paused. "It's ninety-nine percent reliable, but today they couldn't do it."

"Today? Why not?"

"They can't do it in stormy weather. Or nighttime or in the cold. They're apparently planning to start this up sometime next month, when the weather gets even warmer." He paused. "The University of Montana has been working on bees sniffing out land mines for a few years now. This will take the concept to a new venue."

"But does it really work?" I had my doubts.

"That's what they're trying to find out." Again with the condescending attitude. No wonder I hadn't included David Welden in my circle of few friends.

"Listen, Annie, it's Sunday morning. I have to go. But you won't forget that you won't do anything with this?"

"No, I won't —" The dial tone cut me off.

I hung up, trying to put the pieces together: this new bee information, Marisol seeing a body getting dumped in the water, that alleged same body with the possible bee stings. Maybe the Hispanic guy had stumbled onto the bees. But why would someone throw him in the water?

A muffled ringing interrupted my thoughts. I dug through my bag until I found my cell phone. I didn't recognize the caller's number.

"Hello?"

"Miss Seymour?"

"Yes?"

"This is Marisol Gomez." I heard the tenseness in her voice.

"What's wrong?"

"I need to talk to your friend. Right away."

"Are you in trouble?"

"Do you have his number, so I can call him?"

"No, I don't. But I could probably find him." I paused, then, "Marisol, are you in trouble?" I asked again, but I heard a voice in the background. "Who's that?"

"Hold on, okay?" She obviously covered the phone, but I could still hear her. "I'm on the phone, Hector. I'll be off in a minute."

Hector?

"Miss Seymour, tell your friend I'll meet

him at noon at People's Laundromat." With that, she disconnected the call.

I stared at my phone for a few seconds before putting it back in my bag. How the hell was I going to find Rocco to give him the message? I still didn't have his number and didn't know where he lived.

I was a little leery of Marisol; she was a little too squirrelly, but she did sound stressed about something, and I might as well try to find Rocco to give him her message. Maybe I could even tag along.

But I was faced with a real dilemma. The only way to find Rocco was through Vinny. Which meant I was going to have to call him to ask him about Rocco. Somehow, I knew that might not go over well. But did I have a choice?

Vinny had said he was going to his office after breakfast. Maybe he was still there. I didn't want to hang around the paper any longer. It was creepy here alone, long dark shadows in the corners, the rain echoing through the enormous room. Only the bosses had real offices with doors. The rest of us were all out in the open, like goddamn sitting ducks.

I threw on my yellow rain slicker, grabbed my bag, and took off.

■ ■ ■ ■

Vinny's Explorer was parked in the lot behind the brownstone on Trumbull Street. I eased into a spot in front of the building. It would be closer to the entrance, and I wouldn't get as wet. I pulled the hood over my head and made a mad dash toward the door.

I shook the water off my slicker as I pushed his buzzer.

A sliver of light dashed into the hallway as he opened the door. He grinned when he recognized me and let me in, leading me back into his office.

"Twice in one day?" he said, closing the door after me. "To what do I owe this pleasure?"

He walked around his desk and dropped into his chair. I pulled off my slicker and stuck it on the coat rack next to the door before sitting on the couch across from him. His eyes followed my every move; I was feeling very self-conscious, especially since I was here for his brother and not him.

Might as well get it over with.

"I need to find Rocco," I said flatly.

Vinny's eyebrows moved into a frown. "Why?"

I shrugged. "Just need to." I'd already told him Rocco knew Marisol. And Rocco didn't want me to say anything at all.

He was staring me down. I was usually pretty good at staring contests, but with Vinny it was harder. Because as his eyes locked with mine, I started feeling all warm all over, and he knew it. A smile started to play at the corners of his mouth. "You don't expect me to just hand over my brother's phone number to my ex-girlfriend now, do you?"

That was exactly what I expected, but the word "ex-girlfriend" threw me. If he felt that way, why did he kiss me yesterday?

It was my turn to frown. "Ex—" I started, but he interrupted me.

"You should've told me you were back with Tom."

Oh, Christ. He must have seen me and Tom together last night. If so, then why did he kiss me this morning after breakfast? Was it some sort of sick test? Why did my life have to be so goddamn complicated?

I shook my head. "We're not back together. Really. But I need to talk to Rocco. It's important. He has to meet someone at noon. I got a message." I had to get him off the subject of Tom, and this seemed to be the only way.

"Who does he have to meet?" The playfulness was gone; his face was drawn, serious.

"Marisol. She called me, wanted me to tell him to meet her at noon at People's Laundromat."

Vinny nodded slowly. "Okay. I'll make sure he gets the message." He stood up. "Is that all?"

Jesus, he could turn it on and off so fucking fast. I stood up and faced him. "Yeah, guess so."

He didn't move away from his desk, and I put my slicker back on. My hand was on the doorknob and I was about to walk out, but I turned to look at him. "Listen, Vinny, Tom and I are not back together. It's the story about Rodriguez, really. I'm, well, I'm sorry about what happened with us, the way I acted." He still hadn't moved, and I took a deep breath. "I wish I could take it all back and start over."

I didn't even wait for a response. If I stood there one more second I was going to start crying, and he sure as hell didn't need to see that. I didn't want to turn into some sniffling, weak woman trying to get her man back. What the hell was wrong with me, anyway? I stumbled out to my Accord, wondering if I was PMSing. It would explain a lot.

As I rummaged in my bag for my keys, I knew I wanted to be a fly on the wall for Rocco's meeting with Marisol. I wanted to know what was going on. I also knew that I couldn't just show up at the Laundromat.

Pondering my next move, I saw Vinny walking toward his Explorer. From past experience, I knew I couldn't follow him without him knowing I was there. I wasn't trained in covert operations. But every part of me itched to know where he was going.

He waved as he passed me, stopping at the light at Whitney. He was taunting me, daring me to follow him.

Fuck it. I started the car and pulled up behind him.

I lost him somewhere around the Green. He'd managed to get through a yellow light before it turned red, and I was stuck watching him move down Temple Street, then turn left, out of sight. By the time the light changed, he was gone. No sign of him anywhere.

I turned onto Chapel, heading for Ninth Square. I was pretty sure that's where Rocco lived, although Vinny could've easily just called him about the meeting with Marisol. And when I got there, I went in circles, not having a clue where to start and not seeing either Rocco's BMW or Vinny's Explorer. This was ridiculous.

I pulled over to the side of the road next to a fire hydrant. There were no other spots available, and I figured if I was sitting in the car, no one could give me a ticket.

As the rain slapped my windshield, I thought about Marisol and Rocco and the body that washed up in the harbor. And the longer I sat there, the more a crazy idea began to germinate. I glanced at my watch. It was only 11:15; I had forty-five minutes before Marisol and Rocco would be at the Laundromat. Maybe I should check out the park and try to find the place across the river where Marisol saw the guy getting dumped in the water.

I eased back into the road, turned on the wipers, and headed up Chapel Street toward Fair Haven.

By the time I reached the Chapel Street bridge that runs over the Mill River, indicating I was now in Fair Haven, the rain had let up a little. Fair Haven was an interesting neighborhood in that it's on a peninsula, almost completely surrounded by water, making it sort of a city within a city. The Quinnipiac and Mill rivers flank it to the east and the west, respectively, and it opens up to the harbor to the south. A huge swamp is its northern border.

You could say that Fair Haven is pretty waterlogged.

Back in the early days, in the eighteenth and nineteenth centuries, Fair Haven had been known for its oysters, until the beds became depleted and oysters were actually imported to boost the stock. Oystermen moved out into the deeper waters of Long Island Sound, but pollution threatened the shellfish. They were still out there, but in much smaller numbers. I wouldn't eat an oyster out of the Sound, but then again, I wasn't very fond of mucus-like food anyway.

Chapel Street turned into Front Street farther down, where many of the three-story wooden houses still wore their brick facades on the first floors. It was there that the owners had brought in the oysters, shucking them, freezing them, storing them. I'd heard stories about how the river would be saturated with the flat-bottomed boats they called sharpies on the first day of the season, everyone vying for the most oysters from the well-stocked riverbed.

I turned right down James Street and squinted out the window at the Mill River to my right. A swing set sat on a small patch of green that lined the river in Criscuolo Park, but there were no kids out here today.

I spotted a pickup truck and a knot of young men straight ahead on James. They were either dealing drugs or fishing. And while this was my destination, I wasn't inclined to find out which by elbowing my way through them just to check out the other side of the river.

I turned left onto River Street, which was flanked by old, abandoned warehouses. The red brick was faded, the windows boarded up. I wondered if they'd been built with the red sandstone quarried not far from here more than a hundred years ago, like so many buildings around Greater New Haven. It was depressing to see that all these factories had shut down; besides those kids and the pickup, there was no one else around. It felt like a goddamn ghost town.

To my right, I passed a couple of chain-link fences protecting nothing except old pavement with grass growing through its cracks. But spotting one such fence with the gate ajar, I pulled in. Maybe I could check out the other side of the river from here.

I stopped the car, shoved the keys in my pocket, and pulled the slicker close as I opened the door and stepped out.

The wind had picked up now, and I shivered under the slicker even though I had a long-sleeved T-shirt and a fleece pullover on underneath it.

Broken bottles, strewn paper, and cigarette butts crunched under my feet as I made my way along the cracked pavement toward the water. A decrepit warehouse rose a couple of stories high to my right; as I got closer to the water, its appearance deteriorated even further due to graffiti, and the wooden boards covering the windows were falling off in strips.

I reached a concrete block and climbed up on it to get a better view of the water, but I had to keep my hood up to deflect the wind and rain, so my range of vision was poor.

Standing up there like that, swathed in bright yellow plastic, I began to feel slightly uncomfortable, like the whole neighborhood was watching me. I took another look around at the water, a freighter in the distance, and jumped off the block just as something whizzed past me.

I frowned, looking up, wondering if I'd imagined it, but then saw it. A bee.

Chapter 17

It didn't stay in my line of sight for long. It disappeared as quickly as it had appeared. I took a few steps to my left, thinking I might try to follow it, and then admonished myself. How fucking stupid was that?

But still, curiosity was getting the better of me and I took a few more steps toward the back of the warehouse.

The rain was still pattering against my hood, but I could hear it then. Not another bee, but some sort of machinery. I'd thought all these warehouses were abandoned down here. I spotted a window a little farther up, so I made my way across a couple more concrete blocks.

I wasn't tall enough. Even standing on my tiptoes, I needed another few inches. I thought maybe the top of my hood was lined up with the window, and when I heard the shout somewhere off to my right, I knew I wasn't off base on that one.

A Hispanic man built like a tank was coming toward me, his face dark with rage. "What the fuck you doing here?" he yelled.

As he came closer, he looked more familiar to me, until I realized he was the guy who'd picked up Lourdes at my mother's house yesterday. Marisol's brother. Hector. He didn't seem to notice the rain as it soaked through his chamois shirt and jeans, the bandanna on his head dripping into his eyes.

"What the fuck you doing here?" he demanded again, stopping next to me, his hands curled into tight fists. It didn't seem like he'd recognized me, which was a good thing.

I shrugged, trying to look innocent, and thought quickly. "My dog — I had to let him out but he got away. I thought he went this way."

For a moment, he was flustered, glancing around him, then, "No fucking dog here. Get out. Private property."

I nodded. "Okay, okay, but if you see him, he's a small dog" — I couldn't for the life of me remember the breed of any dog at the moment except — "a German shepherd, I mean, a big dog . . ." My voice trailed off and I could see he knew I was bullshitting him. "Sorry," I said, backing up, but I tripped over the concrete and spun down toward the ground. As my back scraped against a block, knocking the wind out of me, my hand plunged down to break my fall and landed on a piece of broken glass. "Fuck!" I exclaimed.

I yanked a hunk of glass out of my hand and grimaced as blood poured out just beneath my thumb. I glanced up, but Hector was gone, and I looked back at my wound.

I needed something to stop the bleeding.

Slowly, I got up and went to my Honda. During the winter, I kept some old towels in the trunk to wipe snow off my car and, since spring cleaning isn't exactly on my "to do" list, they were still there. Dirty, but they'd have to do. I pulled one out and wound it tightly around my hand.

How was I supposed to drive myself out of here with my hand all wrapped up like this? While I could still shift gears with my perfectly fine right hand, I wasn't sure the towel would allow me to steer too well, especially since I hadn't splurged on power steering. I had a hunch that I might need stitches. I didn't exactly feel like knocking on the warehouse door; I wasn't supposed to be here anyway. I doubted Hector would be inclined to help me.

My hand was starting to throb when I saw

an SUV coming down the street toward the T in the road, and I was on the other side, my yellow slicker practically shouting, "Here I am, I'm a white girl in the wrong neighborhood with a bleeding hand. Come and mug me."

My hood had fallen off, and my hair, a mess on a good day, was even worse now that it was wet, flat around my head as the rain rolled off it into the back of my fleece pullover.

I was a fucking crime statistic.

And when the SUV screeched through the gate, my heart quickened. I held my breath and prepared for the worst.

But instead of some gang members, it was Vinny who climbed out of his Explorer.

"Jesus, Annie, what the hell are you doing here?" he asked.

I held up my hand, which was now covered with a very bloodstained towel. "I think I need a doctor."

Fear flooded his eyes, but it didn't distract him. "Is your car locked?"

I nodded as he glanced back at my hand. He shook his head. "I don't want to leave it here; it might not last half an hour. But we don't have a choice."

I looked at my car, hoping I'd see it again. But then I had another thought. I fished around in my pocket for my keys. "My bag," I said. "I need my bag."

Vinny took the keys and got my bag out of the car, locking it again. He held onto the bag as he opened the Explorer's passenger door, and I climbed in. He walked around the back, then got into the driver's seat next to me, dropping my bag on the floor next to me.

As he started the engine, he said. "Tell me what happened. You shouldn't be down here."

"I know that," I snapped, but immediately regretted it when he looked at me like he might be sorry he was helping me. "Sorry," I said, realizing this was the second time today I was apologizing to him.

"You tried to follow me," he said, although not in an accusatory way. He was just making a statement.

"Yeah, but I lost you. I was going to try to meet up with Rocco and Marisol at the Laundromat, but I thought I had time to come down here and see, well, where Marisol saw that body getting tossed in the water."

Vinny frowned. "Why? There was no reason for you to do that. Jesus, Annie, this isn't a great neighborhood."

"Don't you think I know that? Hell, Vinny,

I've only been covering crime in this city for five years. I've been pretty much everywhere by now."

"Okay, okay, fine. Tell me what happened."

So I told him about hearing the machinery and trying to look in the window and the creepy guy and the imaginary dog and then falling onto the broken bottle.

"If nothing else, you probably need a tetanus shot," he said when I finished.

I pulled the towel tighter around my hand. "Is that all you have to say? What do you think's going on over here?"

He stopped at a stop sign and turned to look at me, a small smile teasing me. "Same thing that's been going on here for a while now, Annie. You say you know the city, but you don't know what's going on here?"

Okay, so he didn't have to draw a fucking map for me. The warehouse was probably some sort of illegal sweatshop; Hector was their lookout. But who was the dead guy in the water? Was he one of the workers? And what about those bees?

"What are you doing here?" I asked. It seemed pretty convenient that he showed up when he did.

"I couldn't find Rocco," he said. "So I came over to meet that girl myself. She never showed."

"How do you know what she looks like?" I asked, but he didn't answer as the Explorer started to move again.

"Yale or Saint Raphael?" Vinny asked, ignoring my question.

Mentioning the hospitals brought me back to my hand, which was really throbbing, but I thought it had stopped bleeding.

"Yale," I said without really thinking about it, and Vinny headed there. We missed most of the lights and pulled up in front of the emergency room in record time. Vinny hopped out of the SUV and by the time I opened my door, he was standing next to me, offering a hand to help me out. I could see the worry in his eyes as he looked at all the blood on the towel.

I tried to laugh, but it came out sort of hoarse. "I think it looks worse than it is." But I wasn't sure about that. I didn't want to pull the towel off and see the damage.

He left me at the desk, where I gave them all my insurance information and wondered if I had to sign a contract offering up my first-born child as well. It didn't take him long to park the SUV before he was back, sitting next to me as we waited.

And waited. And waited.

"This was a bad idea," I said after two

hours. Two hours of being very aware of the pain in my hand. Too aware to really concentrate on anything except the fact that I was still sitting there. Every seat was filled with sick and injured people. What the hell did everyone do on weekends to end up here? "Maybe it's not so bad. Maybe I can put one of those, you know, butterfly bandages on it." I started peeling back the fabric, but it was stuck to the wound and as I pulled on it, it started to bleed again. It was only about an inch long, but even I could see it was deep. My head suddenly became rather light; I felt Vinny's hand on the back of my neck, pushing so I found myself with my head between my knees, the floor swirling in front of my eyes.

Somewhere in the distance I heard Vinny's voice calling out that I needed help, that I was passing out, and within seconds I was in a wheelchair behind a white curtain, a doctor about twelve years old flashing a light into my eyes.

I shoved it away. "Jesus, it's not my eyes, it's my hand. I cut it," I growled, holding out the bloody mess so he could see it.

He didn't seem to care that it hurt like a son of a bitch when he probed it. "Stitches," he said. "You need stitches."

Now I'd gotten through almost forty years

without a fucking stitch anywhere. And here I was, in a bright yellow beacon of a rain slicker in a wheelchair with Doogie Howser preparing to stick a needle and thread into my hand. What was wrong with this picture?

Oh, yeah, Vinny wasn't here. "Where's my friend?" I asked as a nurse washed my wound, searching it for any stray shards before they sewed me up.

"He can't come in here," she said grimly, pulling something out of my hand and dropping it in a metal dish.

I must have worked through the pain, or it was the Novocain shot they gave me, because by the time the third stitch went into my hand, I was watching the whole thing like I was on the goddamn Discovery Channel.

The nurse put a big Band-Aid over the wound, trying to shape it a little over the joint. I figured it would last maybe half an hour, if that.

"When was your last tetanus shot?" she asked.

"Beats the hell out of me," I said.

She seemed to take a lot of pleasure in sticking that needle in my arm.

Vinny was waiting for me in the same chair he was in an hour ago. He stood up as I came out, and I could see the relief on his face. He smiled, and I nodded.

"I'm okay," I said as I approached. I held out my hand, twisting it a little so he could see the bandage. "Just call me Frankenstein."

He chuckled and put his arm around me. "Come on. I'll take you home."

I stopped. "What about my car?"

"I'll get Rocco, and we'll go pick it up and bring it around. Don't worry about it."

"I need to pick up a prescription." I waved it in his face. "Percocet. For the pain."

"All you need is a brandy and bed," he said, his eyes lingering on mine as he said "bed."

"Jesus, Vinny, I've been wounded. I'm not sure I'm in the mood." But even as I said it, I knew I'd be able to muster up the energy. It had been a long time, and his five o'clock Don Johnson shadow was looking mighty fine.

He grinned, but didn't say anything. He just leaned over and whispered, "I'm just glad you're okay." And he kissed me, on the sidewalk, and I didn't even give a shit that my hood was down and my hair was getting soaked again.

My phone was ringing as I opened the door to my apartment. I wasn't inclined to answer it, since Vinny already had my slicker off and was working on pulling my fleece over my head. Gently, of course, so it wouldn't hurt my hand.

But when the machine kicked in, Tom's voice made us freeze.

"Annie, if you're there, pick up. Please." His voice was unfamiliar in worry. It threw me off guard, and I picked up the phone, shrugging back into my pullover.

"Yeah, Tom? I just got in." I ignored Vinny's frown.

"Jesus, Annie, what's going on?" The relief was evident.

"What do you mean?"

"We just found your car in a lot on Ferry Street. There's blood everywhere."

I took a deep breath. "I was over there. I fell and cut myself. I've got stitches in my hand, but I'm okay." I didn't tell him it was only three stitches; somehow I thought he might have more sympathy if he thought it was more. "I'm really okay," I repeated.

"No, no, you're not," he insisted.

I hesitated, then, "Why not?"

"Annie, there's a body in the trunk of your car."

CHAPTER 18

The cops were coming to get me. I paced my apartment, Vinny on my heels.

"Do I need a lawyer?" I asked, stopping on the kitchen side of the divider that split my living area in two.

Vinny stopped behind me, and I felt his hands creep around my waist. "Where's your mother?" he asked softly.

I whirled around to face him. "So you *do* think I need a lawyer?"

"Call your mother." He handed me the phone.

"I don't know if she's back yet," I whispered. But a glance at the clock told me she probably was. She'd been due back two hours ago, while I was sitting in the emergency room with my cell phone shut off.

As I listened to her phone ring on the other end, I pondered what Tom had told me, or, rather, what he hadn't told me.

He wouldn't tell me whose body it was in

my car. He wanted to talk to me at the station, officially and all that, and since I didn't have a car, he said he was coming to pick me up. It took me so much by surprise that I'd hung up without telling him I could have Vinny take me over there.

"Hello, Anne." My mother's voice was still full of those tropical breezes and sunshine. I could hear it, really. "The door looks fantastic. I would never have guessed that anyone broke in. You called your father, didn't you?"

"Yeah, Mom, and I really do want to chat about your vacation and all, but, well, I'm in sort of a bind and need you to meet me at the police station."

She didn't say anything for a couple of seconds, then, "Why?"

I knew I didn't have much time before Tom showed up, so I gave it to her in a nutshell: my stupid decision to go over to Fair Haven, the guy at the warehouse, the broken bottle, Vinny rescuing me, and abandoning my car to get to the emergency room for the stitches. Then getting home and Tom's call.

"Do you think you'll have a scar?" she asked.

"Jesus, Mother, do you think I'm worried about that now?"

"All right, I'll meet you over there. But

don't say anything to Tom until I'm there."

"You do know that I didn't put a body in my car, right?" She was acting like I was guilty of something heinous.

She made a sort of twittery sound. "Of course you didn't put a body in your car, Annie, and your detective knows that. But you were right to call me. I'll see you there in half an hour."

Vinny started massaging my shoulders, and my thumb started throbbing. Wouldn't you know the Novocain would wear off now, just when I needed it the most. And we hadn't bothered to stop to pick up the pain medication because we were too hot and bothered for each other. I was seriously fucked. And not in a good way.

The buzzer made me jump. I looked at Vinny, and he went to the door and pressed the button to let Tom up.

It was pretty obvious from the look he gave me that Tom was pissed to see I had company. But I was pissed because he'd brought along a uniform, like I really was some sort of criminal type who would stuff bodies into my car.

"You're not going to handcuff me, are you?" I growled.

He glared back at me, one eye on Vinny. "Why is he here?"

I held up my hand to show him the bandage. "He took me to the emergency room." I was reluctant to tell him the details until we were safely under my mother's watch.

Tom's face softened. "What the hell did you do to yourself?"

"Fell on a broken bottle." I picked my slicker up off the floor where I'd dropped it when we'd come in. "Are we ready?"

Vinny made like he was coming with us, but Tom stopped him by holding up his hand. "Where are you going?"

"I'm her alibi," Vinny said. "I picked her up at the lot, saw her car. Didn't see any blood except what was on her hand. I want to give a statement."

Tom's lips tightened into a grim line. He knew he was going to have to take Vinny's statement, too, since he was there. And he didn't like that. But he just shrugged, nodded, put his hand on the small of my back, and led me down the stairs. I heard Vinny pull the door shut behind us.

My mother had gotten there before we did and was waiting for us. She handed me a Dunkin' Donuts latte. I took it, sort of wishing that she'd give me a hug or something, but she was all business. She'd dressed for the occasion — I didn't think she'd worn the gray blazer and skirt on the plane — and probably didn't want to get rumpled. I was lucky to get the coffee.

We went up in the elevator, got off, and Tom ushered me, my mother, and Vinny into an interrogation room, and even I began to wonder if I'd put a body in my car to deserve this sort of treatment.

The dirty, rain-soaked windows overlooked the train station. The table, just a step up from a folding table, was wobbly, as was the chair I sat in.

Tom turned on a tape recorder and had a pad and pen in front of him. Just as he opened his mouth to say something, the door opened and Sam O'Neill came in, apologizing for being late.

Hell, I'd be late for this party if I could.

"Annie" — Tom looked me straight in the eye — "you'd better start at the beginning. Tell us why your car was there, what happened today."

I glanced at my mother, who closed her eyes briefly and then nodded serenely. Maybe she was still drunk from the cocktails on the plane.

I thought for a second and started from Vinny's office. Tom didn't care what I'd had for breakfast or that I'd spent time alone in the newsroom.

When I was done, I leaned back in my chair and took a sip of the latte. It was still fairly warm, but I could barely taste it.

"Well, you see, Detective, this has all been a terrible mistake." My mother's voice was stern; I recognized it as her official lawyer voice. And then it hit me: My mother had never met Tom before. She knew about him, of course, but she'd never met him.

It was a good thing we broke up. We never would've survived this.

Sam leaned over and whispered something in Tom's ear, and they both stood up. "Excuse us for a moment," Tom said, and they went out into the hall. We could see them through the little window high up in the door. Sam was talking, Tom was nodding, but we couldn't hear them. We tried.

"They have to let you go," Vinny said, but I could tell my mother wasn't convinced. She hadn't looked at me since I'd finished talking.

I started getting worried.

But then Tom and Sam were back, sitting down, looking like they were getting comfortable. Shit.

"Annie, you said you thought you knew who the guy was outside the warehouse." Tom leaned toward me, his elbows on the table between us.

I nodded. I told them about seeing the guy outside my mother's house in the Honda.

"You're sure it was the same guy?" Sam asked.

"Yeah. Looked sort of like Marlon Brando."

Vinny tried to muffle a chuckle, and Tom looked at him like he had forgotten he was there. "Do you know this guy, Vinny?"

Vinny shrugged. "I didn't see him. When I got to the lot, Annie was alone."

"It wasn't him, was it?" I asked.

Sam frowned. "Who?"

"The body in my car. Was it that guy?"

Sam and Tom exchanged a look, then Tom shook his head. "No, Annie."

"Then who was it?"

Another look between Sam and Tom, and it started to piss me off.

"Listen, don't you think I have a right to know who it is?"

Tom nodded. "Yeah, I guess you do. But we don't have an ID yet."

"Detective," my mother interrupted, "you must realize by now that Annie has been terribly cooperative through the whole harrowing ordeal. She's been injured today, and I would like to take her home. She obviously does not know how a body ended up in her trunk. She was gone for several hours, during which time someone could've used the car as a coffin without her knowledge. We all know that neighborhood; that is not out of the realm of possibility."

Tom looked at Sam, and for the first time I saw that this had been Sam's idea all along. Tom knew I wasn't capable of killing anyone, much less disposing of a body, but for some reason Sam wanted him to go through this charade.

I remembered my conversation with Sam the day before. He'd warned me off the Rodriguez story and said I shouldn't talk to Tom. Was this his way of trying to keep me quiet even longer?

Christ, I was cynical.

But before I could say anything, Tom was shaking my mother's hand and thanking her for coming in. He even shook Vinny's hand before turning to me, his blue eyes kind as he leaned over and gently squeezed my hand. "Sorry about this," he whispered in my ear, his breath warm.

Sam was scowling, but he didn't say anything as the three of us left.

My mother was driving. This was not a good thing. My mother is the worst driver in the world. She's gotten into more fender benders than I can count on two hands, because she just doesn't pay attention to what's going on in the road.

I was up front, next to her, and Vinny was in the back. He'd agreed to the ride to Wooster Square before I could warn him. I'd rather have walked than accept the ride, but he didn't know.

He did now. My mother skidded to a stop just as the light on State Street turned red, barely missing a pedestrian about to cross the street.

"So, Annie, is there anything else you need to tell me?" she asked in her best "mother" voice. The lawyer was gone, at least for the moment.

"No, Mom, I told Tom everything." Well, I may have left out the part about why I was in the lot in the first place. I had just said I was following Vinny. I had said nothing about Marisol or the body she'd seen. Maybe I should've, but I couldn't make the connection between what happened with me and what happened with them. Well, maybe one thing. Hector was Marisol's brother.

But Hector couldn't be the one she'd seen with the body, because she said she didn't know that guy.

The light turned green, and my mother

stepped on the accelerator. It was a good thing we were strapped in; I felt my butt leave the seat as she flew over the small incline down Water Street, then careened left onto Olive. Thank God we weren't far now. I just wanted to get home alive.

But as she pulled the Mercedes up in front of my brownstone, it dawned on me: I didn't have a car.

How the hell was I going to do my job without a car?

New Haven isn't exactly New York City or Boston or San Francisco. We don't have a subway system that will cart us all over the city. We do have buses, but hell if I knew any schedules, or even where the bus stops were, not to mention the routes. Only people without cars take the bus, and people without cars were poor, or losers.

Like me.

I pulled my phone out of my bag and dialed. When Tom picked up, I said, "Where the fuck's my car?" Now that I was safely home, or just about, I had a lot more confidence.

My mother and Vinny just stared at me, but I shrugged at them as I waited for Tom's answer. Which I knew I wouldn't like.

"Annie, a body was found in the trunk. Your car's evidence in a homicide. You're going to have to find another way to get around." And then he hung up.

I stared at the phone.

"Annie, you can rent a car," my mother was saying.

"With what, my good looks?" Although I always pretended that I didn't have much money, I had more than anyone knew. I lived fairly frugally and socked as much cash away in the bank as I could. You never knew when that rainy day would come.

And, as the rain splashed against my mother's windshield, I realized that day was here.

Chapter 19

My mother said she'd pick up the Percocet prescription for me and go back to my apartment while Vinny took me to the airport to rent a car. She said she wanted to take care of me, but I knew she really wanted to grill me more about my day, and probably what happened at her house the day before. I was no longer in control. And when I got to the airport rental car counter, it was more bad news.

All they had was a Kia Rio. A fucking Kia. But it was an automatic, not like my car with its stick shift and clutch, and even with my stitched-up hand I would be able to manage it.

I slid behind the wheel and looked at all the unfamiliar dials and gauges. I'd spent fourteen years in my Honda Accord. Which made me wonder about all my shit in the car. Were the cops going to confiscate everything? Hell, my police scanner was in the backseat, along with two months of newspapers I hadn't gotten around to clipping yet.

And what about my cassettes? My Rolling Stones cassettes? I glanced at the radio and the CD player in the Kia. No cassettes here.

Vinny was leaning on the open door, watching me. "I can lend you some music," he said, going over to his SUV and reaching in the passenger door. He came back with two CDs.

"Who the hell are the White Stripes?" I asked, flipping to the second one, "And Our Lady Peace? Sounds like a goddamn convent." I am very unhip when it comes to music. I like the classics — the Stones, Springsteen, The Who, Elton John — and I had never heard of either of these bands.

"Give them a chance, Annie. I figured you'd rather have those than Frank."

He was smiling, and his resemblance to Frank Sinatra again caught me off guard.

"Yeah, okay," I said.

Vinny stooped down and gave me a kiss on the cheek. "Maybe we can pick up where we left off earlier," he whispered. "But right now I have to get going."

He backed away, slamming the car door shut, and I watched as he climbed into the Explorer.

I started up the Kia and put in the White Stripes CD. I couldn't drive without music, and radio usually sucked. I pulled out of the lot, favoring my left hand by steering mostly with my right, and headed home, the beat of the music getting the better of me.

As I reached Chapel Street, I realized I should call Marty before going home. I didn't want my mother eavesdropping, so I pulled into an empty parking spot, turned on my cell phone for the first time in hours and punched his number into my phone.

"What the hell's going on?" He knew it was me; he didn't even say hello. "I've been trying to reach you."

"I had to turn the phone off in the emergency room and forgot to turn it back on. This is the first chance I've had to call." I filled him in on my eventful day.

"Kevin Prisley's been over in Fair Haven, but he's back now. He didn't know it was your car. No one said whose car it was. We don't know anything about the body except that whoever it was got shot."

"Kevin? Where's Dick?"

"I gave you two the day off, remember?" And I could tell by his tone he was regretting it. "Did the cops tell you whose body it was in the car?"

"No." I thought about Hector but didn't mention him, because Tom had said it wasn't him. "All I know is, there was a lot of blood." I paused. "When I got over there, I saw a bunch of guys at the end of James Street. Gang shooting, maybe?"

"I'll have Kevin check it out."

My hand was throbbing. "Listen, Marty, I gotta go. I need to take those Percocets. If I can get anything else out of Tom, I'll let you know, but for right now, that's all I've got."

"I can't believe they used your car," Marty said.

"Yeah, me, too," I said.

"If you're not up to it, you don't have to come in tomorrow," he said.

"Let me see how I feel," I said, knowing that I would have a hard time staying away from this story.

I punched END and I was thinking about those Percocets by the time I reached my brownstone. My mother would be easier to take if I was drugged.

I dragged my ass up the stairs and opened my apartment door. I sniffed. Someone was cooking.

My mother was stirring something on the stove.

"What's that?" I asked, pulling off my slicker and hanging it on the coat rack next to the door.

"Soup."

But how?

"You had a can of chicken broth in the back of the cupboard, and I found some noodles and a carrot," she continued. "There are even crackers."

I knew about the crackers and the carrot. But the noodles? When did I buy them?

"Why don't you go wash up?" My mother peered into my face. "You look terrible."

"Jesus, Mom, I fell on a broken bottle and a body was found in my car. Wouldn't you look pretty bad after that?"

She ignored me and turned back to the makeshift soup. I went into the bedroom, took off my jeans, and pulled on my yoga pants. I gingerly peeled off my fleece and T-shirt, throwing them in the laundry basket after the jeans, and stretched into an oversized sweatshirt that announced that what happens in Vegas stays there. Not a bad idea. A thick pair of socks on my feet, and I was finally comfortable. Well, almost. My mother had left the Percocets next to the sink in the bathroom. I popped one and braced myself for a little mother-daughter bonding. Yeah, right.

My mother put a bowl of soup down in front of me on the counter. I perched on a stool and dipped the spoon in the broth, taking a tentative sip. Pretty good. My mother watched as I ate it all, and about five crackers. I was still a little hungry, but the pill was taking effect and I felt myself relaxing. My hand didn't hurt at all now.

"So tell me what happened with the break-in yesterday," she said after tucking a blanket around me on the couch. All I wanted to do was go to sleep, but she hovered over me, and I knew I had to give her at least the short version.

So I did.

When I was finished, she gazed at me from my rocking chair, her hands folded in her lap. "You said you really didn't look at the fax, but how did you know which warehouse to go to?" she asked softly.

I frowned, my eyelids feeling like lead weights. I struggled to stay awake. "What do you mean?"

She didn't say anything, studying my face for a few seconds. "Are you and Vinny back together?"

Her question threw me off in my Percocet-laced fog. "No. I don't think so."

"Your detective didn't seem happy to see him."

"No. He probably wasn't." It was an effort to form the words with my mouth. "Mom, I have to sleep now," I said.

I vaguely remember feeling her lips on my cheek as she kissed me good-bye.

Instead of waking up feeling refreshed, my neck ached from sleeping funny on the couch and my hand was aching. I'd passed out cold and never bothered moving to my bed. The blanket was on the floor, and I shivered under the sweatshirt. The clock on the wall over the stove told me it was eight a.m.

Even though Marty had said I could stay home, what the hell would I do with myself? I'd be thinking about my car, the body, Rodriguez, and the floater all day. Might as well get my ass to the paper.

Speaking of which, it wasn't on the doorstep. I'd been fighting with the circulation people; they were insisting that I hadn't paid, and I kept telling them that I got a free paper because I worked there. Now, apparently, they had decided to punish me by not delivering it.

It wasn't easy taking a shower. I managed to wash myself and my hair with one hand, but it took forever. By the time I was dressed and ready to go, it was almost nine o'clock. I was hungry. I needed food. I took a couple of ibuprofens before going downstairs.

It was still raining, so I was wearing the yellow slicker again. With all my activity during the last twenty-four hours, I might as well just wrap myself in crime scene tape.

I certainly didn't want any questions from George, so Clark's Dairy was out. This was one day I wanted to go somewhere where no one knew my name.

So I went to the Twin Pines Diner in East Haven, on Route 1, your basic diner with good eggs and hash browns. It was perfect, and I was going to be alone.

Or so I thought. Until Rocco DeLucia walked in and sat down across the table from me. He started perusing the menu, ignoring my glare. Finally, when the waitress filled his coffee cup, he looked up at me and grinned.

"Heard you had an exciting day yesterday, Annie."

"Did you follow me here?"

"Oh, don't get pissed. I was coming to see you when I saw you get in that new car and drive away. Figured I'd just catch up with you."

The waitress came back to take our order before I could say something really nasty. I ordered eggs over easy and an English muffin. Rocco ordered a three-egg Western omelet and pancakes.

Pancakes. Why didn't I think of that?

"It's not a new car," I said. "It's a rental."

"Oh, yeah, but you're going to need a new one."

"Why?"

"Don't tell me you'll still drive that Honda after the cops scrape that body out of the trunk."

I hadn't thought of it that way. Granted, the car was fourteen years old and paid off, but I figured I'd get a new one after selling the Accord and at least get some money toward a replacement. Would the cops clean the car enough so I could sell it and never tell the ignorant buyer why?

Maybe the fact that I hadn't seen the body in the trunk made it unfathomable that it was actually there. Maybe that's why I was in such complete denial about this.

I frowned. "So why did you want to see me bad enough you had to follow me?"

Rocco leaned forward. "Got more information for you," he whispered.

"Oh, right, like the Homeland Security thing?" But even as I said it, I thought of David Welden and the bees. Something else to follow up on today.

"Keep your voice down." Rocco glanced

around us at the other tables of people who obviously had their own lives to worry about without paying attention to ours.

I rolled my eyes at him. "Christ, Rocco, does Vinny know you're into conspiracy theories?"

He leaned back. "Speaking of Vinny, what's going on with you two? You back together?"

Rocco and my mother should get together and talk about us. Maybe Tom would want to join them.

"What's this important information you have?" I asked, ignoring his questions.

The waitress interrupted us with our plates. That was fast. I'd have to come here more often.

I took a bite of my eggs, staring at Rocco's pancakes. Shit, he noticed.

"Want some?" And before I could say anything, a pancake the size of a fucking dinner plate was sitting on top of my eggs.

But I wasn't going to complain, since I now had this incredible craving for it. I dug my fork in. "So what's up?" I asked again.

"My police source says there's going to be a raid at that warehouse where your car was found yesterday."

The minute he said it, I remembered my mother's words from the night before.

Something about her fax, and how did I know to go there. I'd been so doped up, I hadn't thought anything of it.

"What sort of raid?" I asked carefully, taking another bite of pancake but watching his face.

"It's a sweatshop."

I tried to remember what was on that fax. Names. Lots of them. Were they the names of illegals working at the warehouse? And if so, how would anyone know my mother had them? And why would my mother be involved?

But then I had another thought. Lourdes. She was at my mother's house when I got there. She might have seen the fax. She might have told Hector about it. He might have gone back to get it, breaking into my mother's house. But why break in if Lourdes had a key?

And why would my mother want Vinny to know when the fax was missing? What did Vinny know about all this? What was he working on for her?

Too many questions and not enough answers. I hated that.

But the biggest question that I wanted an answer to was who the hell was in my car. I watched Rocco eat, picking at my own food now, wondering how I was going to get rid of him. I had to go see Tom. He had to have an ID by now.

I spotted a newspaper on the table next to us, so I reached over and grabbed it. The story about my car and its body had been relegated to the police blotter on page two. It wasn't even big enough for page one. But a story about a crazy house cat attacking its neighbors stared out at me from under the *New Haven Herald* banner on page one. What the fuck was wrong with this picture?

I scanned the blotter story, which was pretty information-free, like Marty had said. And even though I'd told him it was my car, he didn't put that in the story. But somehow, after I'd spoken with Marty, Kevin had finally gotten the name of the person in the trunk.

Rosario Ortiz. The girl from the mailroom. The sister of the guy who'd tried to gun down Tom and Sam O'Neill.

Chapter 20

The more I thought about it, the more I realized no one had actually told me the body was male. I'd just assumed that. And hell, anyone who ever watched *The Odd Couple* knew what that meant. But I'm dating myself.

I put the paper down, and Rocco picked it up, scanning the story. "That's it?" he asked flatly.

I shrugged. "Not much information."

"You wouldn't go on the record?"

I snorted. "With what? I don't know shit."

"But it's your car."

"I don't know shit," I repeated, glancing at my watch. I had to go to work. But I remembered something, something that I had pushed to the back burner while Rocco told me his "information."

"I want to know why you were in Fair Haven that day Marisol saw the body getting dumped."

Rocco picked the check up off the table and studied it, ignoring me.

"Listen, Rocco, it seems pretty convenient that you were there."

He looked up at me as he simultaneously pulled his wallet out of his back pocket.

"I've got something I have to do now. Can we get together later?"

"Why can't you just tell me?"

It looked like he was going to say something when my cell phone rang. I dug it out of my purse. "Yeah?" I asked after seeing Marty's number. "I'm on my way in."

"When you get here, come to Charlie Simmons' office."

"Am I in trouble?" I asked.

"No." But there was something about his tone that made me wonder if I was.

As I put my phone back in my bag, I knew I'd have to wait on interrogating Rocco. He paid the breakfast tab, and I thanked him as we stood between our cars, the shiny white BMW next to the white Kia Rio. They shouldn't even have been in the same parking lot together.

"Later?" I asked.

Rocco shrugged. "Sure, okay," he said, climbing into his car.

I watched him drive away before getting into the Kia. The seat wasn't uncomfortable, but it didn't have my shape to it. I slipped in the White Stripes — I was getting used to it; it wasn't bad — and figured I'd stop by Radio Shack later for a new police scanner. Who knew when I'd get mine back, if ever.

I couldn't park in the lot. I'd forgotten about the paving project that was supposed to last at least a week. A sign advertising employee parking was propped up at the entrance to the visitors' lot, an arrow pointing down the street.

I ignored it and parked in the visitors' lot. Hell, security wouldn't know whose car this was, since it was a rental and they only had my Accord on record.

Marty and Charlie Simmons were waiting for me. The door was closed, but I could see them through the glass. They saw me, too, and Charlie was beckoning me to join them, like it was a fucking party.

I didn't even take off my slicker, but pushed the door open and stood dripping all over the carpet. Charlie sat behind the desk, while Marty was seated in one of the two chairs in front of him. The empty chair was obviously mine, but standing made me feel more in control.

"What's up?" I tried to ask nonchalantly,

looking from Charlie to Marty and back to Charlie.

Charlie leaned back in his chair, his hands behind his head with his elbows sticking out like he had goddamn wings. "Why was a body found in your car in Fair Haven, Annie?"

I snorted. "It's not like I fucking put it there."

Marty made like he was going to say something, but Charlie held up his hand to stop him. "There's no call for that sort of language."

I plopped down in the chair, and as I did, knocked the base of my thumb against its arm. A thousand needles of pain shot through my hand and up my arm, and I felt tears run uncontrollably down my cheeks.

Marty and Dick just stared. Charlie sat back, a look of astonishment on his face.

"I didn't mean anything by that," he tried lamely.

I held up my hand, showing them the bandage. "I hit my hand on the chair," I said. "Yesterday, while Rosario Ortiz was getting stuffed in my trunk, I was in the emergency room getting stitches after falling on a broken bottle."

"So you don't know what happened?" Charlie asked.

I glared at him. He shouldn't even have asked me that. Marty knew what I was thinking. He was perched at the edge of his chair, and I could see the stress in his forehead. I didn't want to make Marty tense, but Charlie was new around here. He didn't know me yet, didn't know that I didn't lie and that I owned up when I fucked up.

"I don't think Annie would kill someone and put her in her trunk," Marty said slowly, as if to a child.

It was not lost on Charlie. He frowned at Marty, his attention now completely off me as he perceived insubordination.

"You know they were illegal," I butted in, owing Marty one for sticking up for me.

That got Charlie's attention. "Who?"

"Rosario Ortiz and her brother. And something's going on down there in that warehouse. A sweatshop, I hear."

Now all eyes were on me, but they weren't angry anymore. I'd piqued their curiosity.

"Where did you hear that?" Charlie asked.

He was always asking things he shouldn't. I shrugged. "Let's just say an anonymous source."

"But we can't rely on that," he said. "We can't have anonymous sources."

Who was this guy? Anonymous sources

were like gold to journalists, and we should be able to nurture them so they'd continue to talk.

Granted, I'd have to find out if Rocco could be believed, but between his information and my mother's questions the night before, I tended to think he wasn't bullshitting me.

"Let's just say it's a reliable source," I said. "I'll make sure I get it confirmed."

Charlie Simmons leaned back in his chair and studied my face for a few seconds. It was a creepy feeling to have his eyes running all over me, and I shivered on reflex.

"I've heard about you," he said then, breaking the silence. "You'd better be careful."

I wondered if he knew his boss was sleeping with my mother. I figured I had pretty good job security as long as I didn't screw up completely.

"What else do you know, Annie?" Marty asked.

I thought a second. "I know that Tony Rodriguez was working on something with Homeland Security down at the port." David Welden would kill me if I spilled the beans about the bees, so I only added, "But I haven't gotten that confirmed yet. I'm working on it." I glanced at my hand. "Well,

I will be working on it."

I was just about to tell them about Rocco's rumor about the raid, but a tap on the door made us all jump. I looked up to see my mother's boyfriend, Bill Bennett, our publisher, pushing the door open. He looked from Charlie to Marty and then finally at me. He tried half a smile but it turned out as more of a grimace. "Am I interrupting anything?"

Charlie shook his head. "Just asking Annie about why a body was found in her car." He said it so matter-of-factly.

And Bill just nodded, like all his reporters ended up with bodies in their cars at some point. "Okay, but can I have a sec?" he asked Charlie.

Marty and I stood up and filed quietly out of the office. Bill closed the door, and we were safe again.

I took a deep breath. "He doesn't really think I had anything to do with that, does he?" I asked Marty.

Now, finally out of the clutches of his new boss, Marty chuckled. "Come on, Annie, that would be going too far, even for you." He paused. "So can you get it confirmed? You know, about the warehouse being a sweatshop?"

I nodded. "Sure," I said, even though I

wasn't exactly sure how. I also wanted to find out about Rosario Ortiz and whether she was moonlighting over there when she wasn't working at the *Herald.* That could explain why her body was found there. Maybe she knew something about her brother and how he'd shot at the cops. Something that could've killed her.

But Marty's voice interrupted me, throwing me for a loop.

"You know you're off the story, right? Just get this confirmed for us; I can get Dick to work on it after that."

I felt like someone had punched me in the stomach. I knew he was right to take me off it, but it still felt damn awful. "What about Rodriguez?"

Marty shook his head. "The kid in your trunk was the sister of the guy who shot at the cops that night. Maybe he didn't kill Rodriguez, but it's too close for comfort for me. We can't have a conflict of interest like that."

I took a deep breath. "So what am I working on?"

Marty glanced at my hand, then shrugged. "Take a couple of sick days, okay? Rest up and chill out. Dick can do the dirty work. Then, if you come back at the end of the week, maybe some of this will be resolved and you can get back to your job."

I looked around the newsroom and saw Dick on the phone at his desk. Maybe I should just quit now.

But then I thought about Rosario — how pretty she'd been, how young. She'd had her whole life ahead of her. Yeah, she may have been here illegally, but she was working, waiting for her green card like so many were. Maybe I wasn't going to be writing the story now, but I had to find out what happened.

Because whoever killed her had made it personal for me. I may have had some issues with that car, but it was mine.

I wanted to talk to Marisol Gomez again. I needed to ask her about Hector. Since he'd been at the warehouse, she probably knew about the sweatshop, too. And while I didn't have her phone number, I knew where she lived, thanks to Rocco.

The rain was still coming down in sheets. April showers, my ass. More like April monsoon. It had only been two days, but I was beginning to hate that yellow slicker. Not to mention the fact that my hair, unruly at best, was looking like a real rat's nest with the humidity.

Marty had had a funny look on his face

when I left; he knew I wasn't going to go home and learn how to knit or anything while I "chilled out." But he also knew that if I found out anything, I'd call him and let him know. So he hadn't said anything.

The Kia's steering was a little loose. I wasn't used to an automatic; I kept trying to press in the clutch. And the White Stripes were getting on my nerves with all that drumming. I slipped out the CD and put in the other one Vinny had lent me. It was okay, but I missed Mick Jagger. Singing in my car calmed me down, and if I ever needed calming, I needed it today. Unfamiliar tunes meant no singing.

I turned off Grand Avenue and onto Blatchley, but slowed down when I saw another car in front of Marisol's house — a city car, I could tell by the license plate. I eased the Kia against the curb a block up and decided I'd wait and see who was making a visit this afternoon.

I didn't have to wait too long, and that was a good thing because this CD was less entertaining than the other. I was going to have to stop at Cutler's later and restock. It wouldn't be a waste, since I was going to have to buy a new car anyway and I might as well get a CD player this time around.

I squinted as I watched the front door

swing open, and a tall figure stepped out on the stoop. But I couldn't see his face; it was obscured by a rain slicker not unlike my own except that it was olive green. He started down the steps, but suddenly a child darted out and scrambled down the stairs.

Marisol rushed out behind the child, caught it on the sidewalk, and picked it up. I'm not good about kids, guessing how old they are, but I figured this one had to be about two or so. Marisol cradled the child close — I couldn't tell if it was a boy or a girl, either, since it was wearing unisex clothes and had short hair — while the figure met her on the walk. Marisol didn't seem to realize it was raining as she reached up to the figure's face.

In a swift move, the hood fell back and, before he kissed her — it was a pretty intense kiss — I recognized him.

It was Sam O'Neill.

CHAPTER 21

A million questions bounced around in my head. What was up with this? Obviously they had a relationship. Was he also the father of the child? And if they were a couple, why didn't she talk to him after she saw the body being tossed in the harbor?

Sam had been at the Yale Rep that night, too, with Rodriguez and his wife. It was a double date, wasn't it? But Marisol hadn't been dressed for a night at the theatre. Maybe he'd been stepping out on her and she was stalking him.

Problem with being a crime reporter is that I see the worst in every situation.

I didn't like all the loose ends. I also didn't want Sam to see me sitting here, spying on him. I scootched down in my seat, started to pull my hood over my head, then thought better of it. With the bright yellow I might as well just put up a billboard announcing my presence.

The kiss lasted a good couple of minutes, then Sam climbed into the car and Marisol dashed up the stairs and into the house with the child firmly attached to her hip. Sam drove away in the opposite direction; I was happy he wasn't going to pass me.

And, in an instant, I made a decision.

I started up the engine and pulled away from the curb and into the street after Sam.

Sure, he might just be going back to police headquarters. But it wouldn't hurt to find out.

And when he turned left, I knew he wasn't going back. Not yet, anyway.

At one point when I'd been following him, Vinny had told me I'd make a lousy private detective, so I tried to be a little more savvy this time around. Sam was a cop, after all. So I made sure I kept at least four car lengths behind him, and at one intersection even let someone get between us.

A few turns, a few stop signs, and a couple of lights later, I saw we were heading toward East Haven via the Tomlinson Bridge. This bridge ran parallel to the Quinnipiac River bridge, but below it. At this hour, there was little traffic, and I worried he was going to notice me. I stayed back even farther until I saw him hang a right, to the port.

I slowed down, since following him would

be even more obvious here. But I was going too slow. An 18-wheeler pulled out between us, and I lost sight of Sam.

I peered out through the windshield wipers and finally spotted him turning right into a restricted-access parking lot next to one of the terminals. The truck in front of me kept going as the Rio was now at a snail's pace going past the lot. I glanced down through the chain-link fence and saw the back of Sam's car disappear around the terminal building.

I wasn't going to find out shit now. I couldn't get past the gate, and if I tried going into the terminal, Sam might see me or find out I was here, and how the hell would I explain that?

There might be a perfectly good explanation as to why Sam was here. But I still couldn't figure out about Sam and Marisol.

As I drove back out toward the main road, I found myself glancing down toward the water between the terminals and the big fuel-storage tanks that dotted the landscape. A large cargo ship was docked at Gateway, probably unloading the fuel it was carrying. Piles of scrap metal rose like jagged hills.

Movement in the corner of my eye made me turn back to the road, and I slammed on my brakes before I hit another 18-

wheeler — a different one this time — coming right at me. He honked, the sound reverberating through the cheap metal that now surrounded me, and I swerved to one side as he passed me.

I was too distracted, and I certainly didn't want to get myself killed.

I watched the road more carefully as I made my way back over the Tomlinson and headed downtown.

I had no idea what I should do first. I didn't want to go back to Marisol's until I could figure out the Sam situation.

I still had to confirm that the warehouse was a sweatshop. That was really the only official assignment I had. But I wanted more information about Rosario Ortiz.

A gunshot wound, according to Kevin Prisley's story. She didn't deserve that. I went over my conversation with her and remembered she'd mentioned Hector and a woman named Lucille. I wondered who Lucille was and if anyone would be willing to talk about her. Rosario hadn't wanted to talk about her.

It dawned on me that maybe someone found out Rosario had talked to me. Granted, she hadn't told me much, but maybe the third party didn't know that.

While it was my job to get information out of people, I didn't like it that sometimes they got into trouble — or worse — for talking to me. I hoped that hadn't been the case this time. I didn't want to feel responsible for her death.

I decided to go back to the *Herald*'s mailroom and see if anyone could shed any light on why someone would want to see Rosario dead.

I didn't take my usual route into the newsroom when I got to the paper — I didn't want Marty to catch wind that I was here — but followed another hallway around to the back of the mailroom. The machines were running, putting the inserts together, and the din filled my ears. I pushed the door open and it got louder. As I watched the workers silently pulling and pushing and creating piles, I wondered how they could stand it. But as I looked closer, many of them wore ear buds with white wires stretching down under their aprons. Probably iPods.

They'd all be deaf before they turned thirty.

Garrett Poore, the supervisor, saw me, frowned, and walked over to me as I stood by the door.

"What do you want this time?" he asked,

leading me back out into the hall where it was quieter.

"I was wondering if I could ask you about Rosario Ortiz," I said.

He shrugged. "Too bad about her," he said, but I couldn't see any sign that he was really sorry she was dead.

"I heard she didn't have her green card yet," I said.

He narrowed his eyes at me, like he was trying to figure out if I had a tape recorder on me.

"I'm just trying to find out stuff about her, like where she was from, where she lived, what her situation was," I said. "This isn't going into the paper."

Garrett took a deep breath. "No, she didn't have her card yet. But she was waiting. She had a sponsor. In fact, her sponsor has helped a couple of the girls here. But they have their green cards now, so when we hired Rosario, we knew it was just a matter of time," he added quickly.

"Was that Lucille?"

He seemed a little surprised that I knew her name, but he recovered quickly. "Yes, that's the name."

"You've never talked to Lucille?"

"No. I've just heard about her. The girls like her, say she's like their mom here."

"Can I talk to them?" I asked. "The girls?"

He glanced back into the mailroom through the window in the door, then looked at me again and shrugged. "Okay, sure, why not?" And he opened the door, letting me walk through first.

Eyes followed us as we walked across the room, stopping at two young women, maybe in their early twenties. Garrett introduced them as Luisa and Carmen.

"Tell her about Rosario," he told them. I don't think he thought I saw it, but he gave them a wink before he turned away and went back to his post.

Wondering what that was about, I studied the women in front of me. Both sported thick, curly hair pulled up into ponytails, dark eyes, and olive skin. Luisa was painfully thin — bordering on a serious food issue it looked like — while Carmen was thick around the middle. Not in the way a pregnant woman is, but that apple versus pear shape thing you hear about. She probably had battled her weight her whole life.

"Do either of you know any reason why anyone would kill Rosario?" I asked.

They exchanged a look, their eyes coming back to me at the same second. Luisa shook her head. "She just wanted to work, get her green card, and find her own place with her brother."

Carmen stifled a sob at the mention of Roberto. Was he more to her than just someone they worked with?

"Their own place?" I asked. "Where were they living?"

Again with the look between them. They certainly weren't sure just how much to tell me, and I wondered again about Garrett's wink. Maybe it was him I should be pressing for information. He was watching us closely, even though he was pretending to be interested in one of the inserts coming through the machines.

"Where did Rosario live?" I asked again when neither of them answered.

Carmen bit her lip and shrugged. "Lucille takes care of us. She gets us a place to live, a job."

"Does she help you get to New Haven?" I asked.

It was Luisa's turn. "I had a cousin here already."

Carmen nodded. "Me, too."

"But Rosario and Roberto?" I asked.

"We don't know how they got here," Carmen said softly.

"Where can I find Lucille?" I asked.

"She's around," Carmen said. "She's got an office at the church."

"Which church?"

They exchanged another look but didn't say anything. I wasn't going to get shit out of them about Lucille. I figured I'd try another tack. "Did Rosario have a boyfriend or anything?"

Luisa scowled. "He put all sorts of crazy ideas into her head."

"Like what?"

"She say she want to go to college." Carmen said it like Rosario had wanted to rob a bank.

What had happened to the American dream? Immigrants coming to the United States to better themselves, make their fortunes? These girls just wanted to get a green card and then, well, what? Make minimum wage and be happy they weren't back in Mexico where they'd have to live on even less? That was fucked up.

"What's her boyfriend's name? Where can I find him?" I asked, hoping to get something out of these two.

Carmen shrugged. "She never brought him around. We don't know anything about him. We don't know why he was a secret."

"They met at Atticus," Luisa offered up, referring to a café/bookstore on Chapel Street. "Rosario worked the breakfast and lunch shifts there." A glance between the two girls showed that Rosario had trusted Luisa more than Carmen.

"They've got to get back to work now." Garrett had snuck up on us and startled me. He took Carmen's arm and started leading them away from me. "We've got work to do," he scolded. "You can't take up all their time."

I needed more time, but it was obvious he wasn't going to let me have it. "Well, if you don't want me to talk to them, maybe you know how I can reach Lucille, since obviously she must be the contact on their employment application."

Garrett whispered something to the girls and they went back to their places in line along the machines. He turned to me. "These kids need a break. They want to work, and they're good workers. But there are eyes everywhere in their world, and you were talking to Rosario and now she's dead. I don't want them put at risk."

I tried to see behind the bullshit, because I was sure that's what it was, but he was good. He looked me right in the eye when he spoke, his voice measured and slow. He knew damn well how to reach Lucille, and he wasn't going to tell me anything.

I nodded. "Okay," I said. "Thanks."

I made my way out of the room and took

the back way through the loading dock out of the building. At least I'd gotten a tiny bit of information. Lucille had an office at a church. Of course, there were a lot of churches in the city, but I was sure I could narrow it down to those in Fair Haven. I could start cold calling, then thought better of it. No one would tell me anything over the phone. I'd have to go over there and start knocking on doors.

Chapter 22

It was lunchtime. It wouldn't hurt if I stopped somewhere and grabbed something to eat before I went to find Lucille. And why not Atticus? Maybe I could get a line on Rosario's boyfriend there. It dawned on me that the last couple of times I'd stopped in there, I noticed the employees were mostly Latino, so maybe one of them was this mysterious guy who wanted more for Rosario.

Two jobs and possibly working at the warehouse, too? I wondered when Rosario planned to take classes.

The board near the door indicated that they had their mouthwatering black bean soup, so I slipped onto a stool at the counter and scanned the employees. Yeah, they were all Latino. A short, thin guy, probably in his twenties, came over to me, a quick, warm smile on his face.

I ordered the soup and a Coke, then

added, "I was wondering, did you know Rosario Ortiz?"

The smile disappeared and his eyes fell. "Yes."

"I'm Annie Seymour, with the *Herald.* I know she worked here."

Immediately, I could see a wall go up. "She was getting her green card. She had a sponsor."

He thought I was here because she was illegal. I shook my head. "No, I don't care about that." Although I knew I was back to Lucille. But first things first. "I heard she had a boyfriend here. I was wondering if you could help me."

That surprised him. "He didn't work here," he said after a few seconds. His eyes moved back behind me, and he cocked his head. "That's him, over there."

I turned and saw him.

"I'll take my lunch over there," I said, as I picked up my bag and joined the tall young man at the table against the wall.

It wasn't until I was seated that I noticed his face was slack, his eyes a little glazed. It looked like he wasn't getting much sleep. "I was going to call you," he said softly.

"Hi, Dwayne," I said, remembering that I'd met him the night of the shooting just down the street from here. "I've been looking for you."

Dwayne sighed, his big shoulders looking out of place on his long, thin body. "You know? About me and Rosario?"

I nodded as a waitress set my bowl down on the table. I ate a couple of spoonfuls of soup, waiting for him.

Finally, "I keep thinking she'll walk through the door." He made a sort of sobbing sound before he caught himself, sniffed, and got himself under control.

"Did you meet her here?"

He nodded. "We met two months ago. I come in for lunch or coffee pretty regularly; we started talking. She was pretty amazing. She wanted to go to college, get a degree, make something of herself."

"What do you do?" I asked. "Do you go to school?"

He nodded. "I'm a junior at Yale."

Interesting.

"You knew Rosario didn't have her green card?"

He shifted in his chair and took a deep breath. "She was getting it. Someone was helping her."

"Lucille?" Now if Dwayne knew where I could find Lucille, it would make my day.

He nodded. "Yeah, Lucille." It was the way he said it that made me take notice.

"You don't like her?"

"No. She's been making Rosario wait six months now, and every few weeks she asks for more money. I told Rosario she shouldn't give her any more, because she's getting ripped off."

I pondered that as I continued to eat my soup. If Rosario was refusing to make her payments, maybe Lucille knocked her off and had Hector throw her in my trunk. Made sense to me. "Do you know where I can find Lucille?"

Dwayne shifted again, rolled his neck like he had a crick in it. "Not sure. She has an office in one of those churches over there in Fair Haven. Maybe Grand Avenue?"

Shit. "So you've never met her?"

"Once. We ran into her at the deli. She wasn't happy Rosario was with me," he said.

"Because you're black and not Hispanic?" I ventured.

He smirked. "Yeah. And because my father's a lawyer in New York, and I go to Yale. She doesn't want Rosario getting too comfortable with anyone else outside her own kind. Like maybe Rosario'll get some smarts and realize she's being scammed." He paused then, his eyes getting softer. "She was beautiful," he said, so quietly I had to lean closer to hear. He started, like he'd forgotten I was there for a second, and sat up straighter. "I was asking around, you know, to find out how she could get her green card without Lucille. I even went to talk to her boss at the *Herald.*"

"Garrett Poore?"

"Yeah, that's right. But he said the paper wasn't willing to help those girls out there."

No shit. It was admirable of Dwayne to have tried to find out. But his words left me with some more questions for Garrett. He hadn't mentioned meeting Dwayne or having that conversation.

"Did you know Rosario's brother?" I asked.

He bit his lip and nodded. "He was a quiet guy, never wanted to rock the boat. He had three jobs, too, trying to take care of Rosario. He was a decent guy, from what I could see. I had no idea he'd do what he did."

I mulled that over for a few seconds while I finished my soup. Something had certainly pushed Roberto Ortiz over the edge.

"I'm glad I ran into you," I told Dwayne as I put a few dollars on the table for my lunch. I handed him another one of my cards, just in case he no longer had the one I already gave him. "If you think of anything else about either Rosario or Roberto, can you call me?"

Dwayne nodded and got up with me. He followed me out onto the sidewalk, and as he started to walk away, I said, "Hey, Dwayne."

He turned.

"I'm sorry about what happened to Rosario."

He shrugged. "Thanks," he said, turning away again, but not so quickly that I didn't see him wipe the tear from his eye.

Now I knew I had to find Lucille, even though she probably didn't want to be found. But before I could start the car engine, my cell phone rang. I dug it out of my bag, wincing a little as I twisted my wounded hand. It didn't really bother me unless I moved it.

I checked the number on the phone before flipping the cover. "Hey, Marty," I said.

"Have you found out anything about that sweatshop?"

"I got a little off target. But I'm checking it out now," I lied.

"Well, you might not have to," he said slowly.

"Yeah?"

"Yeah. It seems that our publisher gave our executive editor the heads up that the feds are moving in on that warehouse tonight."

I let Marty's words sink in. Bill Bennett could only have found out about this from my mother. My mother, who had some sort of list of names and who had asked me how I knew about the warehouse.

I was going to have to go see her. "It's my mother, isn't it? She's his source, right?" I asked.

"Can you try to find out about this? He only said tonight, didn't have details."

"I'm on my way over to her office now," I told Marty, closing the phone and tossing it on the seat next to me.

My head was swirling with too much information, too many questions, and not enough answers. I hated multitasking, wishing news happened one thing at a time so I'd have time to cover everything properly.

My mother's office is on the fifth floor of a modest office building on Church Street. I went up in the elevator, tapping my foot subconsciously to the Muzak — something Bee Gees — and when the doors opened, stepped into a world of clean rugs, gleaming wood floors, and fresh paint. I didn't think my system could handle it. I was used to dirty carpets with mice running around occasionally, chipping paint, and piles of old newspapers that seemed to attach their black ink to your person even if you just walked by, not to mention how your hands looked after actually leafing through them.

At the end of the hall, I pushed open the door that sported the sign announcing that Hoffman, Giametti, and Cohen were behind it. Carla, the receptionist, sat at a desk arranged so no one could get past without her knowing about it. She raised an eyebrow at me.

"She's busy," Carla said firmly.

She was always busy. I didn't give a shit. "Tell her I'm here about tonight."

Reluctantly, Carla picked up the phone and gave my message to my mother. She listened a second, then put the phone back down. With a sigh, she waved her hand toward the hall. "She'll see you."

I didn't want to gloat, but I couldn't help but grin. "Thanks," I said as I moved toward my mother's office.

Another desk stood sentry outside my mother's office. Angie, my mother's secretary, was absent, the desk spotless, the computer dark. Must have the day off. I pushed the door open.

My mother sat at her desk, her glasses perched at the end of her nose. She looked up at me. "What do you know about tonight?"

I sat in the chair across from her. "Hell, Mom, you told Bill about it. Warehouse raid. Is that what the fax was all about?"

She studied me for a few seconds and pulled her glasses off, putting them on the desk. "Is that it?"

It was the way she said it that made me wonder if there was something else going down, something that maybe Bill Bennett hadn't figured out. But then I had another thought. My mother wouldn't let even Bill Bennett know about something if it was supposed to be top secret. No, she let this slip, which meant she wanted the paper to know about it.

And it led to another idea. "The person who stole the fax; are you setting him up?"

The corners of her mouth twitched, like she wanted to smile, but she kept it at bay. "You might want to talk with your detective. I don't think I'm the person to talk to."

"You're working with the cops?"

Now she did smile. "Good try, but I can't tell you anything." She rustled a few papers around. "I've got a lot of work to do, Anne. Nice to see you." She picked up her glasses and stuck them on her nose again.

I stood up. “Okay, I’ll go talk to Tom. Can I tell him you told me to ask about this?”

Another serene smile. “Go ahead.”

I couldn’t figure this one out. I was mulling it over as I rode down in the elevator and walked back to my car. The chirp of my cell phone interrupted my thoughts on the sidewalk.

I didn’t recognize the number. “Hello?” I asked.

“Miss Seymour?”

“Yes?”

“This is Dr. Moore.”

It took a second before I remembered: the medical examiner. “Yes, Dr. Moore?”

“You wanted me to call on the John Doe floater?”

The Hispanic guy. The one Marisol saw tossed into the harbor. “Yes, thank you. What did you find?”

“He didn’t drown. He died from an anaphylactic reaction.”

“Layman’s terms?”

“A reaction to a bee sting.”

CHAPTER 23

I was back where I started. Wesley Bell was right about the bee stings. Dr. Moore explained that, while it's not very common, there are some people who do die of insect stings. He said symptoms show up within minutes of the sting and would include wheezing, nausea, and vomiting. The person's blood pressure would fall and his windpipe would close, causing death.

"But he probably collapsed before actually dying," Dr. Moore said. "So he probably didn't realize what was happening."

Cold comfort.

When I climbed into my car, I sat for a few seconds, pondering this new information. If the guy died from bee stings, why would someone feel it necessary to throw his body into the water? I mean, it didn't seem like foul play, unless someone sicced the bee on him. Yeah, right, take a bee and somehow get it to sting someone on command.

But then I wondered if you could do that. Hell, if Lin Rodriguez was training bees to sniff out bombs like David Welden said, then maybe you could do it. On a whim, I dialed the hospital to see what Lin's condition was.

"Mrs. Rodriguez has been released," the public information officer told me. The hospital kept everyone at bay and made us all call the same number to find out conditions of patients.

"She's gone home?"

"She's been released." The phone went dead.

I glanced at my watch. One o'clock. I still wanted to see if I could find Lucille, and I was also going to have to find Tom to ask about this warehouse raid. Shit, he wouldn't tell me a damn thing and my mother knew that even as she told me to ask him. But I had to try.

I pointed the Kia in the direction of the police station and within ten minutes found myself going up the stairs. As I pushed the glass door in, it slammed against someone who muttered, "What the fuck?"

I'd hit Sam O'Neill. He glared at me, rubbing his forehead where the door had knocked him. "What do you want?" he demanded. "I've got to get going."

I shrugged, now on his side of the door, but stepped away so I wouldn't get hit the same way if someone came in. I didn't want to tell him I was looking for Tom, since he'd told me to stay away. Instead, I found myself saying, "We have a mutual friend."

I hadn't meant to mention Marisol to him, but sometimes I just say things without thinking. Sometimes it turned out to be a disaster, but sometimes I managed to get some useful information. I hoped this time it was the latter.

"Marisol Gomez," I said quickly, because he was obviously in a hurry and it was the only way I could think to stop him.

And it did stop him. From the look on his face, which grew darker after an initial second of surprise, I could see this conversation might not turn out the way I'd hoped. "What?" he asked, taking my arm and pushing the door open, leading me back outside. "What are you talking about?"

So that was the way it was. Well, two could play this game.

"I heard that you know my friend, Marisol," I said again.

For a second I thought he was going to slug me. I took a step back, away from him. "Sorry, am I wrong?" I asked.

As I studied his face, which was showing a mix of emotions, none of them good, I wondered what he was trying to hide. He wasn't married at the moment, and he and his ex-wife didn't have any kids, so he didn't have to worry about anything like that. If he wanted to date Marisol Gomez, it wouldn't raise any red flags for anyone. Especially since she was rather easy on the eyes and guys can be superficial about shit like that.

"I know her, but not well," he lied, not that I would've known it was a lie other than that I'd seen him locking lips rather seriously with her. "What about her?"

I shrugged. "Just thought I'd mention it." But my curiosity about their relationship was now thoroughly piqued.

"What did you want?" Sam asked now, a bit eager to get me off the subject.

"When?"

"Why are you here?" he tried again.

"Oh, yeah, well" — I thought quickly — "I was wondering if you'd ever ID'd that floater the other day."

He shook his head. "No, not yet. Doubt we will, either. Those guys are a dime a dozen."

By "those guys," I assumed he meant undocumented Hispanics who might not want the cops to know who they are, so when they're found dead, they remain John Does forever.

I nodded, then figured, what the hell. "I heard that warehouse where my car was is a sweatshop," I said quickly. "And I heard there's going to be a raid tonight. Can you confirm that?"

His eyes narrowed, his bushy eyebrows moving into each other so he looked remarkably like Neanderthal man. "No. No, I can't," he growled.

It seemed like an overreaction, but I couldn't call him on it. "Okay," I said resignedly. I started back down the steps toward my car.

"Annie," I heard Sam call.

I turned. "Yeah?"

He was looking at me with a funny look on his face. "Marisol's on hard times right now. You might want to steer clear of her. She's not that stable."

First Tom and now Marisol. Sam sure didn't want me poking around in any of what he perceived as his business. I just nodded and kept walking. It was going to take more than that to keep me from trying to find out what was going on.

I still hadn't gotten any information about the alleged warehouse raid. I settled into the Kia — hated to admit it, but I was getting used to it — and dialed Tom's cell number. I probably should've done that instead of coming over here.

But all I got was voice mail.

I thought again about the bee stings, and realized that I had let something slide the last two days. Tony Rodriguez. I hadn't done too much to find out who might have wanted to see him dead. Rocco's "tip" about the Homeland Security meeting came back to me. That, combined with Lin Rodriguez's bomb-sniffing bees and a sweatshop full of illegal workers, gave me an idea. I punched in another familiar number.

"Hey, Annie, what's up?" Paula Conrad was one of my best friends. The last time I'd seen her, she was knocking back beers at Bar with a very good-looking guy. But I wasn't calling to find out how things had turned out. She was an FBI agent, and if I wasn't mistaken, the FBI was under the umbrella of Homeland Security these days.

"Tony Rodriguez. Heard he was meeting with some Homeland Security people. You know about that?"

"They were talking about beefing up security at the port," Paula volunteered.

I thought about my conversation with David Welden, debated with myself for about a nanosecond, then said, "His wife was working on a bee project that was tied into it, I think. Bees sniffing out bombs or something. Ring a bell?"

She didn't say anything.

"You know about that?" I asked.

"How do you know about that?" she asked.

"It's going to be in the paper in a few weeks," I said. "Why the secrecy now?"

"It's going to be in the paper? Are you writing about it?"

"Not me, our science reporter. Lin Rodriguez told him about it."

"Shit." She said it softly, but I could hear the force behind the word. Lin wasn't supposed to leak this; I could tell.

"This is off the record," Paula said.

"Okay."

"It's not working the way it's supposed to. We had a little, um, accident over there a few days ago."

"Accident?"

She snorted. "Goddamn bees went everywhere they weren't supposed to. Lin finally found them near a freighter that had just come in. We had a shitload of TNT in another location, and only one bee found it."

I couldn't suppress the chuckle. "At least

there was one." But then I sobered up with another thought. "Did you check that freighter?"

"Damn straight we did. Nothing."

I remembered the John Doe. "What about crew?"

"What do you mean?"

"What about crew on the freighter? Did anyone get stung?"

"We don't let them off," Paula said. "Crew stays on the ship at all times for security reasons."

"No one could get off?"

"No." She seemed pretty sure about that, but I was dubious. That guy had gotten stung, and if he was the guy whom Marisol had seen dumped in the river, then he might have come off that freighter.

"Where'd the freighter come from?" I asked.

"I don't know, some Latin American country, I think. They were speaking Spanish."

I was pulling my net a little closer to shore. That guy must have been there; the timing was right.

"Why all the questions?" Paula was asking.

"John Doe, Hispanic, washed up on Long

Wharf. Just found out he died from a bee sting."

"No shit?" I could tell she was putting the pieces together now, too. "I'll ask around, see if someone did get off that freighter after all. Maybe I missed it."

"Thanks," I said. "Can you let me know?"

"Sure. Listen, don't tell anyone that it got screwed up, okay? The bees, I mean. The suits are all hot and bothered about this. Maybe by the time your reporter writes his story things will have gotten better."

"What about Lin Rodriguez?"

"What about her?"

"She was released from the hospital. Is she okay? I mean, after the overdose?"

Paula didn't say anything.

"Paula, what's going on? Is she okay?"

Finally, "It wasn't an overdose."

I let the words sink in before I asked my next question. "What was it, then?"

"You can't tell anyone. This is so off the record."

I crossed my fingers. "Okay, fine. What is it?"

"Really, I mean it. Off the record."

"Okay, okay."

"She was checking on her bees. She keeps some of them on the back patio at her condo in boxes. Someone knocked her out as she was leaning over the hive, took off her protective headgear. She fell right into the hive, got stung a shitload of times. It's amazing she's not dead."

Chapter 24

If it weren't for Lin Rodriguez's sister, who showed up just minutes later, Lin might have died. Paula told me Mei spotted a cop car and flagged it down; the cop got her to the hospital in record time. But since there wasn't a 911 call, no one had found out exactly what happened. Paula said in light of what happened to Tony Rodriguez, the cops were being tightlipped about Lin's "overdose."

"So no one has a clue who killed Tony or who tried to kill Lin?" I asked. "Do you think it has something to do with the bees?"

Paula sighed. "I have no idea."

"Why the hell does she keep bees at her condo? That doesn't seem safe. And aren't beehives pretty big?" I had no clue about bees.

Paula chuckled. "They're like a dog or a cat to her. And the hives are really just three small wooden boxes that she stacks up. You wouldn't think anything if you saw them." She paused. "She's a little crazy, I think, but I saw the setup myself. It's not like there are swarms of bees everywhere. Just one or two going in and out at a time. She gave me some honey. Fantastic."

"Bet her neighbors don't know, otherwise they'd run those bees right out."

"You're probably right. Hey, I have to get back to work. You promised, right? You're not going to write about this."

There was no way I could get this confirmed by anyone. Tom would keep mum, I knew, and without getting it confirmed, I couldn't use it. "I'm not going to write about it," I promised again, meaning it this time. But that didn't mean I wouldn't try to put the pieces together using it.

It's too bad the bees couldn't talk.

But before she cut me off, I said, "Wait."

"Yeah?"

"There's a warehouse in Fair Haven. I heard it's a sweatshop with illegal workers and there might be a raid tonight. Know anything about that?"

She was quiet for a couple of seconds, then, "I might."

"So there will be a raid tonight?"

"Might be. But you can't quote me on that. I have to go." And before I could get anything else, she hung up.

I closed my phone and started the car. At least I knew this raid wasn't a figment of Rocco's imagination. And even though I couldn't say on the record who told me about it, we could be there tonight to cover the whole thing.

I twisted my hand slightly as I moved the steering wheel, and pain shot through to my elbow. My thumb had been throbbing all morning, and I'd been working through it. I wanted to go home, take a Percocet or two, and lie down, giving myself some time to try to figure out what the hell was going on. Already there were three dead bodies and one attempt on Lin's life. But I had to talk to Marty first.

I pulled over to the side of the road and flipped the cover on my phone, dialing Marty.

"What'd you find out?" he asked without saying hello.

"Got it confirmed from my FBI source there will be a raid at that warehouse tonight." I paused. "I don't know what time or anything, but we could go over there and wait."

"We?"

I took a deep breath. "I really want to go. I want to cover this."

He was silent for a few seconds. "Charlie'll have my ass if you're out there, Annie. I'm going to send Dick. If he needs some help putting it together, you can do that." He paused, knowing I was getting ready to argue. "That's the best I can do, okay?"

I didn't have a choice. "Okay," I said slowly.

"I'm sorry, Annie." I could hear in his voice that he really was. He hung up and I threw the phone on the seat next to me.

I turned onto Olive before I noticed the car behind me. He was right on my ass, too. I sped up a little, and he sped up, until the next thing I knew, I was being thrown back against my seat and the Kia was careening toward a tree. In a second of panic, I swung the steering wheel as far to the left as I could, and I both felt and heard the tree scrape along the side of the car as I slid against it.

The side airbag exploded; I couldn't see the tree anymore, but I could still feel the car behind me pushing the Kia toward the road.

An SUV was coming toward me. There wasn't a damn thing I could do about it. I threw my hands up over my face as I heard the screeching of brakes.

Then silence. I'd stopped moving, and I

let out the breath I'd been holding. Slowly I moved my arms away from my head to stare at the Lincoln Aviator in front of me and saw a guy in a suit and tie jumping across the hood of the Kia and pulling my door open.

"Are you okay? Are you okay?" His voice was trembling, like my entire body.

I shook my head, uncertain if I could speak. There was a knot the size of my fist in my throat.

Finally, "Where did he go?" I asked.

The guy shook his head. "The other car? He took off. Are you okay?" he asked again.

I thought for a second. I wasn't sure I was, but a flashback slammed into my brain. "It was a Honda," I said softly. "It looked like Hector's Honda."

The guy's name was Paul. He was some sort of salesman, and he wanted to call the cops. I wanted to find Hector and ask him what the fuck his problem was with me. The last time I'd seen him, Rosario Ortiz's body ended up in the trunk of my Accord, and now this.

But my plan was flawed. The number one problem was, the Kia didn't seem to be in very good shape, and number two, Paul wasn't inclined to let me leave the scene without getting a police report. Figured I'd get a real Good Samaritan who was a law-abiding citizen. Paul also hinted that perhaps I needed to be checked out at the hospital. I already had Percocets at my house; fat chance I'd sit around the hospital all day again. But I was a bit shaken up, so I didn't argue too much.

We waited for the cops.

Ronald Berger climbed out of his cruiser and surveyed the damage. "What happened here?" he asked me, taking out his notebook.

I told him about the Honda, and as I did, his partner, Mike Mancini, crept around the Kia, taking his own notes. When he came around the front of the car, he stood next to me and nodded at Berger. "She's telling the truth. Someone crashed the shit out of it. Other car was green — there's green paint all over the white. And it looks like the other car will have some white paint on it, too." He paused. "Like that tree."

We looked at the old, tall maple. Yeah, it was branded for life.

I wasn't quite sure just what my rental agreement said about accidents. But I was willing to bet that it wouldn't be good.

Shit. I'd managed to lose two cars in just two days. I'd be lucky if the rental place would even give me another one.

". . . not her fault," Mike was saying.

Okay, so if the cops said it wasn't my fault, then maybe, just maybe, I wouldn't have to replace the Kia. Christ, putting down good money for a Kia just wouldn't be right. Even if I *had* started getting used to it.

"I think I know who was driving," I said, telling them about Hector. I gave them the address on Blatchley where I'd seen him with Lourdes and Marisol. I assumed he lived there with them, but I wasn't 100 percent sure. He could've just been visiting.

Berger said they'd check it out.

I heard my phone ringing. It was Vinny.

"Just checking in," he said.

I let the sound of his voice soothe me for a second before saying, "I had an accident."

Immediately, I heard concern. "Are you okay?"

"Yeah, don't worry. The cops are still here."

"Where are you?"

"Olive and Court."

"I'm at my office. I'll be there in a few minutes."

As I closed my phone, I glanced over at Berger and Mancini. Mancini was on the radio, putting out the call to look for the Honda. Paul was giving a statement to Berger.

Vinny and the tow truck showed up at the same time. As Vinny put his arm around me, I admitted I wasn't sure where to send the car. Should I send it back to the rental place? Vinny told me he'd take care of it. I felt cold as he left my side, watching him as he spoke to the tow truck guy.

"Are you doing okay?" Paul asked for the umpteenth time.

I nodded. "Yeah, I'm fine," I said, although I wasn't quite sure. He squeezed my upper arm as he said good-bye and shook Vinny's hand.

"Seems like a nice guy," Vinny mumbled absently.

"He stopped before he hit me," I said. "I really thought he was going to hit me." I shivered with the thought.

Vinny and I watched the tow truck take the Kia away, and after Berger and Mancini said they'd be in touch, Vinny helped me into his Explorer. We weren't far from Wooster Square, so it only took us a few minutes to pull up in front of my building.

As we climbed the stairs to my apartment, I felt Vinny's hand on the small of my back. He wasn't urging me forward; it was just a light touch that brought back some memories.

He followed me inside after I unlocked

my door.

The pot from the soup my mother had made still sat in my sink, along with the bowl and a mug. I hadn't washed them yet; I hadn't been sure if my hand could deal with washing dishes.

Vinny helped me off with my slicker, then led me into the bedroom, grabbing the yoga pants off the floor. "Put these on," he said.

I raised my eyebrows and he grinned. "Jesus, Annie, I've seen more of you than that."

He had a point. I stripped off my jeans and slipped on the sweats, more than aware that he was watching, and wondering if he'd try something. But he just stood there until I was done.

"Where are your painkillers?"

"Bathroom."

He disappeared, and when he came back, he was holding out his hands.

Two Percocets and a glass of water.

I shook my head. "I don't want to take them. At least not two. I took one yesterday and passed out."

"In just a little while, you're going to start hurting. With the way your car hit that tree, there's no way you're not going to feel it."

He had a point. I mulled over the choices: massive pain or passing out until morning.

It wasn't like I had anything to do, either, like cover a raid on a sweatshop. Life just wasn't fucking fair. I took the pills and washed them down.

Vinny took the glass back into the bathroom, and when he came back he patted the bed. I raised my eyebrows again, and he chuckled.

"I've had four months to think about what I'd do the next time we were in your bedroom, Annie, but I certainly don't want you drugged."

I didn't want to be drugged either, and as I crawled under the comforter it struck me that Vinny had been thinking about me for four months. I wanted to ask him what he'd been waiting for, but thought better of it. Now was not the time to start a discussion that I should most likely be sober for, since the pills were already starting to take effect. I could feel all my muscles relaxing.

Vinny settled down next to me, pulling my comforter around both of us. He put his arm around me, and I scootched down so my head was against his shoulder. He stroked my hair just above my forehead.

"So tell me what's going on, Annie. Why did someone try to run you off the road?"

The Percocet was crashing against my memories, pushing them out of the way.

Damn they were strong suckers.

"I saw Sam O'Neill. He's got something going with Marisol Gomez," I said, yawning, my eyes drooping. Everything started to meld together, until my head felt like a goddamn Jackson Pollock painting. Vinny's hand stopped moving. I wanted to tell him he could turn on the TV while I slept — God knew I would be pretty boring, probably start snoring at some point — but I couldn't form the words. Instead, I slipped into a drug-induced sleep.

He was gone when I woke up. The day had turned grayer, and raindrops slid down the windows. But a glance at the clock let me know that it wasn't yesterday anymore; it was seven thirty a.m. Shit, I lost a day and a half.

I sat up and immediately regretted it. Vinny had been right: I did hurt. The ache ran from my ass all the way up through my neck and into my shoulders, vying with the throbbing pain in my hand. I was still woozy from the Percocets, but they didn't seem to be living up to their reputation as a painkiller at the moment. I'd have to take another one.

The phone was off the hook on the nightstand, and I put it back in its cradle as I headed toward the bathroom. Vinny must have done that, not wanting me to be disturbed. But within seconds it rang loudly, scaring the crap out of me.

"Hello?" I asked, aware that my mouth was too dry to say much more.

"Annie? Are you okay?"

It was my mother.

"I'm a little under the weather."

"Are you okay?"

I debated how much to tell her, then figured she'd find out eventually. I might as well get the inquisition over with.

"Had an accident yesterday."

"Another one?"

"Someone rammed into my car just a little ways from here. I'm okay, but the car really isn't."

I heard my mother take a breath. "Why didn't you call me?"

"Vinny came to get me. He was here, but I slept and now he's gone."

"Oh," she said slowly. "That's what I was calling about."

"What?"

"Vinny. What time did he leave?"

Fear crept into my stomach, turning it into knots. "I don't know. I was asleep. Why the twenty questions?"

I could hear her hesitate, then, "I'm on

my way to the police station. He's been arrested."

CHAPTER 25

Vinny told her to call me. She was his phone call, and he wanted to make sure I was okay. He didn't want her to tell me anything, but the only thing she didn't tell me was why he'd been arrested. After going around in circles for about three minutes, my mother finally agreed to pick me up on her way to the station. She didn't want me tagging along, but I think she could tell by the tone of my voice that I'd manage to get there one way or another, and this way she could keep an eye on me.

It took me a long time to get dressed. I eyed the prescription bottle, but I couldn't take another Percocet or I wouldn't be able to function. And I had to go see Vinny and see what was going on. Whatever he'd been arrested for had to be a mistake. He hadn't started out as a private investigator; he'd been a marine biologist studying whales when funding got cut for his program and he ended up back on Wooster Street, working for a friend of his father's before starting his own business.

I noticed the bandage on my hand was flopping around a little, so I pulled off the part that was still sticking. What was a little more pain? I assessed the stitches, wondered if I could maneuver dressing the wound again — it was pretty red around the edges — but decided I just wasn't that coordinated. Anyway, shouldn't I keep it exposed to air so it would heal better? I'd heard that somewhere, and that was good enough for me.

My mother looked disapprovingly at the yoga pants, long-sleeved T-shirt, and jean jacket. Her eyes lingered longer on my new shoes, funky slip-ons with thick rubber soles that I'd splurged on because they were like wearing slippers.

"You're not going out like that, are you?" she asked.

I picked up my bag and slung it over my shoulder, immediately regretting it. "I feel like shit, so I'm going to be comfortable," I said, herding her out the door before I could change my mind. I felt like a goddamn truck had run over me.

Yeah, that was me. Roadkill.

I settled into the seat of the Mercedes,

happy that my mother had money and could afford a car that could double as a heating pad when I needed it.

"So, what'd they arrest him for?" I asked as she started the car.

"Assault and trespassing."

"Jesus," I whispered. "It must be a mistake."

She shook her head. "I'm not so sure, Annie, but that's between you and me." I recognized her "lawyer" voice and I nodded. She smiled, indicating we had an agreement that when we got to the station I wouldn't say anything that could jeopardize Vinny's fate. "He's been accused of going to a house on Blatchley Avenue and going after a man who lives there."

A flash of Marisol Gomez standing on a landing.

"Do you know anyone named Hector, Annie?"

We were stopped at the light at Chapel and State, and she was staring at me expectantly. I bit my lip and nodded. "Well, I don't really know him, but I've seen him."

He tried to kill me, or at least hurt me, yesterday. And Vinny had gone after him, because he knew that, too.

"Hector's okay," my mother said. "But he's insisting on pressing charges." She paused as she turned left onto State Street. We were close to the police station now.

"You can get Vinny out of there, right?" I asked. She was pulling into a parking spot near the station, and when the car stopped, she smiled at me. "I think I can."

They wouldn't let me in to see him. My mother went through the glass doors and up the elevator with a uniform escort, and I paced in front of the dispatcher, who frowned at me.

I guess I really pissed him off, because before I realized he'd called him, Tom was standing in front of me.

"Guess you're here about DeLucia."

I expected him to be a little more annoyed about it, but he looked pretty relaxed. I nodded. "Yeah. Is he okay?"

"Looks like shit." Tom seemed to enjoy telling me that, if the grin was any indication. But then it softened into a slight frown as he surveyed my own appearance. "Like you. I heard about your accident yesterday, tried to call you, but didn't even get your machine."

"Took the phone off the hook," I said quickly. "I needed some sleep."

"What was he doing over there?"

"What?"

"What was DeLucia doing over there, on Blatchley, I mean? Couple of patrol officers went there after your accident and talked to that guy you said could've been driving the car that hit you."

I was trying to wrap my head around why Tom was calling Vinny "DeLucia," then figured it was a stupid guy thing. I shrugged. "It was Hector's car that hit me. He's the one who should be answering questions, not Vinny."

"We talked to Hector about that, and he denies it. Said someone stole his car yesterday. He doesn't know where it is."

"Did he file a police report?" I asked sarcastically.

Tom grinned. "Okay, you've got me there. But those guys in that neighborhood, most of them don't file police reports and you know why."

"Is Hector legal?"

"He's got a green card." Tom cocked his head at me. "Why did DeLucia go over there later? Why didn't he just leave it to us?"

This had to be some sort of trick, a trick to get me to say something I wasn't supposed to, and then Vinny would end up in jail. Tom would like that, getting Vinny out of the way so there was no competition.

I frowned at Tom. "Can we find a more private place to go?"

He grinned, a leer crossing his face. "Okay."

I slugged him on the arm. "You know what I mean."

"Let's go get a cup of coffee. Your mother'll be in there with them for a while."

We went to the train station. It was catty-corner to the police station and housed a couple of Dunkin' Donuts, every reporter and every cop's favorite place. The station had been renovated to its glory days' appearance and the long wooden benches in the back were rarely crowded. Tom bought me a latte and himself a black coffee, and we went to the very last bench, where we were set back a bit from the hustle and bustle of a rush hour that was almost over. I found myself wanting to buy a ticket to Grand Central and spend the day in the city with my best friend, Priscilla — we went to college together and now she's a copy editor at the *New York Daily News* — and forget everything that was going on.

But Tom was waiting for something. Me. To tell him what I knew. But I'd be damned if I knew what that was. So I decided to start with one of the least odd things that had happened in the last two days.

"Sam O'Neill's having an affair with a woman who lives at that house on Blatchley Avenue. The one where Vinny was arrested. Marisol is Hector's sister," I said, then took a sip of my latte.

Tom's left eyebrow got a little higher. "How do you know Sam is having an affair with her?" he asked.

"I saw him kissing her in front of the house. There was a kid there, too, little kid, I dunno, two or three maybe."

"Marisol?" Tom seemed be a little slow on the uptake, but he was now catching up with everything I'd said.

"Marisol Gomez. I met her the night Rodriguez got shot, after Roberto Ortiz shot at you and Sam. She was one of my witnesses, but she wouldn't give me her last name and she got cut out of the story." I thought a second. "Was Marisol the woman Sam was with at the Yale Rep that night? I mean, she was there, so she must have been, right?"

Tom bit his lip, and I could see him struggling with how much to tell me. Finally, "No, Annie, she's not the woman he was with that night."

I frowned. "So then who was it? Can you tell me?"

He shook his head. "No. She doesn't know anything. We've already talked to her. And she and Sam, well, it was just a date. It was nothing serious."

"It looked serious with Marisol."

"You of all people should realize that a kiss doesn't necessarily mean a relationship is serious."

Ouch.

"I think it would be best if you just forgot about seeing Sam with her." Tom finished his coffee and toyed with the plastic top. Something was bugging him, but before I could say anything, he asked me, "How do you manage to be in the wrong places at the wrong times?"

Hell if I knew.

"Did you tell DeLucia about any of this?"

I shook my head. "No." But then I wasn't so sure. I thought I had said something in my drug haze. And something else dawned on me. I should have a goddamn lightbulb sitting on top of my head. How did Vinny know where to find Hector? Tom was staring at me. "What?" I asked.

He shook his head.

"What about that warehouse raid last night? How did that go?"

He couldn't hide the look of surprise. "How the fuck do you know about that?"

"Did you shut down the sweatshop or not?" I asked.

Tom shook his head back and forth so many times I thought he'd had a hinge attached to his neck. "Annie, there are some things I just can't tell you."

"Aw, come on, sure you can. I won't say who told me. I can get my other source to tell me." I wasn't sure Paula would tell me anything on the record, but if I had something I could start with, you never knew.

Tom just stared at me.

I had another idea, a complete non sequitur that might throw him off so I could get in the back door. "It's Lucille, isn't it? Is she running the sweatshop?"

Now I thought his eyebrows would shoot right off the top of his head they were so high on his forehead. "How do you know about Lucille?"

I shook my head slowly. "Tom, doesn't everybody in Fair Haven know about Lucille?" I didn't have a fucking clue what I was talking about, but he didn't know that.

"What else do you know?" Tom demanded, his eyes dark. I wasn't quite sure why he was so pissed.

I had a lot of pieces, but the puzzle was still evading me. "So what about the warehouse?"

He shook his head. "I can't tell you anything."

"What about the bees?" I no longer gave a shit about David Welden and my promise to him. I was going to get something on the record if it killed me.

"Bees?" Tom started toying with his cuticle.

"Yeah, the bomb-sniffing bees at the harbor. The ones Lin Rodriguez has been training and Homeland Security's all hot and bothered about."

Tom was staring at me like I had three heads. "Where do you get your information?" he asked, although he seemed more in awe of my talents than angry at the moment.

I shrugged. "My natural charm."

He smiled then, an involuntary smile, but a smile nonetheless. "Jesus, Annie."

"Did Marisol Gomez ever call you?"

Tom frowned then. "Why would she call me?"

"I gave her your number a few days ago. She had some information about the floater who washed up at Long Wharf." Although, now that I knew about Marisol and Sam, I couldn't help but wonder again why she hadn't spoken to Sam about what she'd seen. Or maybe she had.

Tom was shaking his head. "I never heard from her."

I started to ask him something else when he blurted out, "Listen, are you still dating DeLucia or do you want to go out sometime?"

He caught me so by surprise that I got flustered. "Oh, well, no," I started.

"No, you're not seeing DeLucia or no you don't want to go out sometime?" He looked so serious, so sincere, that all my questions started melting away.

I shrugged. "I'm not really seeing Vinny, well, not officially, but I don't really know what's going on, so maybe it's not a good idea we go out until I can get everything sorted out." I wasn't sure if I was making sense, but Tom started nodding and got up.

"Well, then, I have to get back to the station," he said.

This wasn't going the way I wanted it to. I hadn't gotten shit out of him, and now I was all fucked up about him and Vinny again. I followed him out of the train station and back across the street. He was about two steps ahead of me and didn't look back as he went through the door at the police station, barely holding it open for me as I scurried through. He disappeared behind another door and I found myself staring at the picture of the mayor on the wall while I waited for my mother.

But it didn't take too long. Only about ten minutes passed before my mother came out with Vinny. Tom was right. Vinny did look like shit. His right eye was swollen shut, and he had a huge gash on his left cheek. He grinned at me, and I felt like I was Adrian to Sylvester Stallone's Rocky.

Between the two of us, we might as well open our own clinic.

"What does the other guy look like?" I asked.

My mother herded us out of the building and down the sidewalk without a word, and Vinny slung his arm around my shoulders as we headed to the car. I winced with pain, but figured he didn't want to hear it, considering, so I kept my mouth shut.

"Actually, the other guy doesn't look like anything, which is how your mother was able to get me out of there. He can't prove that I even touched him."

"Did you?"

"Did I what?"

"Touch him? Hit him, you know."

My mother shot me a look that said I should shut up, but it was too late.

Vinny shrugged. "I tried."

"So what about the charges?"

Vinny gave me a wan smile and indicated my mother. "She's good. She's really good. Hector decided not to pursue it after all. My record remains squeaky clean."

My mother pursed her lips into a thin, tight line but she didn't say anything.

Within minutes we were careening back to Wooster Square, holding onto the seats to make sure we didn't go flying out the window as my mother cluelessly put our lives in danger. We were back in front of my brownstone in no time. I opened my door to get out at the same time Vinny did. My mother kept the car running.

"You're leaving?" I asked her, now out of the car and leaning down through the open passenger door.

She nodded, glanced at Vinny, and said, "Stay away from there."

Vinny shut the back door and I shut the front, and my mother shot out of there like a fucking rocket. I raised my eyebrows at Vinny. "What'd we say?"

He shook his head.

"So what happened?" I asked as we climbed the steps to my apartment.

"I went over there. I knew it was him; he's the one who hit you yesterday. I was pissed." He said it so matter-of-factly. "I banged on the door, he came out, I tried to hit him, but he was too fast for me. He ducked and then slugged me. I had no idea he'd be that fast."

I turned on the light as we got into my living room; Vinny shut the door behind me. "Marisol called the cops, they came, Hector said I hit him, even though I was fucking bleeding and he didn't have a goddamn scratch on him." His voice got louder; he was getting pissed again. "Said I was trespassing, assaulted him, so the cops carted me away. End of story."

He had been pacing in front of my couch and suddenly stopped, staring at me. "We have to go back over there."

I frowned. "Do you think that's a good idea? I mean, he already had you arrested."

"No, I have to get my Explorer."

It wasn't until after we called Rocco for a ride that I realized Vinny had mentioned Marisol. By name.

"You know, you shouldn't go over there," I reminded him again. "Rocco and I can go."

"I'm not going to go bust up Hector or his house. I'm just going to get my SUV. It's parked in the street. Last I looked, that was public property," he said. I couldn't argue with that.

Rocco's BMW pulled up against the curb. Vinny opened the back door, and I ducked inside, again breathing in the scent of fine leather. Vinny got into the front passenger seat.

"Want heat back there?" Rocco asked, looking at me in the rearview mirror.

"Sure." And, within seconds, I could feel the heat through my thighs in a very intimate way. I looked at Vinny and felt myself go even warmer. This wouldn't do. It wasn't the time or the place for me to get frisky. "No, you should turn it off," I said. Rocco turned a knob and I settled back, hoping that Hector wasn't home and that there wasn't going to be another altercation.

Again it was bugging me: How did Vinny know Marisol? I'd told him about Marisol and Rocco, but never said where Marisol lived or that Hector was her brother and lived with her. All I knew for sure was that he had been going to meet her in Rocco's stead at the Laundromat. Which raised another question: How had he known whom to look for that day?

I started asking him questions when we were still at my place, but he'd managed to evade answering by asking for an ibuprofen, and by the time I'd gotten him the bottle and some water, Rocco was laying on the horn downstairs like there was no tomorrow.

A newspaper was on the seat next to me, and I picked it up. Today's *Herald.* I scanned the front page and the city pages to see about the warehouse raid, but nothing. Maybe they didn't do it.

My stomach growled. Loud enough for those in the front to hear.

Vinny twisted around a little to look at me. "Once we get the Explorer, we'll go get something to eat, okay?"

"Sure." I paused. "Vinny, how did you know who Marisol is?"

"Marisol?" he asked innocently.

"Jesus, Vinny, you said she called nine-one-one. How do you know her? I know Rocco knows her."

But in an instant, with just one look from Rocco to Vinny, I knew. It wasn't Rocco. Vinny knew Marisol, and because they looked so much alike, she must have gotten them confused from a distance when Rocco and I had been there on Saturday.

"Jesus, why didn't you tell me?" I demanded. "Why did you let me think she knew Rocco and not you?"

The brothers shrugged at the same time. Sort of like those annoying Doublemint gum commercials with the twins.

"Assholes," I muttered.

They both snickered, and I ignored them, looking out the window but not really seeing anything. My hand had started hurting again, interrupting the throbbing pain that followed my spine from my neck down to my ass. I looked at my thumb and saw it was even redder now than it had been this morning. Somehow I didn't think that was a good thing.

We turned onto Blatchley Avenue and I saw Marisol's house up the block. I glanced around for Vinny's Explorer, but didn't see it.

"Where's your SUV?" I asked.

"Shit," Vinny muttered.

CHAPTER 26

While I'd lost two vehicles within the last couple of days, now Vinny had lost one. Rocco nervously patted his steering wheel.

Before any of us could say anything, however, Marisol stepped out onto the stoop and made her way down the stairs.

A car pulled up, a green Honda that was a little too familiar and a little banged up, with a long white streak along the side. It had scalped the Kia and was wearing its war paint proudly.

Marisol opened the door and climbed inside. We were too far away to see who was driving, but I was willing to bet it was Hector.

"Do we follow them?" I asked as the car did a U-turn and headed in the opposite direction.

Vinny nodded. "But slowly," he told his brother. "We can't let them know we're here."

We were in Fair Haven in a bright white, brand-new BMW. We were goddamn targets as far as I could see, but who was looking?

Something caught my eye, and I leaned forward a little more. Vinny's hand was clutching his gun.

"Do you think you'll need that?" I asked, uncertain what he thought we were going up against.

"Never know." His eyes remained on the Honda, which now turned and disappeared to the right.

We were nearing the water and the warehouse that housed the sweatshop. I squinted ahead, looking for signs that the cops had been there, but didn't see anything.

"Damn," Rocco muttered. "I don't know where they went."

Vinny and I looked down the couple of streets we were passing, but the car had vanished. Now we were right next to the warehouse and the lot where I'd last seen my Honda Accord. It was gone, but something familiar was lurking there.

"Stop," I said. "Stop right here."

The car screeched to a halt, with both brothers watching me. "What's up?" Rocco asked.

I pointed.

Dick Whitfield was squatting in the middle

of the lot, touching something on the ground.

Rocco backed up a little, and I rolled down my window.

"Hey, Dick, what did you find?" I called out.

He looked up, waved, and got to his feet. The three of us were out of the car already and jogging toward him.

Dick frowned at Vinny. "What happened to you?"

"Did you find something?" Vinny asked, ignoring his question.

Dick shrugged. "I don't know." He held out his hand. "What do you think?"

It was an ID card, with an official-looking insignia that indicated Carmen Perez — the picture looked like the same Carmen I'd talked to in the mailroom at the *Herald* — was in the U.S. legally.

Vinny took it from Dick and held it close, inspecting it with his good eye. "Fake," he said flatly.

"How do you know?" Dick asked.

I didn't want to admit it, but I couldn't see anything wrong with it, either. I'd seen some pretty piss-poor fake IDs in the past, but this looked legit, down to the holograms and fingerprint.

Vinny shrugged and stuck it in his jacket

pocket, looking at the ground. "Do you see any others?"

We walked around, our heads bowed as we searched, but didn't see any more. When we congregated back near the fence, that's when we noticed Dick was no longer with us.

"Where the hell did he go?" I asked no one in particular.

Vinny was one step ahead of me. He was already to the spot where I'd fallen the other day, and Rocco and I followed him around the back of the building. A door stood ajar.

There were a lot of words to describe what it was like inside, but cavernous was the first that leaped to mind.

It was empty. Not a stick of furniture, not a scrap of paper, no signs of life anywhere. The electricity was still pumping its way inside, however, because when Vinny hit the switch, the lights illuminated the space and cast weird shadows across the floor.

The ceiling was high, and I spotted stairs leading up toward the back. Vinny bounded across the room and up the stairs before any of us could move. I took a couple of steps and heard him shout, "Nothing up here, either."

"Something was going on here just two days ago," I insisted when Vinny joined us downstairs again. "Hector was keeping watch."

"They probably caught wind of the raid," Vinny said. "They moved it somewhere else."

I thought about the card in Vinny's pocket. "What do you think they were doing here?" I asked. "Was it really a sweatshop, or were they making fake green cards here?"

Vinny shrugged, but he didn't say anything. I thought I saw something cross his face, like he knew but wasn't going to tell. He flicked the light switch off.

Dick was standing in the doorway, his skinny frame a dark silhouette against the gray sky outside. "Annie, I thought you were in a car accident," he said.

"Yesterday, Dick. I'm okay today." Although my back was screaming that it wasn't okay. I ignored it. "Why are you here?"

"Marty told me to come check out the warehouse. Wesley and I came by last night, but no one was here. There was no raid. I figured maybe they'd just moved it to another time. I didn't know there wouldn't be anything here."

Vinny put his hand in between my shoulder blades and nudged me toward the door. "Well, since nothing's happening here, we've got some stuff to do. Nice to see you, Dick," he said as we squeezed past, with Rocco on our heels.

Dick scampered out after us. "Where are you going?"

"We're taking Annie home so she can get some rest," Vinny said as Rocco unlocked the car doors. "You might want to get out of here. Considering the body in Annie's car and all."

Dick's head swiveled as he checked out the environs. I spotted his Prius parked just outside the fence.

"Tell Marty I'll call him later," I said. "I have to get myself a car." And as I said it, I knew I was going to have to go back to the rental place and report the accident. I'd need the police report, so when we were settled back in the BMW, I asked Rocco to take me to the station so I could get it.

He nodded, glancing in the rearview mirror. "You know, he's watching us."

I turned around to look out the back window and immediately regretted it. My back felt like it was going to split in two like a goddamn twig. But Rocco was right. Dick was moving around the fence, heading toward his car, but still staring at the back of the BMW, looking like an idiot.

Suddenly, at the next intersection, a car

whooshed past us without even stopping.

It was as if it were in slow motion, the back of a green Honda, as it moved away from us and closer and closer to Dick.

It didn't slow down.

CHAPTER 27

Rocco slammed on the brakes as I screamed, seeing Dick's body bounce against the chain-link fence, the green car speeding up, careening up a side street, and disappearing.

I don't remember running to Dick, but suddenly I was there, with Vinny and Rocco next to me.

Dick had slumped down against the fence, his head hanging between his knees, which were pressed against his chest.

Vinny stooped down next to him and patted his back. "Dick, Dick, are you okay?"

Dick raised his head, his eyes glassy as he looked from Vinny to me to Rocco and back to Vinny. "Yeah," he whispered. "What the fuck?"

My sentiments exactly.

Vinny was standing now, his hand out to Rocco. "Give me the keys."

Rocco didn't want to give Vinny his keys.

There had already been three vehicle casualties and I didn't really blame him for not wanting to see his pristine Beemer in any shape except perfect. But Vinny was the older brother, and the look on his face told Rocco that he'd beat the crap out of him if he didn't do as he was told.

The keys fell into Vinny's hand, and he raced back to the car. Rocco stared after it wistfully as it followed the same route as the Honda.

I looked at the Prius. Rocco and I were going to have to get Dick out of there. Dick had started hyperventilating.

I wanted to tell him to buck up. But I'd probably be a wreck, too, after being almost sideswiped by a car. So I couldn't really fault him.

"Come on, Dick, let's get out of here," I said as Rocco helped him up. "Where are your keys?"

Dick sobered up pretty quickly at that. "I can drive."

Rocco smiled condescendingly. "No, Dick. You're too shaken up. We'll give you a ride. We shouldn't stick around here, just in case the guy comes back to finish the job."

I was glad Rocco said that and not me.

Dick's eyes narrowed as he studied Rocco. "Okay," he said finally, pulling the keys out of his pocket and handing them to Rocco.

"Are you sure you're okay?" I asked Dick. "Do you need to go to the emergency room or anything?"

Dick rolled his shoulders and stretched out his neck. "No. He didn't hit me. I'm okay. Do you know who it was?"

Rocco and I exchanged a look.

"We're not sure," I said slowly.

We climbed into the Prius, which was a pretty damn nice car. It was almost as spotless as Vinny's Explorer, and it still had that new-car smell. How much *were* they paying him?

A few CDs were on the backseat, and I picked them up so I could sit down. No Rolling Stones or White Stripes here. No, Dick had Norah Jones and Josh Groban. Figured. I was surprised he didn't have the CD by the latest American Idol. But then, it might be in the glove box up front.

Rocco was having a hard time with the fact that the Prius didn't make any noise when you turned on the ignition, it being an electric/gasoline hybrid. He kept turning the key, until Dick pointed out that the car was on and he should just start driving.

Rocco turned carefully up a side street, heading back downtown. "Annie needs to stop at the police station for her police report," he explained to Dick. "From there, we'll go to the airport for a new rental car, and you can head back to the paper. Is that a plan?"

I could see Dick was starting to figure out that we needed transportation, and that was why we'd commandeered his Prius.

I wondered where Vinny had gone, if he'd managed to find the green Honda. I hoped he wasn't going to get himself arrested again.

Dick was trying to figure out what was going on.

"So who was in that car that almost hit me?" he asked as we pulled up to the police station.

I opened the door and got out, leaving Rocco to deal with Dick. I went inside and told the dispatcher what I was there for. Fortunately, the report was waiting for me — with a note from Tom.

"When you get the car thing straightened out, go home and stay there. I'll come by this afternoon."

I glanced at my watch. It was this afternoon already, and I wasn't sure just when Tom thought he was going to find me home. I took the report and went back to the Prius, where Rocco was trying not to answer Dick's questions. He knew, like I did, that the less Dick knew, the better.

The Prius sailed over the Q bridge and down Townsend Avenue toward the airport, where I'd rented the Kia.

Tweed New Haven Airport had a terminal that was about the size of one of the new McMansions along the shoreline in the suburbs. I'd never flown in or out of here, and judging from the weeds growing between the cracks along the runway, I doubted I ever would. There was a feud going on between the city of New Haven and the town of East Haven, which owned some property adjacent to the airport that it was holding hostage so the city couldn't expand the runways and bring in bigger planes.

The rental car companies had a couple of rows ear-marked in the parking lot, and I began to wonder if they'd even rent me another car. As I stood at the counter, the middle-aged man in charge of the rentals wasn't so sure, either.

I handed him the police report and the rental car documents that I'd had in my bag.

He inspected all of them, tsk tsking a little before finally looking up at me. "You don't have collision insurance."

I had a fucking 1993 Honda Accord with over two hundred thousand miles on it. Why would I need collision insurance? If I got into an accident with it, I'd call it a day.

I forced myself to remain calm. "But, sir," I said firmly, "I purchased the collision insurance your company offered when I rented the car."

He rustled through the paperwork and finally saw it and nodded. "And where's the car now?"

It had been towed to a garage in East Rock, and I gave him the address and phone number. I didn't even want to think about how much my insurance premiums were going to go up with this on my record.

He was still looking through the documents. "Everything looks in order. Have you contacted your insurance company?"

In between Percocets and watching Dick Whitfield almost get run over, it had slipped my mind. But somehow I figured this guy would think my excuses would be akin to saying the dog ate my homework. I shook my head.

"You're going to have to call your agent immediately so we can get this filed," he admonished.

I hesitated.

"Yes, Miss Seymour?"

"I sort of need a car."

"I'm afraid that's impossible." The man's eyebrows were arched so high and his squint so pronounced that he looked like Mr. Magoo.

I glanced at Rocco, who shrugged.

"I need a car," I told Mr. Magoo again, but he shook his head sadly.

"I'm sorry," he said, "but our policy is not to provide a replacement vehicle in a situation like this."

Dick was pacing, distracting me. "How long is this going to take?" he asked. "I have to get back to work."

I didn't want to deal with his shit, but I needed his car. "Just a few more minutes, okay, Dick?" Mr. Magoo had put some papers in front of me that I had to sign, so I picked up the pen he offered and started skimming the fine print, ignoring Dick's heavy sighs.

Rocco must have gotten sick of hearing Dick sigh, too, because he pulled out his phone and went across the small waiting area. By the time he came back, I'd finished signing and Mr. Magoo had made more copies of my insurance card and driver's license.

"We've got to go," Rocco said impatiently.

I stuffed my copies of everything into my bag. Rocco was pacing now. "What's up?"

Dick had gone outside to wait, and he was hovering around his car, precariously close to leaving without us. Rocco and I went out to meet him, Rocco a few steps ahead of me. Something was bugging him.

"Take us to Annie's apartment, okay, Dick?" Rocco said. "Just drop us there, and then you can get going."

Dick looked from Rocco to me. "What's going on?" He wasn't as oblivious as I'd thought.

I wanted to know what was going on, too. But Rocco kept mum as Dick pulled the Prius out of the parking lot and maneuvered the side streets until we came back out onto Townsend Avenue again.

Dick drove like my mother as he careened back across the bridge, pulled off at the Hamilton Street exit, and took his right on red down toward Chapel without even looking to see if cars were coming. When he finally eased against the curb in front of my building, I was glad to be rid of him and happy I was still alive.

"Are you going to be in later?" Dick asked sarcastically, like I usually blew off work.

"Marty gave me a couple of days off," I said reluctantly. "But tell him I'll call him," I added.

Rocco and I watched as he peeled out of the parking spot.

"Didn't think those hybrids could do

that," Rocco said thoughtfully.

"Want to trade in the Beemer?" I asked.

He grinned, a lopsided smile that took over his whole face. "No way."

We noticed his white car at the same time. It was parked catty-corner to my building, in front of Vinny's brownstone. Rocco and I walked over as Vinny came down his steps.

"Did you catch him?" I asked.

"No," he said, pushing a curl out of my eyes. His finger was warm against my skin. He winked at me and turned to his brother. "Cops found my SUV down on Ferry Street, near the bridge. They said it's okay, just looks like someone took a joyride."

"No bodies inside?" I asked, trying to keep my tone light, but didn't really pull it off.

Vinny chuckled. "No, not this time. But why don't we take the Beemer over there. What about another rental?" he asked me.

"They think I'm some sort of risk."

Vinny laughed then. "No shit."

"I'm not quite sure what to do."

"I know a place where you can rent a car. But I have to warn you, it might not be the most beautiful car."

"Right, like that's a big deal," I said.

Vinny nodded. "Okay. I'll take you there when we get the Explorer." He tossed the BMW's keys to Rocco and we all climbed into the car again.

This was getting to be worse than a game of musical chairs.

"How're you holding up?" Vinny asked.

I was in the backseat again and Vinny had twisted around so he could talk to me. Even though he looked worse than I did, I could see in his good eye that he was thinking impure thoughts. And it was turning me on.

Jesus, I was fucked-up.

"So was it an accident that you ran into Marisol after she saw the body getting dumped in the harbor?" I asked him, trying to get my mind out of the gutter.

"What are you implying?"

"It seems so convenient that you were there right then. Why would you be at that spot? It's not like a place where you'd hang out for no reason." But as I said it, I remembered my mother and that fax with the names on it. And her question about how I'd known about the warehouse. "It's my mother, isn't it? She's involved somehow in that warehouse. What are you working on for her?"

Rocco snorted and looked at Vinny. "She's like a pit bull, isn't she?"

Vinny smiled and gave me a wink. "But in a good way."

"Christ, Vinny, I don't know why you

can't just tell me."

"I can't violate a client's confidentiality," he said.

"But what about this: Did you see the guy who dumped the body?"

"No."

"Did Marisol say if she knew who it was?"

Vinny shook his head. "No, I don't know if she knew him or not."

"Did you follow her at all after that?" Vinny had been at Rodriguez's shooting later that evening, and so was Marisol. And then I remembered how Marisol had been nervous at IKEA. I hadn't seen Vinny there, but maybe she had.

Vinny raised his eyebrows as if to say "I'll never tell." I wasn't going to get shit out of him. I changed gears. I was worse than a goddamn yo-yo.

"So, what's been going on at the warehouse?" I asked.

"I don't know."

My memory flashed back on the green card we'd found in the abandoned lot. "What about the fake green card? Do you know anything about that?"

Vinny's lips curled into a smile, but he didn't say anything.

"Come on, Vinny. You've got to give me something."

Vinny glanced at Rocco, who nodded. Jesus, they were both in on it.

"Okay, but this can't go anywhere." He was telling me it was off the record. Shit.

But what choice did I have? I nodded. "Okay."

"There's a counterfeit green card operation going on. We're trying to track it down."

"We?" But as I said it, I knew. Vinny was working for my mother. "My mother knew about the green card scam, didn't she? And she had you check it out. Who's she representing?"

Vinny shook his head, but the small smile that played at the corner of his lips told me I was right.

"Those names on the fax — were they victims of the scam?"

He still didn't say anything.

It was starting to make sense. But I was still a few clowns short of a circus. Vinny was keeping mum; it was almost worse than Tom. For a second, I debated how much I could get out of Vinny using my "feminine wiles," so to speak. Even as I thought about it, I knew it wouldn't work. It hadn't ever worked with Tom, either, although there were some pleasant payoffs.

It didn't take too long to get over to Ferry Street. A lot of the houses on this street were being renovated, since the river view was considered pretty desirable. Even still, Fair Haven was dicey as far as crime went, and I doubted I'd sink any money into real estate here until it was fixed up a bit more and I'd be able to take a walk at night without taking a risk that I would be mugged.

We spotted Vinny's SUV up ahead, parked near the Ferry Street Bridge, which was still under construction. The project had been stalled so long that I was beginning to doubt whether this bridge would ever be open again.

No one was around. Vinny got out, and we followed.

"Do you want me to take you to get a car?" he asked as we approached the Explorer.

"Sure." What the hell else was I supposed to do? Sit around my apartment and wait for Tom? I needed a car; that had to be priority and Tom was just going to have to deal with it.

Vinny took his keys out of his pocket and was reaching toward the door of the SUV when suddenly he pulled his hand away and took a step backward. Rocco and I were just behind him.

"What's wrong, bro?" Rocco asked.

Vinny shook his head. "Get her out of here," he said, quietly but firmly.

I knew he was talking about me, but I wasn't going to go unless there was a damn good reason.

"There's not a body in your car, too, is there?" I asked.

He shook his head and backed up further. I peered more closely at the Explorer and saw some sort of shadow in the window. I took a step toward it, and as I did, the shadow moved and I jumped back. "What the hell is it?" I asked.

Rocco, who was standing to my left, had a better vantage point. "Bees," he said.

Chapter 28

Vinny stepped around the back of the SUV and looked inside. "There's a hive in there."

"A hive?" I asked. "Don't they usually just make hives in trees or under gutters on houses or something?"

Vinny chuckled. "Those are natural hives, Annie. This one's man-made. It's a small wooden box, and it's been dismantled."

"Didn't the cops see this when they found it?" I asked.

Vinny shrugged. "Maybe, maybe not. Maybe someone put the hive in there between the time the cops found it and now."

"But why?"

Both Rocco and Vinny rolled their eyes at me. Okay, so that was a stupid question. "Wouldn't whoever put it in there know you'd see it before you opened the door?" I asked after a second.

I could see he'd thought of that but didn't have an answer, either.

"So who would do this?" I asked. "How pissed is Hector at you?" And as I said it, I wondered how the hell Hector would get bees. The only person I knew who had bees was Lin Rodriguez, and she was out of commission because someone tried to kill her with the bees.

As I mulled this over, I heard Vinny ask Rocco, "Do you have time to take us to the car place?" He didn't seem all that concerned about his Explorer or the obvious message that had been left for him.

"Aren't you worried about this?" I asked him.

Vinny chuckled. "Not a whole helluva lot I can do about it, is there?"

He must do yoga or meditate or some shit like that.

Rocco cocked his head toward the Explorer. The bees were moving across the front windshield. "What're you going to do about that?"

"Call an exterminator."

Made sense to me. We piled back into the Beemer, and Vinny gave Rocco directions to a used car lot on Main Street in East Haven. We weren't very far, but it meant going back over the Q bridge again and dodging the construction on Interstate 95. The ten-year project to widen the highway and build a new bridge was under way and causing innumerable problems for anyone who had to go east of the city on a regular basis. Thank God I didn't have to.

Vinny knew the owner at the lot, but since I wasn't prepared to actually purchase a car on the spot, he was willing to rent me a car at half the price I'd gotten the Kia for, but only for a week. After that, I was on my own. And I didn't get a choice of vehicle.

The Ford Taurus was as old as my Honda and probably had more miles on it, even though the odometer swore it had only seen thirty thousand miles. But beggars can't be choosers, so I plunked down my credit card and got a key.

I ignored the rust spreading along the undercarriage and shrugged when Vinny asked if it was okay.

"Sure," I said, just happy I'd have wheels now. And if someone decided to crash into this one, well, I wouldn't feel quite as bad.

I climbed into the driver's seat. Remarkably, the car was clean, even though a little worn around the edges. As I started the engine, Vinny opened the passenger door and got in. I frowned at him.

"What're you doing?" I asked, although I hadn't thought about where I was going to go once I got out on the road.

He was looking around the car. "Hey, pretty good, huh?"

I shrugged. "Yeah, sure. Where to?"

"Lunch?"

Seemed like a plan, so I pulled out onto Main Street. The Taurus didn't handle too badly. Rocco was a few cars ahead, going in the same direction. "Where should we go?" I asked.

"Scupper."

I glanced down at my jeans and then at his fleece pullover. "We're a little under-dressed, aren't we? How about somewhere a little less, well, you know." The Rusty Scupper wasn't that fancy, but it was a "fine dining" restaurant as opposed to my usual haunts. It was the only restaurant in the city that sat on the harbor. "How about Louis' Lunch?"

Louis' Lunch on Crown Street invented the hamburger. And because of that, they believe you should enjoy said hamburger on two slices of white toast. You can get tomato and onion and cheese if you want, but absolutely no ketchup. They were the hamburger Nazis, but they were pretty good hamburgers.

Vinny was knocking down my idea. "Let's just go to the Scupper. It's right over the bridge."

"Why didn't you get a car, too?" I asked, not having the strength to argue. "I mean, it might not be easy to get those bees out."

"Temporary setback," Vinny said. "It shouldn't be too difficult to get rid of the bees, so I won't be without a car for too long. Anyway, this way I can ride with you and I can keep an eye on you at the same time."

"I don't need a bodyguard," I argued. I wanted to call Paula and see if I could get her on the record about the green card counterfeiting, since I was sure the FBI would be involved in the investigation. Maybe I could get my mother to tell me what her role in this was. And if I could get any information from anyone, maybe Marty would let me come back to work.

As I pulled into the parking lot at the Scupper, I glanced across the harbor at the port, but a freighter was blocking most of the view.

Vinny and I went into the restaurant, and he asked for one of the tables lining the floor-to-ceiling windows overlooking the water.

I sat down, dropping my bag on the floor next to me. I picked up the menu and scanned it, finding an open-faced crab-and-shrimp sandwich on a croissant. The waitress hovered, and I pointed to it. "That, I'll have that," I said, and when she asked for my choice of drink, I glanced at Vinny and said, "Heineken."

Vinny grinned as he ordered the fried fish sandwich and a Heineken of his own.

I looked out over at the port.

"What do you see?" Vinny asked softly.

I shrugged. "Ship. Fuel-storage tanks. Usual shit."

"Nobody pays attention, really, to what goes on over there."

"No."

"Then that guy gets dumped, washes up."

"And still no one pays attention." It was a shame that guy was a John Doe, but no one did give a shit about him. I wondered if he had a family somewhere. "Do you think anyone misses him?"

"What do you mean?"

The waitress came over, set our beers down in front of us, and moved away silently. I took a sip before saying anything. When I put my glass down, I sighed. "Does anyone in Fair Haven miss that guy?"

"Why do you think he's from Fair Haven?"

"Why not? That's where his people are." My people were in my own Wooster Square neighborhood, deemed New Haven's "Little Italy," where my dad grew up, and over in

Westville, where my Jewish mother lived. We all had our places.

"Why do you think no one has claimed him?" Vinny asked.

I thought for a second. "His people can't draw attention to themselves because they're here illegally. Can't tell the cops someone's missing who doesn't exist."

Vinny nodded. "You're right. But maybe no one did know him."

I took another drink, looking at him from the corner of my eye. "Maybe," I said, although I wasn't quite sure what he was getting at.

Vinny pulled his cell phone out of his pocket and punched in some numbers. I leisurely drank my beer as I listened to him talking to an exterminator after calling directory assistance. Our sandwiches came just as Vinny hung up, and we both dove in without a word. Breakfast had been a long time ago.

We were done in record time. Vinny refused to let me pay, and it made me a bit uncomfortable, knowing that our relationship situation hadn't been completely worked out. Were we friends now? Did he want it to be more? Did I want it to be more?

I had to admit he was looking pretty damn

good in the jeans and fleece, despite his Rocky-like face. But then Tom's kiss nudged my memory, and I wondered if I shouldn't just swear off men completely until I could figure this shit out.

Vinny was excusing himself to go to the men's room. As he walked across the restaurant, I figured this was a good time to touch base with Marty.

"Dick told me what happened," he said. "What the hell's going on?"

"There's something going on with green cards. A scam. But I'm not sure how it works yet and I'm not sure exactly what's up. I have to do some more checking." I knew if I could break open this story about the green card counterfeiting, Marty would name me employee of the month.

Well, maybe I wouldn't go that far, but he'd be pretty happy.

"Green cards?"

"Yeah. I'll try to find out something as soon as I can and let you know."

"Does it have anything to do with that warehouse?" Marty asked.

"I'm not sure. I'll see what I can find out."

"Can you find out sooner rather than later?" He seemed to have forgotten that he'd given me time off. Which was just fine with me.

"I'll see what I can do and get back to you when I know something."

He was quiet for a second, then, "Be careful, though, okay?"

"Yeah, sure, I will."

Vinny was standing next to me as I closed the phone.

"No one's going to tell you shit on the record," he said.

"I have to try."

"Suit yourself."

"I will." We were behaving like children, but that wasn't anything new.

And as I thought about what I needed to do — talk to my mother, Paula, and even Tom — I knew. I knew I was going to have to get rid of Vinny or I really wouldn't get anything.

We went back out to the car and, as I got in, I shifted in my seat a little and managed to actually put myself in some real pain. I caught my breath.

"You okay?"

I shook my head, trying to keep back tears. I shouldn't have put that much into it. "You know, my back's fucking killing me."

Vinny studied my face for a second and apparently decided I was telling the truth. "You should go home and take another Percocet and get some rest."

I nodded, pulling out of the parking lot and heading toward Wooster Square. "What about you, though?" I asked. "You need a car."

He gave me a sidelong glance. "I'll take this one. You don't need it anyway."

I opened my mouth to argue, then shut it again. He did help me get the car, and I couldn't say anything without him knowing I was lying. "Okay," I said slowly. "But I want it back in one piece. I'm not going to have an insurance record worth shit if I lose another car."

I pulled into a parking space just across from my brownstone. I got out of the Taurus and waited for Vinny to come around to the driver's side. I handed him the keys.

"Be careful," I said.

He nodded and put his fingers under my chin, raising my face to his. His lips found mine and I closed my eyes as I felt his tongue.

He pulled away too quickly. I was about to ask him to forget about everything, to come up to my bed and spend the afternoon with me. It had been too long; I didn't care about any story anymore. But his eyes were resting on something behind me, his lips now in a grim, tight line. I turned to see what he was looking at.

Tom stood on the sidewalk at the bottom of my brownstone steps.

CHAPTER 29

I don't know how it happened, but in what seemed like an instant, Vinny was driving away in my rental car and I was climbing the stairs to my apartment with Tom, who still hadn't said a word.

When we finally got into my living room, I turned to him. "What's going on?"

He scowled. "I told you I'd come by this afternoon. You could've told me you'd be with DeLucia."

"Why the hell are you calling him by his last name now? Jesus, Tom, it's like we're in high school all over again."

"And you're the high school tease."

Okay, maybe I deserved that, but it really pissed me off. "He helped me get a new rental car and he was just dropping me off so I could get some rest because I was in a goddamn accident yesterday and I hurt like hell." My voice got higher with each word until I felt like a fucking shrew.

"So why is he taking your rental car?"

"Because there are bees in his."

"Bees?"

So I told him about the Explorer. Tom's face changed slightly as I finished, and he bit his lip thoughtfully.

"Someone took one of Lin Rodriguez's hives while she was in the hospital. She came home and found it missing."

I sat on my couch, and Tom dropped into my rocking chair across the room. We stared at each other for a few seconds.

"I know about the green card counterfeiting," I said.

He nodded. "Figured DeLucia — um, Vinny — would tell you."

"You know that he knew?"

"He works for your mother, right?"

Again my mother. "Who is she representing?"

He shook his head. "Can't tell you. This is out of our hands, really."

"Feds?"

He nodded.

"Are you guys doing anything?"

"We've been told to stay out of the way." And from the way he said it, it was his turn to be pissed.

"So what's going on?"

"Tony knew everything, and Sam knows,

but he's not telling me too much."

"Do you think Rodriguez was killed over this?"

Tom took a deep breath and rubbed at his eyes; he was tired. "Yeah. Yeah, I do. Nothing else makes sense."

"But what about Roberto Ortiz? Is he awake yet? Did he kill Rodriguez? Can he tell you why he shot at you and Sam? And what's up with his sister? Why was she killed?"

"He's still in a coma. And I don't know anything else." He wasn't bullshitting, either. I could see in his face that he was truly perplexed by this.

"Rosario talked to me in the mailroom at the paper, but she didn't say anything much," I said. "You don't think someone saw us talking and thought she said more than she did, do you?"

"You talk to everyone," Tom said.

"Yeah, but one day I talked to her and the next she was taking up room in my trunk."

"Do you think that was deliberate?"

I didn't know what the hell I thought. "Maybe, maybe not." I didn't want to feel responsible for causing Rosario's early demise. Dwayne didn't blame me, which was good.

"I talked to a couple of other girls, too," I started.

"Are they dead?" Tom interrupted.

"Jesus, Tom, no."

"So maybe Rosario Ortiz wasn't killed because she talked to you."

"Okay, maybe not. But those other girls, they told me about Lucille. They said she helps everyone who comes here. What's her story?"

Tom shook his head, but it wasn't because he was saying no; it was because he thought I was pitiful. Really.

"Maybe you should just stay out of it now," Tom said condescendingly, pointing at my hand. "First you have to get stitches and then you get in a car accident. Maybe someone's telling you to mind your own business on this one."

"You think someone tried to run me down because I'm asking questions?"

"Christ, Annie, of course. You do tend to get on people's nerves."

So sue me. That wasn't front page news.

Tom got up and started pacing. "I guess I should be happy DeLucia took your wheels so you can't go anywhere," he said, finally stopping in front of me. "So now I can leave and I won't feel like shit like I would if you go back out there looking for trouble."

Tom didn't have to know that I was already trying to figure out how to get transportation back over to Fair Haven. Hell, at this point I'd walk. It wasn't too far.

"So you're leaving?" I asked, trying to sound like I wasn't trying to get rid of him.

He nodded, and I stood up. Together we moved toward the door. I opened it for him, but he stopped at the threshold and turned back to me, his face close, about as close as Vinny's had been just minutes ago.

"I can't forget about you," he said softly, then disappeared down the black stairwell.

I closed the door when I heard him slam the front door downstairs. I was in a real fucking pickle, that was for sure. And I wasn't talking about not having a car this time. Here I was again, thinking about two men whom I'd thought were completely out of my life and who'd both shown up at the same time to force me to make a goddamn decision.

And I thought life was a pain in the ass before.

A honk echoed through the air, and I moved to the window, looking down to see Rocco's familiar BMW parked across the street. I smiled, happy to be able to put off any real introspection about the Vinny versus Tom situation as I put on my jean jacket. On impulse, though, I picked up my rain slicker on the way out; the sky was looking pretty ominous again.

Rocco said he had something to show me. He said he couldn't get Vinny on his cell, thought he was with me, but since he was going to show both of us anyway, he'd be content with just me.

I wondered why Vinny wasn't answering his phone, but a ride was a ride, and Rocco was going my way.

We headed toward Fair Haven.

"What's up?" I asked after a few minutes of silence.

Rocco was tapping the steering wheel with his thumbs as he drove. I wondered if it was a habit for him or just a nervous tic caused by all the crazy stuff going on around us.

"I think I found something interesting."

I sat up a little straighter. "What?"

"You won't believe it."

"Try me."

"I think I found that Lucille you've been looking for."

Now that was definitely something interesting.

"How?" I asked.

"I was sort of just driving around, and I

saw this woman come out of one of those churches, you know, the storefront churches with the name of the priest, or whatever, and the phone number painted on the outside wall. It was mostly in Spanish, and Arnie doesn't do Spanish."

I frowned. Arnie? Shit, he was channeling his book character again. This could be a wild-goose chase. But on second thought, I didn't have anything to do this afternoon, I was in the right place, and I had a ride. So I figured I could play along.

"Was she alone?"

Rocco shook his head. "She came out all covered up in a big trench raincoat with a hood, so I couldn't see her face, but she was with that guy we saw, the one you think slammed into your car."

"Hector?"

"Yeah. And they walked down here to the McDonald's." Rocco pulled into the parking lot as he said that.

I stared at the golden arches and frowned. "What should we do?"

Rocco was one step ahead of me. He had his door open and, as he stepped out, said, "Wait here."

I watched as he went inside. It was just a few minutes before he came out, carrying a bag and a soda. He climbed back into the car, grinning. “They’re in there,” he said.

“Should I go in?” I asked.

Rocco pulled a French fry out of the bag and stuck it in his mouth as he shrugged.

I pulled at the latch in the door, but before I could open it, movement made me freeze. A woman came out, her hood down, exposing her face.

It was my mother.

Chapter 30

As she walked away from us, I almost started to breathe again, until I saw Hector come out of the McDonald's, right behind her. She paused as he said something to her, then she continued on her way toward the Mercedes that I hadn't even noticed parked a few spots away.

"Shit, Rocco," I said loudly, my voice startling me. "That's my mother."

He stared at me. "Your mother?"

"Yeah, and let's follow her. I want to get to the bottom of this right now."

As Rocco pulled the Beemer out into the road, I pulled my cell out of my bag and punched in my mother's number. She answered on the second ring.

"Annie, I can't talk right now."

"Yeah, I know. You're going down Grand Avenue."

I saw the Mercedes brake suddenly as she looked in the rearview mirror. I waved. Her hand went up automatically. “What the hell are you doing?” she demanded.

“Why don’t we meet at my apartment and you can tell me what you’re doing,” I said.

“Who’s that with you?”

I glanced at Rocco. “Oh, it’s Vinny’s brother.”

“The writer? What are you doing with him?”

“What are you doing with Hector?” This must be big. Fast food and my mother were like oil and water.

“Okay, I’ll meet you at your place.” She disconnected the call, and the Mercedes sped back up.

We lost her somewhere around State Street, but she was waiting for us at my brownstone when we arrived.

My mother got out of her car, smoothing her black slacks and pulling her trench coat closer. She held a hand over her eyes, shielding them from the few drops of rain that had started to fall.

Within seconds, the sky stopped spitting and let go buckets on us. The three of us dashed up the stairs and I fumbled awkwardly with my key before finally releasing the lock and letting us inside, where it was dry.

I put a kettle of water on for coffee, even

though no one had asked for any. But it was the only way to gather my thoughts before I started firing questions at my mother.

"So what's your business with Hector?" I asked. "Does it have to do with Vinny?"

My mother's eyes slid from me to Rocco and back again, her eyebrows arched, asking me if I wanted Rocco to be there. I nodded. "You can talk to Rocco, too. He's Vinny's brother."

She frowned and pushed a brown curl off her forehead. "All right," she said after a couple of seconds. "But this can't leave this room. You can't write about it. Not yet."

Just as she said it, I began to itch to call Marty. She saw that, too, and waited until I nodded. "Okay," I said.

"Hector came to me three months ago, not long after Lourdes started cleaning for me. He's been driving her to my house, and I met him one day as I was leaving for work. I'd represented someone he knew in a robbery case, pro bono, and he recognized my name. A few days later, he called me, wanted to know if I could help some of his people who are being exploited."

"The green cards?" I asked.

She hesitated, then nodded. "Yes. He told me about a woman who's taking money from these people, promising them green cards, but what they're getting are counterfeits."

"But those people are illegal anyway," I started, and my mother put a finger to her lips.

"Yes, but this cannot be tolerated. They don't know any better, and they're being taken advantage of. I've been trying to get Hector to educate them that they don't need this Lucille — that they can do this legally without repercussions."

"But it can take a long time," Rocco said quietly from his perch next to the island between my galley kitchen and the living room.

My mother nodded. "Yes, but it's legal." Her voice was firm, and I knew she thought she was doing the right thing, pointing these people in what she knew was the right direction.

It was too bad they weren't so sure and took their chances with Lucille instead.

"Have you seen Lucille?" I asked.

My mother shook her head. "Hector has been very secretive about her. He doesn't want to tell anyone where she is right now, because he's afraid she'll leave town."

"Is she real?" Rocco asked. "I mean, he's not bullshitting you, is he?"

Before she could answer, I said, "No, I

think she's real. A couple of girls at the paper talked about her." I paused. "So what was that fax I saw?"

"The names of the people who have been scammed," my mother said.

"But I saw Hector there that day. He picked up Lourdes. I thought he might have gone back to get the fax, and that's why your house got broken into."

Distress crossed her face and her lips tightened into a straight line before she spoke. "Hector asked me from the start to keep everything he told me confidential, not even tell Lourdes. He is afraid someone will find out what he's doing and there will be reprisals. He said the only one who knows he's talking to me is his sister, Marisol, and he trusts her completely. She has helped him get information that I need for my case."

Marisol?

"Why did Hector beat the shit out of my brother?" Rocco was asking.

My mother shook her head and looked at me. "Because Vinny started it. He accused Hector of trying to run Annie down. Hector says it wasn't him."

"Then who the hell was it?" I asked, vaguely aware that my hand had started itching and I was picking at the stitches. I glanced down and saw it was even redder than it had been. Damn, it was probably infected.

My mother noticed it at the same time. "You need to put some peroxide on that and wrap it up," she said, getting up before I could respond. She was gone for literally seconds, during which Rocco just shrugged at me, and came back with my first aid kit from the bathroom. "Come over here," she instructed as she took the kettle off the stove and hovered next to the sink, twisting the cap off the peroxide bottle.

This was going to hurt like a son of a bitch and I didn't want anything to do with it, but even though I was almost forty, my mother was still my mother and if I didn't do as she said, I'd be in deep shit.

I let her pour the peroxide over my stitches, and I bit the inside of my lip until I could taste blood.

Within minutes, she'd dried the wound and wrapped my hand in gauze and tape. Now, instead of Frankenstein, I looked like the Mummy.

"So where were we?" she asked as she neatly packed everything back in the kit.

I surveyed my hand and glanced up at Rocco, who seemed more confused by my mother's Clara Barton routine than anything else.

"So you knew who Hector was when you went to help Vinny?" I asked.

She nodded. "It helped, you know. Hector trusts me. He hadn't seen Vinny before, didn't know Vinny works for me. He agreed to forget about the whole incident."

It would take Vinny longer to forget, I figured, because he'd have to see that shiner in the mirror for a while.

"So what's your next step? Do you have enough to have Lucille arrested?"

"I've spoken to Sam O'Neill and Jeff Parker at the FBI, but because of the bureaucracy with Immigration and Homeland Security, it's going nowhere right now." I could see she wasn't happy with that, but it sounded like the right chain of command to me. She hated this, waiting for someone else before she could take action.

The nut didn't fall too far from the tree.

My mother glanced at the clock and picked up her bag. "I have to get back to my office. I have some things to do."

I barely heard her as I ran through all the information she'd just given me and mentally kicked myself that I'd promised I wouldn't use it. I wondered if I could get Paula on the phone.

My mother was one step ahead of me.

"You can't write this now, even if you get it confirmed by someone else. We're not ready yet."

"Does this have anything to do with that warehouse?" I asked.

I could see her debating with herself about what she should tell me. Finally, "Many of the people on that list worked at what they called the factoria, which we assumed was that warehouse. They said they were making cardboard boxes there. We don't know if it's connected to the green cards, but it's the one thing the authorities said they could do something about right away. But when they arrived, there was no one there. It was as if nothing had ever occurred there. Someone tipped them off."

She moved toward the door, but as her hand touched the knob, she faced me and Rocco. "Neither of you do anything tonight. I'm going to call Jeff Parker and tell him we need to move on this tomorrow. I'll try to get Hector to tell me where Lucille is. I know I can't expect you to sit on a story too long."

I went over to her and kissed her on the cheek. "Thanks, Mom," I said.

"I owe you that much," she said, "for taking care of the door at the house."

I watched her go down the stairs before

turning back to Rocco and closing the door.

"So now what?" he asked.

I shrugged. "I promised I'd hold off." I held up my hand. "There's not much I can do with this, either, right now. You might as well take off. Vinny'll be back at some point."

Rocco hesitated. He didn't completely trust me; if I was going to sneak out, he obviously wanted to go along for the ride. But it had been a long day, and my body was screaming at me to take another pill and let it rest. I didn't know where Vinny had gone, although my mother's revelation about Marisol knowing what she was doing tugged at me. I pushed my worry aside.

"I need to get some sleep," I told Rocco. "Really." As I said it, my eyelids literally started drooping.

He nodded. "Okay. I guess I'll see you tomorrow." He let himself out, and I locked the door behind him before going over to the couch and collapsing on top of it.

I stared at the ceiling, uncertain if I could even move to go get a Percocet. I willed my muscles to be completely still and somehow it worked.

Maybe I'd take up meditation.

Not.

Out of the corner of my eye I could see

the afternoon turning to dusk. I wondered where Vinny had gone with my car. Or, rather, the rental car. I wanted the things that I'd left in the Accord. Maybe if I asked Tom nicely, he'd get them for me. My tapes were in the front, my scanner was in the backseat; they couldn't possibly have any evidence on them since Rosario was found in the trunk.

Rosario's face drifted in front of my eyes as I closed them, and it turned into the faces of those girls in the mailroom. And then I pictured Dwayne, whom I'd first met when I saw Marisol at the shooting on Chapel. It seemed a million years ago. Why was Marisol there? I asked myself again before I drifted to sleep.

Someone was hammering. I opened one eye, then the other, and stared at the ceiling. It was dark now; the glow of the streetlight hung eerily across the room like a ghostly clothesline. I shifted on the couch — I was in the same position I'd been in when I'd fallen asleep — and my muscles had settled and stiffened, causing me to catch my breath.

The hammering wouldn't stop.

Slowly I pulled myself up into a sitting position. It wasn't coming from above me, but definitely downstairs. What the hell were those new tenants doing in the middle of the night?

And then the buzzer screeched through my ears.

I shot up, ignoring the pain, and looked down at the street below. Vinny was standing on the landing. I buzzed him in and opened the door, waiting as he climbed the stairs and came inside.

He shook out his jacket — he'd traded his leather one for a basic nylon and fleece — spilling raindrops across my rug. I frowned.

"What the hell's wrong with you? What time is it?" I demanded, glancing across at the clock on the stove.

Eleven o'clock. Hell, I'd been asleep for seven hours. In the same position. No wonder I was stiff.

"I don't think your buzzer is working," he said. "I've been down there for ten minutes."

"Well, it worked just now," I said grumpily, sitting back down on the couch and pulling my afghan across my lap.

"What happened with your hand?" Vinny asked, dropping next to me.

"My mother wrapped me up. I think it was getting infected."

"You saw your mother?"

"Yeah, earlier. She was here; so was Rocco."

Vinny sat up straighter. "Do you know where Rocco went?"

I shrugged. "I've been asleep since they left."

Vinny leaned forward, his elbows on his knees as he ran his hands across his face and through his hair.

"What's wrong?"

He shook his head.

"Why didn't you tell me Marisol knew about my mother working on the green card scam? That Hector is the one who brought this to my mother's attention?"

Vinny lifted his head slowly and stared at me. "Marisol? I knew about Hector and the scam, but Marisol? She wasn't involved in that."

"My mother said she helped get information."

Vinny's head swung back and forth like a goddamn pendulum. It was making me a little dizzy. "All I was doing for your mother on this was verifying names."

"Then what's your connection with Marisol? I don't buy it that you were conveniently around the corner when she saw that body getting dumped."

He sat back and looked at me for a few

seconds before answering.

"It was Lin Rodriguez. Lin hired me to follow Marisol."

CHAPTER 31

It took a minute before his words registered.

"Lin Rodriguez? Why?"

Vinny hung his head back and sighed as he stared at the ceiling. "Marisol and Tony had a past."

I immediately thought about the phone calls that Lin's sister had mentioned. "She's the old girlfriend who had been calling them?"

"Not so old, really."

"Well, yeah, she's young —" The look on his face stopped me. "Jesus, Vinny, don't tell me he'd been cheating on Lin."

"Tony told Lin it was over about a year and a half ago."

It was my turn to sigh. "That kid, her kid — it's Tony's, isn't it?"

He nodded.

Shit. They had seemed so in sync with each other, Lin and Tony, so in love. "Lin thought Tony was lying about it being over?"

I asked softly.

Vinny took my hand, not the one that was hurt, and massaged the palm. "Yeah."

"Had he?"

He shrugged. "We may never know now, will we?"

We both thought about that for a few seconds before he spoke again.

"Marisol wanted money. For the kid."

I nodded. "Makes sense."

"He paid her, was paying her. Lin wanted him to stop. Marisol stopped calling, but Lin found out Tony was still giving her money, supporting her and the child. That's when she hired me, to see if they were still seeing each other, having an affair."

"But what about Sam O'Neill? What's Marisol's relationship with him?" I asked.

"They've been together," Vinny conceded. "But I'm not sure just how long." He paused. "Lin doesn't know about Sam, as far as I know. At least I haven't told her. I figured I'd write it up in my formal report, but with everything that's happened, I just haven't had time to pull it all together."

I thought about Lin and her accident with the bees. "Do you think Marisol would ever hurt Lin, I mean, besides having an affair with her husband?"

"How?"

"Physically hurt her, like, well, try to kill her."

Vinny's fingers pressed deeply into my palm as he contemplated that. "I don't think so, but you never know. I never saw her go near either of them, well, except . . ." His voice trailed off.

"Except that night at the theatre," I finished for him. "You were there following Marisol, weren't you? She was stalking Tony and Lin, wasn't she?"

"She didn't approach them, but she was hanging out across the street. Like she was waiting for the bus." Vinny sighed. "She was watching them."

Vinny's fingers were lightly moving along my wrist now, and I was more than aware of how erotic it felt. I forced myself to concentrate on our conversation. But as I opened my mouth to ask another question, Vinny cut me off by shifting around so he could kiss me.

I forgot all about Marisol Gomez, Tony Rodriguez and his fucked-up marriage, and the fact that I still didn't really have wheels. It had been four long months and we were both healing from our injuries, so we took our time.

At some point we'd moved to the bed, so I

pulled the comforter over me, watching Vinny get dressed on the other side of the room.

"Get up," he said. "There's work to do."

One glance at the window told me it was still raining. The last thing I wanted to do was go outside, but I dragged my ass out of bed and put on a pair of jeans, a T-shirt, and a fleece pullover. Vinny was in the kitchen by then, and I followed the scent of coffee.

He handed me a cup and grazed my cheek with his lips. I felt the roughness of his hours-old beard.

"Want a razor?" I asked as I sipped my coffee.

He ran his hand over his cheeks and chin and grinned. "Do I need one?"

I was sorry I'd mentioned it. He looked so damn sexy. I shook my head and grinned back. "I like it."

Christ, we were going to turn into one of those sappy Viagra commercials if we weren't careful.

"I have to go to work today, talk to Marty, tell him what's going on," I said. "My little mandated vacation is so over."

Vinny pointed at my hand, which had lost its bandages at some point, but the redness had turned a faint pink, indicating that perhaps it was actually healing. It itched like hell, too, which was another sign it was getting better.

"Can you work with that?" he asked.

"Yeah. I'm pretty good one-handed."

He winked. "I can vouch for that."

I blushed. Shit, this wouldn't do. "Where are you going?" I asked to get us off this track.

"Staking out Marisol Gomez."

"Why?"

Vinny shrugged. "Hunch." He downed his coffee and put the mug in the sink. I was still only halfway done with mine.

"No breakfast?" I asked, hungry as usual.

Vinny picked the car keys up off the counter.

"Hey," I said. "Isn't that my car?"

He came over to me and put the keys in my hand as he leaned toward me and kissed me, a deep, long kiss. When he finally pulled away, I was ready to lunge at him again, but I could see he had somehow collected himself and was ready to leave.

"You've got your SUV back?" I asked.

Vinny nodded, and pointed out the window at it on the street below. "After the exterminators got the bees out of my car yesterday, Rocco took me to go pick it up. Thought I'd die from the fumes of that shit they used, but it should be gone by now," he said.

"Why would someone put bees in your Explorer?" I asked. "It must have something to do with you following Marisol for Lin, because they must be her bees."

Vinny shrugged. "Who the hell knows." But I could see by the expression on his face that he wasn't as nonchalant as he appeared. This was bugging him, too. He took his jacket off my coat rack. "I'll call you in a couple hours. We can have lunch."

Vinny put his jacket on and threw me a kiss at the door. It wasn't until I heard the downstairs door slam shut that I realized Marty might not be happy when I showed up at the paper. But since I had some information about the warehouse and the counterfeiting scam, maybe he would be cool about it.

The Ford Taurus was, surprisingly, not as smooth as the Kia. Maybe I'd have to start writing auto reviews, since I was unfortunately becoming an expert.

Dick Whitfield was at his desk when I came in, tapping on his keyboard, but not immersed enough in what he was writing not to notice me. He scowled as he looked up.

"What?" I asked, waiting for him to say something.

"I heard you're taking vacation."

I glanced over at the editor's office and saw the back of Marty's head. "What's up?" I asked Dick, ignoring his comment.

He shrugged and turned back to his computer.

What the fuck was his problem? We practically saved his life yesterday; he should be more appreciative.

Charlie had spotted me and was waving me toward his office. Uh-oh. I wasn't sure I wanted to get into it, but I didn't have a choice now. I made my way to Charlie's office, and both he and Marty looked up when I opened the door.

Charlie's eyes started at my face and ran down the length of my body. It creeped me out.

Marty closed the door behind me without even getting up. "Do you have anything on the green card scam yet?"

I shifted from one foot to the other. "My mother's involved, but she won't talk on the record. I need to get what she said confirmed."

"Which was?"

I told them about the list and that she was getting help from someone in the community to try to nail Lucille.

"Can you get something from your FBI source?" Marty asked.

"Hopefully." It would probably be a miracle if I did, but they didn't have to know that.

"You don't look so good," Charlie said.

My face had a bit of rug burn from the impact of the airbag during my accident, and the bandage on my hand was askew, since I'd done a poor job of covering it up after Vinny left. "I'm okay," I said.

"Are you going to continue to work on this?" Charlie asked.

I glanced at Marty. What the hell was going on here?

"I'd like to," I said.

"You look like hell," Charlie said again.

"It doesn't matter what I look like," I said. "Listen, if I don't have something by the end of the day, I'll stay home, like a good girl. But I'll have something. I'll have the whole damn thing, okay? Don't worry about me."

Marty started to get up, but I swept out of the room as fast as I could before either of them could stop me. I managed to get to my desk and pick up my bag, ignoring Dick's raised eyebrows, and ran through the newsroom and down the hall, stopping only briefly to take a couple of deep breaths outside the building before making my way to my car.

I'd told them I would have something today. I was fucked. I had broken one of the biggest unwritten rules: Never tell your editor you've got a story when you really don't.

I sat in the Taurus in the visitors' parking lot and assessed what I had to do to get a story. But which one? The bees? The green card scam? The floater? Tony Rodriguez?

The easiest one would be the green card scam, I figured. I just needed to get someone on the record about what was going on, and possibly find Lucille.

I glanced over at the building. My best bet would be to talk to those girls in the mailroom again. They were still waiting for their green cards and they both knew Lucille. As I climbed back out of the car and into the rain, it seemed too easy somehow.

But Garrett Poore wasn't going to make it any easier. He stopped me at the door.

"What are you doing?" he asked.

"I'd like to talk to those girls again, you know, Carmen and Luisa." My eyes scanned the room, but I didn't see them.

He moved a little, obviously not wanting me to see past him. "Sorry, neither of them work here anymore."

I frowned. "What do you mean?"

He shrugged and snorted. "Someone" — and he emphasized this word as he stared me down — "told someone out there" — his arm swept toward the newsroom — "that some of the workers here didn't have their green cards yet. So they were told to leave."

"Well, it wasn't me," I said firmly, even though I remembered telling Marty that Rosario Ortiz had been illegal. But Garrett didn't have to know that. "Do you know their addresses? I do need to talk to them. It's about their green cards."

Garrett gave me the once-over. "I can't do that. You'll have to go to human resources."

I wouldn't get shit out of human resources, and he knew that. "Come on, Garrett, let me talk to someone who's still here who knew them."

"Maybe you just need to mind your own business," he said, heading back to his office.

I stood in the doorway, trying to decide if it was worth pissing him off even more by defying him and just going over to talk to someone. But as I watched him watching me from his glassed-in office, I decided it wasn't.

I went back out to my car, dodging the rain, and as I sat there pondering what the hell I should do next, the employee entrance door opened and Garrett Poore scrambled across the parking lot like the rat he was. What was he doing? It wasn't time for lunch yet, and he wasn't just stepping out for a smoke break. He climbed into a nondescript brown Buick and screeched out of the lot.

I turned the key in the Taurus' ignition, put the car into drive, and followed him.

Chapter 32

I had spent a good part of the last few days following people in cars. I liked to think I was getting good at it. But as I got stuck at a light and watched Garrett turn a corner and go out of sight, I reminded myself that I wasn't actually personally driving much of that time.

When the light changed, I figured I might as well give it a shot, and was happy to see that Garrett had been stopped at another light up ahead. Thank God for timed lights.

He was heading for Fair Haven, and while I had been familiar with the neighborhood before, I was getting downright chummy with it these days. I wondered how much those houses on the river went for; maybe it was time to get my own house. Yeah, right. With my luck, the river would run right through the basement the first time it rained.

Even with the rain, Grand Avenue was

bustling with activity. Women pushed strollers with plastic covers and a couple of knots of young men, hunched over in their oversized jackets and jeans, moved along at healthy clips. I knew that most of the immigrants, legal or not, lived close to the main drag because they didn't have cars.

Garrett eased his Buick up against the curb in front of one of those storefront churches. It wasn't the one where Rocco had seen my mother. This one was farther down toward the river on Grand Avenue. I doubted Garrett was here to take communion. He got out and went around the back of the building.

I wondered if Lucille had her base in this particular church, where Garrett was taking a little spiritual leave during his workday. Interesting. He did know those girls; he did know they didn't have their green cards yet.

As I stared at the church from across the street, I realized I didn't have a plan. Should I just barge in, hoping to find Garrett and Lucille and a stack of fake green cards on the table?

A tap on the window near my head scared the shit out of me.

Sam O'Neill's face was almost pressed up against the glass. "What are you doing here, Annie?" he asked.

I could've asked him the same question, so I pushed the button and let the window descend a few inches. "Nothing much, Sam. You?"

"Looks like you're staking out the church. Any reason?"

"Why would I do that?" I asked.

"There's an AA meeting going on in there now," he said. "Unless you're going to join them, I think they might not like it that someone's watching them."

AA meeting? How would he know that? Is that why he was here?

"This is a no parking zone." Sam added, indicating the fire hydrant just past the hood of the car. "If you don't move, I'll have to give you a ticket."

"Jesus, Sam, you're the acting police chief. Do you do that sort of thing now?" I knew I was being a wiseass, but that was nothing new. I wanted to ask him about Marisol and how he could be with someone who was the mother of his dead friend's kid, but that would be a little much. Even for me.

But maybe, just maybe, I could use this little encounter to help my cause. Which was to get enough information to write a damn story this afternoon.

"Hey, Sam," I said. "I'm glad I ran into you. I want to ask you about the green card scam that's going on."

He looked like I'd hit him with a two-by-four. For a couple of seconds, he just stared at me with the wind knocked out of him before saying, "I don't know what you're talking about."

"Officially," I said, like he hadn't even said anything. "I need something official for the paper."

I opened the car door and got out, ignoring my stiff limbs. I glanced back at the church, but Garrett was still inside. The rain had let up, but I still felt a few drops hit my forehead.

"Annie, I told you I don't know what you're talking about." Sam's eyes were shifting from me to the car with the lie.

"Come on, Sam. My mother told me she'd spoken to you."

I hadn't meant to use my mother like that, but hell, I was desperate. And he stopped looking behind me and stared straight at me. "It's out of my hands. You need to talk to the feds." He paused. "What did your mother tell you, anyway?"

I might as well come clean with him. "She told me about Lucille and the green cards," I said. "But it was all off the record. I need something I can write. She said she was hoping for an arrest warrant soon. She's got names of people who've been scammed."

Sam sighed. "It's not that easy, Annie. None of those people really exist."

I knew what he meant: None of them were on the books legally, which meant their statements might not hold up in court. If they even showed up in court. "But you have to do something, right?"

Sam hung his head for a second, then looked back up at me. "You have to talk to the feds. Jeff Parker at the FBI — he knows what's going on. His crew's in charge."

I thought about Paula and what she knew and what she wouldn't tell me. I couldn't write a fucking word until there was an arrest, because no one would tell me anything on the record until then. "So you're just going to keep letting these people get exploited like that?" I asked.

"They're not legal, Annie. I really don't give a shit if they're stupid." Sam barked the last word a lot louder than he obviously intended, because even he looked startled.

My thoughts shifted in another direction. I had to get something; I had to get a story.

"What about Rodriguez?" I asked. "Do you have any leads on who killed him? Do you know who tried to kill Lin Rodriguez? Are the crimes related?"

His eyes grew dark with anger. "Goddammit, Annie, where did you hear that about Lin?"

I couldn't give up Paula. I shrugged. "I can't say."

He wasn't going to tell me shit now. He took a deep breath and hissed, "Can you just stay out of our way so we can do our jobs? When we arrest someone, anyone, we'll let you know, okay?"

I watched him turn and walk away from me, but I wasn't really bothered by it. Hell, I'd heard worse from other officials who wanted me off a story. Sam was actually pretty restrained.

Garrett still hadn't come out of the church. Sam was walking up Grand Avenue. I watched his back as he sauntered away, the rain spitting on my head. I pulled my hood over my hair, but I knew it was too late. If my hair were shorter, I'd have an Afro by now.

I opened the Taurus' door, but as I started to get in, I stepped back out again, looking over toward Sam.

He was at the intersection with Blatchley. And he was getting into a green Honda that had slowed to a stop next to him.

CHAPTER 33

I had a quick decision to make, but it was complicated further by Garrett Poore, who decided at just that second to come out of the church and get into his car.

I glanced from Garrett's Buick to Sam in the Honda, hesitating. Maybe Garrett's visit to the church wasn't sinister after all. Maybe he was here for that AA meeting, but I didn't really think that was possible. He certainly hadn't been in there long enough for an AA meeting. Not that I was an expert on AA meetings. As I pondered this, the Honda crossed Grand, still on Blatchley, until I couldn't see it anymore. The Buick moved down Grand in the direction my car was pointed.

I wanted to go after Sam, but my hesitation had lost him. So I got in the Taurus and followed Garrett.

Right back to the newspaper.

My cell phone rang as I watched the Buick

move around the gate and the paving project to the temporary employee parking lot. I pulled into visitors' parking and dug the phone out of my bag, glancing at the number.

"Hey, Vinny."

"How you doing?"

"Sam O'Neill."

"What about him?"

"I just saw him get into a green Honda in Fair Haven. Looked like it could've been the Honda that hit my car."

Vinny was quiet for a second, then, "So where is he now?"

I sighed. "Lost him. I was following someone else, but it was a dead end." I thought about the church. "I think I know where Lucille might be."

"Then you know more than anyone else."

"Why do you say that?"

"She's vanished. Like the stuff in the warehouse."

"You knew where she was?"

"I got a tip about half an hour ago from one of the people on your mother's list. But when I showed up at the building where she supposedly did her business, there was nothing there."

I thought about those girls in the mailroom, waiting for their green cards, hoping to really start their lives here. I hoped my mother could help them now.

"You said Sam O'Neill got in a green Honda?"

"Yeah."

"Well, a green Honda just passed me. And it's got a white streak on the side."

"Where are you?"

"On Chapel Street."

"Which direction?"

"The wrong direction. I'll turn around, and I'll call you back."

He hung up before I got a chance to ask him if I should head for Chapel Street, so I made an executive decision. I was just pulling out of the parking lot when the phone rang again.

"He's on the Tomlinson Bridge," Vinny said without saying "hello." And a few seconds later, "The car's turning down toward the port."

"I'll meet you there, in front of New Haven Terminal," I said, disconnecting the call.

The road was deserted except for Vinny's Explorer. It was facing me. I pulled up next to it and rolled my window down just as his window came down. This was typical cop position, a real sixty-nine.

Vinny smiled at me. His eye was better today, not that it wasn't still black and blue, but at least it was open more than a slit. "Hey, beautiful," he said. "Fancy meeting you here."

"Where is he?" I asked.

He chuckled. "Always have to get to the point. What about a little foreplay?"

"Shit, Vinny, where is he?"

"I don't know."

"Did he leave?"

"Didn't see him. No one passed me. He must be in there somewhere." Vinny's hand swept the air, indicating the chain-link fences that kept the regular people like us away from the freighters. "Have any sources over here who could let us in?"

Didn't I wish. "We haven't covered the port in years," I said. "No one really knows what goes on over here." I cocked my head toward his SUV. "Bees all gone?"

Vinny grinned. "I have to keep the windows open a bit to air it out, but, yeah, just like new."

"Did you find Marisol?"

The grin faded. "That's the funny thing."

"What is?"

"Marisol left her house in a green Honda this morning."

We were quiet for a few seconds, "Is it the

same Honda, I mean, the one that hit me?" I asked.

Vinny nodded. "Yeah, I think so. It's got a long white streak on it, and it's a bit bashed up. What about the car you saw Sam get into?"

"I was sort of far away," I said, "but it could be the same one, too. I couldn't tell who was driving." I paused, thinking for a second. "Hector said the car had been stolen. If that's true, why, then, would his sister be driving it? She couldn't be the one who hit me, could she? But then again, if she was, maybe Hector was trying to protect her by saying the car was stolen. But why would Marisol try to kill me?" Even I was confused, so it was no wonder Vinny didn't say anything.

And before he could share his thoughts, motion caught our eyes. A car was coming toward us, or, rather, a black SUV, similar to Vinny's but not quite. They all looked alike to me. As it passed, I caught a glimpse of the driver.

It was Lin Rodriguez.

We watched as she honked her horn twice and the gate on the other side of the road swung wide to let her in. The SUV turned a corner to the left and disappeared.

"We have to get in there," Vinny said.

Damn straight.

I pulled the Taurus up a little farther and parked, rolled up the window, grabbed my bag, and got out of the car. Vinny was two steps ahead of me.

"What're we going to do?" I asked.

"We can make it up as we go along."

Sounded like a plan to me.

We walked across the street toward a short, squat, gray building. The New Haven Terminal building was just to our right, and this one, with the gate Lin and Sam had both gone through, was to our left, looking like sort of an afterthought as the United Illuminating terminal hugged its fence a little too closely, like a blind date who wouldn't get a fucking clue. There was no sign on it; it was fairly nondescript, painted gray, with no windows — on our side at least — and a couple of glass doors up a few steps from the street.

I had an idea.

"Do you have your camera with you?" I asked Vinny.

He frowned. "How do you know I have a camera?"

"You're a private dick, aren't you?"

He grinned and went back to the SUV. I watched as he pulled a big camera out of the backseat. It was one of those fancy, high-tech digital cameras I've seen at Circuit City. Me, I like to just point and shoot.

While he got the camera, I dug in my bag for my notebook and a pen. When I had them, I went to the Taurus, unlocked it, shoved the bag under the front seat, locked up the car for a second time, and put the keys in my pocket.

"What sort of story are you going to say you're working on?" he asked as we crossed the street.

I liked it that he was quick — well, as long as it was only in the sense that he could pick up where I was going with this. "I'm not sure. I'll think of something."

The closer we got, the clearer I could see small frosted letters on the glass door: EAST SHORE TERMINAL. At least I had a little something to work with.

We climbed the steps and pushed the door open.

I was first surprised that the door actually opened without having to ring a bell; second, the security guard who jumped out in front of us scared the shit out of me.

"What's your business?" he growled, demanding this of Vinny. Obviously he considered Vinny in charge because he was a man. That pissed me off.

"I need to see whoever's in charge," I said

loudly, forcing him to take his eyes off Vinny and study me for a second.

"Why?"

The rumor about the scrap metal theft at the port popped into my head. "I'm Annie Seymour with the *Herald.* We're doing a story about the missing scrap metal down here at the port. How much has been stolen from East Shore?"

Vinny's eyebrows rose slightly and a smile played at the corners of his lips. I concentrated on the guard, because I couldn't keep looking at Vinny or I'd give us away.

The security guard, whose name tag branded him as SPRINGER, stared me down. "How do you know about that?"

I actually had a story here. Go figure. Maybe Marty would let me write about it now. "I can't reveal my source," I said conspiratorially. "But I thought someone here might want to go on the record."

The guard shifted his gaze from me to Vinny. "Who's he?"

"My photographer. We hoped we could get some pictures down at the dock, you know, to illustrate the story." I was going to hell for all these lies, but then again, I didn't exactly believe in hell, so it shouldn't be a problem.

He bit his lip. "Not sure about that, but

let me see if someone can talk to you." He moved away from us, went behind a tall security desk, and picked up a phone. Vinny and I took the opportunity to check out our surroundings.

It was a very small, plain room, about as interesting as the building's exterior, done up in early concrete. A huge bulletin board was stuck to a wall to our left, with all sorts of union and policy memos dangling from thumbtacks. I itched to go over and take a closer look, but Springer's eyes never left us as he spoke softly into the receiver.

A door was behind him, but there was no window so I couldn't tell what was going on in the rest of the building.

Springer put the phone down. "Mr. Hartley will be here in a moment." His face scrunched up like he was pissed that someone would actually deign to speak with us. If he smiled, he might actually be good looking in a Vin Diesel sort of way.

Within seconds, the door swung open, and a short, bald man with a really bad comb-over sped into the room. His eyes were darting all around, resting on me for only about a nanosecond before seeing Vinny, then swinging back over to me. It was a little disconcerting.

"Miss Seymour?" he asked.

I nodded. "Mr. Hartley?"

He held out his hand, first to me and then to Vinny. "Roger Hartley. I'm the manager here. Come back to my office."

Springer didn't give us another glance as Hartley whisked us out into the hall and into an office that was only slightly more warm than the concrete foyer. Hartley went around behind a metal desk overpowered by an old Compaq computer, file folders, piles of papers, and an overturned pencil holder that bled pens and markers. He indicated we were to sit across from him in two straight-backed chairs. A couple of metal bookshelves completed the decor, spilling over with blueprints and three-ring notebooks stuffed with even more paper.

An IBM Selectric typewriter rested on a side table next to Hartley's desk, possibly a backup to the ancient computer. It was worse than at the *Herald,* if that was possible.

"Mr. Hartley," I began, "you wouldn't by chance be willing to show us around the dock, would you? I've heard about the scrap metal thefts here, and I'd like to be able to get a real picture of what it's like out there and how someone could get in."

Hartley shook his head back and forth so fast he looked like a bobblehead doll. "I'm sorry, my dear" — I cringed, but said nothing — "but the police are aware of the situation, and we shouldn't put anything in the paper that could encourage any more problems."

He had a point, but that wasn't what I was here for, although this could be a good story, too.

"We thought we saw the acting police chief drive in just before us," Vinny said. I shot him a look, but he ignored me. "Is he investigating?"

Hartley gripped a pencil and, even though his expression stayed neutral, I could see his knuckles grow white. He was going to lie. Big-time.

"Yes, he's investigating," he said. "That's right."

"What about the bees?" I asked. "Are they using your dock to test the bees?"

His face turned white now. Another thing I wasn't supposed to know. "I — I don't know what you mean," he stammered.

I nodded conspiratorially. "Oh, Mr. Hartley, we know about the bomb-sniffing bees. We're doing a separate story about that next week. I just thought I would ask about that while I was here."

"A story?" He didn't like that idea at all.

"Oh, yes." I paused. "You know, Mr. Hartley, if we could go out there and see how it works, that would be great for the story."

"But, well, you need to talk to —"

"The police chief?" Vinny interrupted. "Yes, and since he's here, maybe you can just ask —"

"I can't do that," Hartley said, jumping up. "Listen, I don't know what you're looking for, but I can't give it to you." Beads of sweat had formed on his forehead and were threatening to drip down into his eyebrows. "I have to ask you to leave. Now."

Vinny stood up, and I followed suit. Something was making this little guy nervous, and I had a feeling it was more than the bees, or even the scrap metal theft.

"How much scrap metal has disappeared?" I asked.

He licked his lips and ran a hand over his head, disturbing the wisps of sparse hair. "I can't talk about it." Hartley stared at me, and for a second I thought he was going to say something else, but finally he said, "You have to leave."

I nodded. I'd tried. "Okay, Mr. Hartley."

There was no way we could see out to the dock — there were no windows — so Vinny and I allowed Hartley and then Springer to see us to the front steps. The rain dripped down on us, not unlike Hartley's sweat.

"He's scared about something," I said.

"Yeah, but what?" Vinny asked. He grinned. "You were good in there."

"It's a gift," I said.

We went down the stairs, but as we were about halfway across the road, we heard a creaking and a whirring behind us. The gate was opening, and the green Honda was barreling right toward us.

Chapter 34

Vinny grabbed me around the waist, dropping the camera, and pulled me out of the path of the car. We landed on the sandy ground with a thud as the car careened past, me on top of Vinny. I heard him grunt.

"I don't weigh that much," I muttered.

"It's my back," he groaned, then saw the smashed camera. "Goddamn."

I pulled myself up, noticing that Springer was watching us through the door.

"What the fuck's his problem?" I asked. "Didn't he see that?"

Vinny was sitting, assessing the damage to the camera. "Why the hell would Sam O'Neill try to run us down?" he asked.

"How do we know it was Sam?" I asked. "Marisol could be driving. Or Hector. Sam could still be back there, with Lin."

I eyed the gate, which was still open. Springer was no longer standing sentry at the door. I glanced at Vinny as the gate started to slowly close. He was watching it, too.

"How fast are you?" he asked, the camera forgotten, as we both got up at the same time and ran toward the gate.

Vinny got there first, so he had more room. I felt the gate start to press on my shoulder as I squeezed through, gasping for breath.

"There are probably cameras here," I whispered.

Vinny nodded, leading me to the edge of the building. We hugged it as we crept along it, going toward the back, toward the dock.

As we reached the corner, we surveyed the landscape. Wide, white fuel-storage tanks, six or seven stories high at least, were to our right. Because of their girth, I couldn't see how many there were, but I counted three right in front of us. It looked like there were several more behind them. To our left, beyond a small driveway, piles of scrap metal rose above us, and a crane hovered overhead, a long piece of metal dangling in its hook. The driveway seemed to lead down to the dock, where a freighter sat silently, its black hull a sharp contrast to the white tanks nearby.

We didn't see any people.

"Why isn't anyone here?" I whispered. "Isn't today a workday?"

"Maybe Hartley gave everyone the day off."

Right. For the bees. Because why the hell else would Lin Rodriguez be here? And God knew the bees were a fucking secret. Until David Welden's story. Or mine.

I saw movement farther down, between the piles of scrap metal. How the hell did Hartley know any was missing? Seemed like there was plenty. I started toward one of the piles, but Vinny pulled me back.

He pointed up. On the back of the building, a camera was focused on the area I was headed for. I nodded. "Okay, but how do we get over there?"

As I spoke, a back door swung open and Hartley ran down a few steps and disappeared behind one of the piles.

But instead of heading toward the dock, we saw him go past the scrap metal and toward the crane. We held our breath, wondering what we should do next, and as we waited, a roar filled our ears.

"Fuck," Vinny muttered. "He's started the crane."

He grabbed my arm. "Come on," he shouted and we ran down between the scrap metal and the fuel tanks, not caring about the camera anymore as the hook reached closer.

I heard a crash and stopped, staring. The huge piece of metal was hanging precariously over our heads.

"Run, Annie!" Vinny shouted, and he didn't have to tell me again.

We raced toward the freighter as the metal slammed onto the ground where we'd just stood.

Lin Rodriguez's SUV was parked just at the beginning of the dock. A couple of boxes were toppled on the ground next to it, and even from where we were I could see the swarms of bees hovering.

But stopping wasn't an option. The crane was coming toward us, a larger piece of metal in its claw now. What the hell had possessed us to do this?

We veered around the side of the SUV where the bees hadn't congregated and found ourselves on the dock next to the freighter. Suddenly the whine of the crane ceased, and we stopped, watching the metal swing back and forth like a pendulum over Lin's SUV.

"What's going on?" I whispered between deep breaths.

Vinny shook his head. But before he could

say anything, Lourdes stepped out in front of us.

She had a gun in her hand.

Chapter 35

Vinny was in front of me, facing me, as we lay on the ground, our hands bound together with duct tape.

"If we weren't in trouble, this might be fun," he quipped.

"Fuck you," I mumbled, but my heart wasn't in it. We were seriously screwed.

Lourdes was Lucille. The crewman who provided the duct tape called her Lucille before she slapped him upside the head with the gun. Without a word, she had herded us toward the freighter, up the gang-plank, and along the walkway to the back of the ship.

I don't know much about ships or freighters, but she seemed to know her way around. Enough to grab two crewmen who didn't even blink as she asked them to take us "to the room" as she continued to hold the gun on us.

The "room," such as it was, was little more than a deep closet with piles of blankets inside.

At least we weren't on bare floor.

All Lourdes said before she left us there was, "This should teach you that you shouldn't ask questions."

Hell, it was my fucking job to ask questions. She'd been cleaning my mother's house long enough to know who I was and what my job was about.

She'd shut the door after her, bathing us in darkness. I could see a little crack of light under the door, but that was it. All I could hear was that crane. I was trying to come to grips with the fact that my mother's cleaning lady was the mastermind behind the counterfeit green card operation. Jesus, what a great cover.

But what did she need to clean houses for if she was making a mint off the illegal immigrants?

I felt Vinny's breath on my cheek.

"You didn't think to bring your gun?" I asked.

"Lapse in judgment. What can you do?"

Crying over the proverbial spilled milk wouldn't do much good now.

"What do you think they're going to do with us?" I asked.

He didn't say anything, but I could feel his hands moving beneath the tape, pulling on my wrist.

"It's tight," I said.

"No shit," he muttered, but his heart wasn't in it, either.

Our hands and feet were tied together. To each other.

"You don't think they're going to dump us in the harbor?" I asked, thinking about the floater last week, the guy who'd started all this. While I wanted to spend more time with Vinny, I hadn't made up my mind that I wanted to spend eternity with him yet.

I felt his legs moving against mine.

"Jesus, Annie, can you help?" he barked.

"Shut up," I whispered as I started moving my hands and feet against his.

The tape was fucking tight. I knew without looking that my stitches had come out, but there was so much of me in pain right then that I couldn't pinpoint exact spots.

All of a sudden, my hands were very close to Vinny's crotch.

"What are you doing?" I hissed. "This isn't the time."

He chuckled. Actually chuckled. "Dammit, Annie, I've got my keys in my front pocket. If we can get them out, maybe we can use one of them to rip the tape."

He was goddamn MacGyver.

Carefully we made our way to Vinny's

pocket. My fingers touched the front.

"Can you get your hand in there?" he asked.

A nervous laugh escaped my throat. "Let's not try this at home," I said, stretching my fingers as far as they could. My fingertips felt something hard. I hoped it was the keys. Vinny didn't make any sudden movements, so I figured it was.

I pulled on the tape to get my hand closer.

"Shit," Vinny growled.

"I'm doing the best I can," I said loudly.

"Sssh."

"No one can hear us in here," I said, reaching farther into his pocket. My fingers tickled the keys and I managed to get underneath them, sliding them up along the fabric. Deftly, I managed to pull my thumb around and grasped one of the keys. It popped out of the pocket.

"Got it," I said, then felt Vinny's fingers slide over mine as he took another key, on the opposite end of the key chain.

"You use yours, I'll use mine," he said. I felt him jabbing at the tape.

I took a deep breath and wrenched the key around, but I couldn't make contact with the tape without seriously injuring my wrist. "I can't," I said.

A jab into the back of my hand caused me

to catch my breath. "Fuck, Vinny, what are you doing?"

"I think I've got it."

I moved my hand a little and felt the tape give way a little. Seconds later, Vinny practically dislocated both my wrists by yanking down quickly, but since my hands were free, I couldn't really be too pissed about it. Fortunately the tape had caught on my shirt sleeves, so I was pretty sure skin loss was minimal.

I was glad it was dark in here. I didn't want to see the condition of my thumb. I'd have to go back to that emergency room and get restitched after this.

Vinny was working on the tape on our ankles, and within a few minutes, our legs were free again, too.

We sat, getting our bearings.

"So how are we getting off this ship?" I asked.

"Can you get up okay?" Vinny asked, and we got to our feet. I took his lack of an answer to my question to mean that he didn't have a clue how to get out of this.

I was afraid we would be locked in, but when Vinny moved the latch, the door creaked open, letting more of the day's gray light inside. He peered around the corner.

"See anything?" I whispered.

He shook his head. "Come on."

What did we have to lose? The worst that could happen now was that Lourdes would shoot us and then dump us in the water. We stayed against the wall, looking over the railing at the harbor beneath us. I wished we were on the other side, so we could see what was happening on the dock, but it was probably better this way. I doubted there were any cameras that could see us over here.

We heard footsteps and froze. We were leaning against another door, and Vinny reached around, quietly pushing it open. We went inside, not expecting to see anyone else.

Lin Rodriguez was on the floor.

She wasn't in any better shape than we'd just been in, since she, too, was bound in duct tape. Vinny quickly used his keys again and managed to free her as she stared in disbelief.

"What are you doing here?" she asked.

"Long story," I said, "and I might ask you the same thing. But we should get going now."

Vinny pulled her to her feet, but she was in worse shape than we thought and stumbled.

"Just hang on a little while, okay?" Vinny whispered. "We'll get you out of here."

More footsteps outside the door stopped us. I looked around the room, which was filled with unmarked cardboard boxes. A door on the opposite side seemed the best place to go.

"Vinny," I whispered, cocking my head toward the door.

He nodded, and the three of us tiptoed out into a hallway, obviously in the middle of the freighter somewhere. It was so narrow that we had to go single file, with Vinny leading the way. But we had no idea where we were heading. Stairs both up and down greeted us around a corner.

Vinny started down as someone clambered above us. I didn't like the idea of being in the bowels of a goddamn ship, and if I had my way, I would've run the whole afternoon in reverse and gone out for lunch instead of trying to trick Roger Hartley at East Shore Terminal. My stomach growled as I thought about it, and Vinny glanced back with a sly grin, like this was the most normal thing we could be doing, skulking around a freighter, running from a little woman with a gun.

Lin Rodriguez was keeping up pretty well, in between me and Vinny. I saw the red marks on her neck and face from where the bees had stung her. She was still a bit swollen.

The bees. I thought about the bees hovering near the front of the ship as we went down the dock. I hoped they hadn't found a bomb or anything.

We came to another door at the bottom of the stairs, and now I could hear something, something that wasn't the crane.

It was chatter. A lot of chatter. On the other side of the door.

The door swung wide and a roomful of faces stared at us.

Chapter 36

I felt like I was in *Titanic.* The part where Leonardo DiCaprio and Kate Winslet are running around in steerage and all the third-class passengers are cramming themselves up against the gates trying not to drown.

Not that there was all that water in here, but there were that many people. Must have been a hundred, at least.

And it stank. Someone wasn't cleaning out the chamber pots. If, in fact, they even had them. I didn't want to stick around long enough to find out, but the three of us were glued to the floor.

It had gotten eerily quiet as we all stared each other down.

Vinny looked at me. "Do you speak Spanish?"

"I took it in eighth grade. I can say hello."

His eyebrows rose at Lin, who shook her head sadly. It was too bad there weren't any

Chinese here. They were all obviously Hispanic, and I thought about the floater. Who the hell were these people?

"Say hello, Annie," Vinny said.

My eyes moved from face to face, all of them dirty, men and women alike. I didn't see any children. Most of them were expressionless, as if they were used to having to pretend to be invisible. I focused on one man, whose black eyes glittered with what could've been tears. "Hola," I said.

A small smile appeared, but before anyone could respond, Vinny put his finger to his lips, indicating they shouldn't say anything. He shook his head. "Wish we could tell them we'll be back," he said.

Back from where? I didn't have time to ask. We were going up the stairs, the door shut behind us, closing off those people again.

Somehow Vinny found a door to the outside. Lin and I were blindly following him. If it were me, I'd probably be leading us in circles, but Vinny really did seem to have his head about him. Maybe he'd been an Eagle Scout. Those kids knew everything, how to follow stars and make fire and shit.

I used to make fun of them. Now I wanted to know where I could sign up.

My heart jumped into my throat as a face

appeared at the door. But then it was gone. I looked down, and the guy was on the ground, Vinny standing over him with his fist clenched.

We were going to feel like crap once we got out of here. Good thing I had those Percocets.

"Come on," Vinny whispered, and the three of us ran along the railing, not bothering to see if anyone was after us, just hoping we could get as far away as possible.

A gangplank was up ahead, leading back to the dock. Lin's SUV still sat there and, as we got closer, I could see the bees swarming, a few of them near the gangplank. I didn't think I was allergic, and this really wasn't the time to stop and be cautious.

But then I pulled on Vinny's sleeve and pointed toward two men with guns walking up the dock below us. As the three of us stopped, they saw us, pointing their weapons in our direction.

I heard the gunshots as we threaded our way around a stairwell and out toward the railing on the other side of the freighter. Movement down to our left caught my eye. It was another guy with a gun. We ran along the edge, away from him, but hit the dead end at the back of the ship. Something whizzed by my head, and Vinny pushed me over, out of range. He was watching the water below.

"We have to jump," he said.

I didn't even have time to think. Vinny had Lin up and over the railing, until she was out of sight. Blood was pounding so hard in my ears that if she made any noise hitting the water, I couldn't hear it.

I was on top of the railing, a fear of heights constricting my chest.

"It's just water," Vinny whispered. "You can dive; just do it."

And I felt my body falling, the water coming closer. An old instinct kicked in and my arms moved over my head, my fingers hitting the surface first as I plunged into the icy harbor.

It was fucking cold. I felt like I'd drunk a bottle of ice; I was freezing from the inside out.

I opened my eyes, and it wasn't much better than having them closed.

My arms pulled the water back behind me, and in three strokes my head broke the surface. The freighter was right in front of me, and I kicked to move away from it. I looked up at where we'd jumped from the ship, expecting to see the men with guns. But they weren't there.

Something grabbed my waist, and Vinny

was guiding me away from the freighter to the dock at the next terminal. Lin was next to us, keeping up. She was a helluva lot stronger than I'd given her credit for.

Finally we were huddled together under the wooden dock. My teeth started to chatter as I treaded water.

"Hypothermia," I gasped.

Vinny shook his head. "Don't think about it. We're going to go up there" — he indicated a wooden ladder just behind me that led up to the dock — "and run like hell."

Sounded like a plan to me. If I could feel my feet once they hit land. I doubted it.

"Why did they stop shooting at us?" I asked.

Vinny shook his head, and I could see he was perplexed by that, too.

"I'll go first, make sure it's okay," Vinny said.

"Yeah, right, and if it's not?" I asked. "Will you leave us here to die?" Suddenly that *Titanic* image loomed large. I certainly didn't want to go down with the goddamn ship.

Vinny pointed toward another dock, the last one we could see. "If I don't give the signal to come up, you guys have to get over there."

It sounded good, in theory.

Vinny climbed up the ladder and in what seemed like hours later but was probably only seconds, his hand came down and we heard him say, "Come on."

Lin's face was blue, so I did the right thing and let her go next. It worried me a little, because I was getting used to the cold water and I didn't want to get too comfortable.

The footing was slippery, so I was glad when Vinny's hand wrapped itself around my forearm and helped me onto the dock. I could still feel my feet, but just barely.

I glanced over toward the East Shore Terminal dock, but it was concealed by the freighter we'd just jumped from. We didn't see anyone anywhere.

Vinny was nodding. "Okay, let's go."

My legs were like rubber, and I moved in slow motion. My wet jeans clung to my legs, and water squished in my shoes. I'd lost the yellow slicker in the water, and my fleece was soggy, as heavy as my hair, which was so saturated it hung straight.

We managed to make it up the dock and across the concrete lot toward a door in the gate that we hadn't seen before. Vinny pushed it, and it swung open. We stepped out onto the street and could see the Explorer and the Taurus up ahead, just where we'd left them.

But as we reached the corner of the East Shore Terminal building, where our adventure had begun, a black Chevy Impala swerved out of the gate and slammed on its brakes, skidding to within inches of us.

Shit.

Sam O'Neill got out.

What the fuck was he doing?

"Sam!" I said, but the word caught in my throat.

He had a gun in his hand.

Before anyone could react, there was a click behind us, and as I swung around to see what it was, an explosion crashed in my ears.

Lourdes tumbled down the steps of the terminal building, as if she'd just taken a wrong step. But as she rolled to a stop at the bottom, we could see her chest was a bloody mess.

CHAPTER 37

"She was going to kill you," Sam said flatly, and I saw the gun in her hand; remarkably, she hadn't dropped it.

Vinny's hand snaked into mine as we stared at her.

"Why?" I asked Sam.

He'd slipped his gun into his waistband — I thought they only did that on TV — and walked over to Lourdes, standing over her and shaking his head slightly. "Isn't it obvious?"

Since I had no clue until today that my mother's cleaning lady would want to kill me, I didn't see what could be so obvious. "No, it isn't," I said, ignoring the slight squeeze of Vinny's hand that I was sure meant "shut the fuck up." But somehow I just couldn't. "Why did she have us tied up and thrown on the boat? Did she think we already knew about the people down there?"

Sam's head lifted and his eyes narrowed.

"What people?"

"There are people on that boat, down below. I think she was smuggling them in."

He didn't say anything, continuing to stare at me.

Lin was looking at Lourdes with a curious expression on her face.

"What is it?" I asked her.

"She cleans my house," she said softly. "I was so surprised to see her here. But all I remember is seeing her on the dock and then, the next thing I knew, you were there, helping me."

Before I could respond, Roger Hartley and Springer bounded through the gate. In the same second, we heard sirens approaching.

Sam frowned, turning slightly toward the sound.

Hartley barked, "What's going on out here?" as he reached us, huffing and puffing. Hell, he needed exercise worse than I did.

Sam held up his hand. "Sorry, Roger, but she pulled a gun."

Hartley and Springer gaped at the sight of Lourdes' body.

"She was running the counterfeit green card operation," Sam said to no one in particular.

Vinny was still holding my hand and still hadn't said anything.

"You'll need to come down to the station and make a statement about what happened here," Sam told us, oblivious to the fact that we were soaking wet.

I started shivering and noticed Lin was, too. Vinny's hand tightened around mine. He wasn't shivering. He must be some sort of fucking Aquaman.

Oh, yeah, he was a marine scientist in his other life. Maybe he was used to swimming in freezing water.

"Sure," Vinny said. "What about Tom Behr? You'd better make sure he takes your statement, too." He indicated Sam's gun.

Sam glared at Vinny. "It was self-defense. You saw her. She had a gun."

"I never said it wasn't," Vinny said, and I couldn't figure out what his problem was. While I knew he and Tom had a tenuous relationship at best, I didn't realize he could be hostile to all cops. Maybe it had something to do with being a private detective; there was just an automatic dislike on both sides.

The cruisers came around the bend, their lights flashing to announce their arrival. They eased themselves against the side of the road, and I saw Sam punching in numbers on his cell phone, turning as someone obviously answered, and talking with his back to us for a few seconds before facing us again. He raised his eyebrows at Vinny. "Tom's on his way." He paused. "And so's the coroner." Another pause, and I followed his gaze to my hand. The one Vinny wasn't holding.

I yanked it up. The stitches were gone, the wound uglier than it had been when I'd first gotten cut. The duct tape had left a red band around half my wrist, and the skin was raw — red, but not bleeding. It didn't hurt. I was numb; it had to be hypothermia setting in.

"A couple of ambulances are coming, too," Sam said.

I couldn't figure out why Sam was here. The last time we saw him, he was in the green Honda, the same green Honda that we'd followed here. But we hadn't seen him here earlier, and now he was in a black Impala. I tried to chalk up my questions to being dunked in cold salt water, but something didn't feel right.

When the officers got out of their cars, Sam went to greet them. I heard more sirens in the distance, probably the ambulances, but I moved a little closer to the cops, hoping to hear what Sam was telling them.

It was a jumble of voices, then, ". . . monitors . . . saw them jump . . . what the fuck's going on over here?"

Just what I wanted to know.

But I didn't have time to think too much, because Ronald Berger, the cop who'd responded to my car accident, was coming toward us with blankets in his arms. Within seconds, Lin, Vinny, and I were wrapped in wool. Now, instead of being Popsicles, we were like soggy tomatoes on dry bread and I just knew we'd be soaking through that heavy fabric pretty quickly.

"We'll get you warmed up," Berger said to Lin, then turned to me. "Why are you always getting into trouble?"

"Why do you think this was my fault?" I tried to ask in a defiant manner, but my teeth were chattering so much it didn't really work.

"Dispatcher at the station saw you jump off the boat. What the fuck were you doing?" Berger's eyes traveled from me to Vinny and back again.

"Someone was shooting at us," Vinny said matter-of-factly. "And how did the dispatcher see us?"

Good question. I should've asked that, but I was too waterlogged at the moment. I felt like I was one step behind the conversation.

"We've got a camera here and a couple on the Maritime Center across the way" — Berger indicated the tall, green building that stood next to the Rusty Scupper restaurant — "with monitors at the station showing the port from different angles. Good thing the guy looked up when he did and saw you, otherwise we never would've known to come out here."

"So he called Sam?" I asked.

"Sam?" Confusion crossed Berger's face.

"Yeah, Sam O'Neill. He was here when we got out of the water."

"Sam? He probably heard the call on the radio."

I pulled the blanket a little closer, but it wasn't doing a damn bit of good. Lin didn't look too well, her face was too white, and I wondered where the ambulance was.

As if in response to my unspoken question, one pulled into the lot. Tom's car was right behind it.

I watched Tom climb out of his car, and he met my eyes as he approached us.

"Are you okay?" he asked me.

I nodded, even though I wasn't sure.

He looked at Vinny next, and then Lin. "Are you both okay?"

"Yeah," Vinny said gruffly.

Lin looked agitated. "I have to go get

them. Put them back." She started walking toward the gate, her blanket trailing on the ground behind her.

We took a few steps to catch up. Tom touched her arm, stopped her.

"Where are you going, Lin? You need medical help."

"My bees," she said softly. "I have to get them."

Tom frowned. "Where are they?"

"They're on the dock, like Sam asked."

Vinny and I glanced over to where Sam was talking with a few of the uniforms. He didn't seem to be paying attention to us.

Tom asked Lin gently, "What did Sam ask?"

"He said to bring the bees. We were going to try again." She sighed. "But when I got here, no one was here. Mr. Hartley let me in — he knows me from before — but there was no one else."

I glanced at Vinny. We'd seen the green Honda go through the gate before Lin's Pathfinder.

"I started getting the bees out of the back of the SUV. And then Lourdes showed up," Lin was saying.

Maybe it was Lourdes in that car. But I'd seen Sam getting into it. I felt like I was in the middle of a really weird David Copperfield illusion.

Sam had walked over and was taking in every word she was saying. "When I got here," he said, "Lin was nowhere to be seen. One of the hives was in pieces. There were bees everywhere. But I didn't see anyone." He paused. "I was late. I'd gotten held up, and I didn't have Lin's cell number on me so I couldn't call her. I was worried when she wasn't here and the hive was broken."

No one said anything as he paused.

"I didn't think she'd gone far, maybe to the bathroom or something," Sam continued. "I was walking around when I saw these three" — he indicated me, Vinny and Lin — "going around the side of the terminal next door. I got in the car to meet them, and when I came out of the gate, I saw her" — he indicated Lourdes' body now — "coming down the steps with a gun."

I was digesting his story when I had another thought.

"Tom, you might want to get on that freighter," I said. "There are people on it. I think they're being smuggled in."

All eyes swung over to me.

"What?" Tom asked.

I told him about the people we'd seen below as we were trying to get off the freighter. Tom's expression was a mixture of incredulity and shock. He called Berger over. "Take a couple of men to that freighter. Do a full search. There may be people aboard."

He turned to me then. "Start at the beginning. I want to hear what happened."

I pulled the blanket closer. I was starting to dry a bit, but I was still chilled so deeply that I wondered if I'd ever be warm again.

The crime scene guys had arrived and were buzzing around Lourdes' body, taking their pictures and securing the scene. A couple of cops were climbing the gangplank onto the freighter. Everything seemed so surreal.

I started telling Tom about how Vinny and I duped Roger Hartley and, as I continued, Vinny came over and stood next to me, nodding.

When I was done, Tom was frowning, staring at Lourdes. "Jesus."

Two more ambulances screamed their arrival, but the sirens were cut as they slammed to a stop just past the police cruisers.

I felt a twinge in my hand and looked down to see pinpricks of blood starting to ooze out of the wound. "I think I need to get some stitches," I said, holding it up for Tom to see.

He nodded. "The paramedics can take a look at it on the way to the hospital." He looked from me to Vinny to Lin. "All three of you need to get there. We can finish this discussion at the hospital."

"But what about my bees?" Lin asked. "I have to get them contained."

Tom shook his head. "Sorry, Lin. Your health comes first." He took her arm above the blanket and started leading her toward the ambulances, indicating that Vinny and I should follow.

A shout from the freighter made us all look up. Berger was leaning against the railing, cupping his mouth as he yelled, "They're here, all right. We're going to need more ambulances."

Tom frowned. "Did you know about this before?" he asked me. "Is this why you came out here?"

Vinny and I shook our heads. "No," I said. "We had no clue."

"Then why did you come here?"

"You might want to ask Sam —" I started, but before I could finish, Sam was standing next to me.

"Ask me what?" he said. "What do you want to ask?"

It was now or never. "I saw you get into a green Honda that looked like the car that hit me," I said quickly. "And Vinny and I followed the car here. It showed up before Lin did. Because we saw her arrive, too."

Sam nodded slowly before saying, "A friend picked me up earlier and dropped me at the service station to get my car, where it was getting a tune-up." He indicated the Impala. "I don't know where she was heading after that." His tone indicated he was pretty pissed that I was giving him the third degree, but I didn't give a shit.

She? "Was it Marisol?" I asked. "Was Marisol giving you a ride?" But why would Marisol come to the port? And if she did, where was she?

Sam looked at Tom, who sighed. "Annie," Tom said, "can we give it a rest?"

I didn't want to "give it a rest," but I was familiar enough with the look on Tom's face to know that he wasn't going to let me continue. I was going to give it one more try, but before I could, Ronald Berger sprinted toward us. "We're going to need as many ambulances as we can get," he said.

Tom opened his mouth to say something, but Sam interrupted, turning to Vinny and saying, "Why don't you take Annie to the hospital so we can free up an ambulance."

"Sure," Vinny said. "What about Lin?"

Lin was still standing next to the gate,

looking down toward her SUV and her bees. "I really need to contain them," she repeated.

Tom looked at Berger. "Take Lin over there, see if you can help her get the bees together as quickly as possible, then you can have one of the guys take her to the hospital, okay?"

Lin's face showed her relief. She smiled. "Thank you," she said as she and Berger went through the gate.

"I have to go see what's going on over there," Tom said to me and Vinny, "but I want to talk to both of you later. So when you're done at the hospital, just come to the station."

We agreed, and turned to go to the Explorer across the street. I looked back once to see Sam watching us. I shivered under the blanket.

"I don't think Tom would mind if we stopped home to get a change of clothes," Vinny said, noticing.

The Taurus sat next to the Explorer. "Can we leave it here?" I asked.

Vinny glanced around at the police cruisers. "Probably the safest place in the city right now," he said. He popped open the back of the Explorer. A gym bag sat there, and Vinny unzipped it and pulled out a towel, handing it to me. "Wrap your hand up."

I did as I was told, grabbed my bag out of the Taurus, and we climbed into the SUV.

As we turned onto the Tomlinson Bridge, I glanced over and saw the commotion from a different angle. The red lights from the ambulances danced against the black hull of the freighter, and I could see ant-sized people being herded down the gangplank.

"Jesus," I whispered.

Vinny didn't say anything.

"What's wrong? You've been really quiet."

He licked his lips. "Something's not right."

"No shit."

He hit the brakes at the light and we stopped abruptly. I shifted a little in the seat, then settled back.

Vinny turned to me, his hands on the steering wheel. "The feds were the ones who were doing this bee thing with Lin Rodriguez, right?"

"Yeah, what about it?"

"Then where were they? Why would the acting city police chief call her and ask her to bring the bees without having the feds there?"

Chapter 38

I dug my cell phone out of my bag as we crossed the bridge, punching in Paula's phone number. She answered on the first ring.

"We heard you were involved in an incident over at the port," she said without saying hello. "Jeff Parker's on his way over there now with a couple of guys. We heard there are people on the freighter, possibly being smuggled in. Is that right?"

"It sure looks that way," I said. "Listen, Paula, were you guys going to do another bee trial over at East Shore Terminal today?"

She snorted. "No way. The last one was such a disaster, we've been getting a lot of shit about it and there's talk that the program might not continue. Why?"

I told her about what Lin had said about Sam. She was quiet for a few seconds, then, "I don't know why he'd call her."

"Have you worked with Sam O'Neill on this?"

"He's been briefed, but we really only worked with Rodriguez."

I thanked her, promised that I'd let her know if anything else came up, and ended the call. As I told Vinny what she'd said, he gripped the wheel tighter, but he didn't say anything.

He stopped in front of his brownstone first, telling me to sit tight. Within minutes he was back and threw a duffel bag into the backseat before driving the block to my brownstone, where we both got out. He reached back for the bag and carried it up the stairs.

"We could've just walked over," I said as we got into my apartment. I'd left the heat on, and for the first time in hours I could feel myself thawing.

"Let's just get dressed," he said. "You need to get that hand fixed up."

I really wanted a shower. A long, hot shower. And when I suggested it, Vinny's mouth curled into a sexy smile.

"Might be better than sitting in an emergency room waiting for someone to tell us we don't have hypothermia," he said, running an icy finger along my jawbone.

I pulled his face to mine, wanting to feel

something other than cold, and the intensity of the kiss surprised us both as we clung to each other. His fingers ran through my hair, then down, slipping my pullover over my shoulders, his tongue moving across my neck, caressing my bare skin. I slipped my unwounded hand under his shirt; his chest was cold, but I could feel his heart beating fast under my palm. We didn't speak as we undressed each other, then stepped under the steamy, hot spray of the shower. Every nerve ending was on fire as Vinny touched me; my skin was crimson from the heat. I closed my eyes and felt Vinny's mouth on me, washing away the salt and the fear.

When we were once again swathed in fleece pullovers, jeans, and thick socks and sneakers, sure that we had survived our April swim without any ramifications and figuring out our next move, the phone rang.

"Annie?"

Christ, it was Dick.

"Yeah? I'm on my way to the hospital, Dick. What is it?"

"I'm over here at the port, and, well, your name keeps coming up. What the hell happened? No one will tell me anything."

I didn't want to tell him anything, either, but Marty would have my ass if I didn't.

"Listen, Dick, when I get back from the hospital, I'll come by the paper and talk to you. But I have to go get my hand stitched up."

"It's going to be hours," he said.

"What?"

"They've got four ambulances going over there now."

"All to Yale? What about Saint Rafe's?"

"Who's in the ambulances, Annie? I know you know."

I thought again about those people on the ship. "It has to do with the green card scam, the warehouse, everything, I think. I don't even know the whole story yet. I'll come in after I get stitched up." I hung up the phone and grabbed Vinny's arm, pulling him out the door before the phone could ring again.

When I told Vinny what Dick had said about the ambulances headed for the hospitals, he decided we couldn't go there unless we wanted to bring sleeping bags and a picnic lunch.

"We'll go to the medical center in Guilford. They'll fix you up there," he said as we got onto the Q bridge and took Interstate 95 east to the suburbs.

It was a slow day in Guilford. I got in to

see a doctor right away.

He tsked when he saw my hand. "How did those stitches get ripped out?" he demanded, pulling a black thread from somewhere in the recesses of the wound.

"I got abducted and duct-taped together with my boyfriend on a freighter," I said matter-of-factly.

He stared at me. "What are you, some sort of comedian?"

I shrugged. "No, really, that's what happened."

His eyes went back down to my hand. "Did you get a tetanus shot?"

"Yeah."

He put four stitches in. I guess he didn't think three would be enough this time, and he was probably right. He stuck a bandage over the top of it. "Keep it clean," he said. "You know, you're pretty lucky."

"Why?"

"If you're going to cut your hand, that's the place to do it. Anywhere else, you might have gotten a tendon and you wouldn't be able to use a finger or two."

He was a fucking Pollyanna, that's for sure. I thanked him and headed back out to see Vinny leaning back in one of the chairs in the waiting room. I held up my hand. "Good as new," I said.

Vinny grinned. "We'll have to see about that."

I punched him on the shoulder with my good hand. "Asshole," I said.

The nurse looked up, and we both started giggling as we went out into the darkness.

"I'm hungry," Vinny said, and the minute he said it, I felt the familiar rumble in my stomach. When the hell had I last eaten?

Within half an hour, we were seated at Guadalupe la Poblanita on Chapel Street, right back in Fair Haven, with two cervezas — besides saying "hello," I did remember the word for beer — and devouring chicken gorditas. Four little paper Dixie cups sat in front of us, one filled with guacamole, the other three with different kinds of salsa. I dunked a crunchy tortilla chip into a sort of pureed tomato liquid and savored its flavor, happy that I was finally warm again.

I took a sidelong look at Vinny, wondering if there would be a declaration of any type of feeling after what we'd gone through, after our intense lovemaking. Granted, it wasn't really in my personality to do that sort of shit, and obviously it wasn't in Vinny's, either, because after taking a long drink of his Corona, he said, "We need to see Tom."

Talk about breaking a mood.

"You're still hung up on Sam, aren't you?" I asked.

"Damn straight."

"Jesus, Vinny. What do you think he's into?"

Vinny put his fork down and looked at me for a few seconds without speaking. Then, "I'm not sure. I've just got a feeling. It just seemed too convenient that he was there, that he called Lin to be there."

My phone rang, startling us. I pulled it out and flipped up the cover. Tom.

"Where are you?"

"Went to Guilford because we didn't want to wait at the hospital."

He was quiet for a second. "That was a good idea. When can you come to the station?"

"We're having some dinner." I paused. "What's going on with Sam?"

"He's on leave pending an investigation. Because of the shooting. But it seems pretty clear-cut."

To him, maybe. "So now that Sam's on leave, who's in charge?" I asked.

"Me. The mayor made that decision twenty minutes ago."

Tom, as chief of detectives, was now the acting police chief. Marty wasn't going to like that very much — his police reporter the ex-girlfriend of the new acting chief. It looked like my worst nightmare might come true. Marty might give Dick my beat because of a perceived conflict of interest.

"We need to talk to you and Vinny," Tom said. "We need your official statements."

"Tom, I'm curious about something."

"What's that?"

"Sam. He tells Lin to bring her bees, but I talked to Paula. He didn't invite the feds along, and it's their project. And then, why was he still there after we managed to get off the freighter?"

Tom didn't say anything for a few seconds, then, "Jesus, Annie. Do you know what you're saying? Let's just talk when you get here."

Tom obviously didn't share our concerns about Sam, didn't see anything wrong with the picture presented him at the dock earlier. Maybe we were wrong. Maybe there was nothing odd about Sam except that he was involved with Rodriguez's old girlfriend. I promised Tom we'd be in as soon as possible and put the phone back in my bag.

"I thought you wanted to go to the paper now," Vinny said.

I was quiet.

"What's wrong?" Vinny asked.

I shrugged. "Dick. He's probably going to

get my job now that Tom's acting chief." Damn if it didn't make me feel like shit to say that out loud. It made it more real, and butterflies started gathering in my stomach as I thought about how Marty was going to tell me.

My phone rang again. Speak of the devil.

"Hey, Marty."

"What the hell is going on with you?"

I found myself telling him everything, keeping my voice monotone and soft so the other diners wouldn't hear. Not that many of them spoke English anyway. When I was done, I heard Marty sigh.

"Dick's over at the port. He told me you were involved."

"Yeah, he called me. No one's telling him anything."

"Then you come back here and give it to me, and we'll write it up."

I hoped Tom would understand why I wasn't going to show up right away. It wasn't like my story was going to change between now and then anyway, I reasoned with myself.

"I'll be right there," I said, punching END on my phone. "Take me to the paper," I told Vinny, grabbing my bag and standing up.

Chapter 39

When we got there, the visitors' parking lot was blocked off now because of the paving work. I directed Vinny around the back of the building to the employee lot, but half of that was blocked off, too.

I didn't see any choice but to go through the entrance at the loading dock. It was late, there were no tractor-trailer trucks dropping off anything, so I didn't have to worry about getting hit by one of them, which is sometimes a concern during the day.

Vinny studied the building warily. "In there?" he asked.

I pointed to the door next to the loading dock. "I'll be fine," I said, getting out of the car.

I frowned as Vinny got out, too.

"This is my turf, Vinny," I said. "I don't need a fucking escort."

"It's dark," he tried.

"Hell, I can find my way around this

building with my eyes closed," I snorted, walking toward the steps.

A cell phone rang. I glanced at my bag, but then saw Vinny put his phone to his ear. He stopped walking, and I heard him say, "Hey, bro."

I waited as Vinny talked to Rocco, but a shadow just ahead made me catch my breath. A cigarette glowed red at the top of the steps. Someone was having a smoke break. As he moved slightly, the parking lot light caught his silhouette. It was Garrett Poore. And he was watching us.

The guy gave me the creeps. I started wondering again about Rosario Ortiz and his connection to her and her brother. He knew about Lourdes — had to when he hired them. And then I remembered the brown car. His brown Buick that he drove to the church that day I followed him. And the brown car that was seen in my mother's driveway the day her house was broken into.

Suddenly I wanted Vinny to walk me into the building. But he was still on the phone, and as I waited, Garrett's cigarette fell like a shooting star, disappearing on the concrete as he ground it under his boot. He gave me a short wave and went inside.

"Annie, I have to go," Vinny said, closing his phone. "That was Rocco. He locked himself out of his car." He snorted. "Fancy shit car like that; you'd think there'd be some gadget that'd keep you from locking yourself out."

"How can you help?" I asked, wondering how to keep him here.

"I've got a key." He held up his keys and jangled them as he looked up at the building, a big, hulking box. "You're right, you'll be okay."

I wasn't so sure now, but Garrett was gone and I was going into familiar territory. It wasn't far to the newsroom. Just to make sure, I pulled out my phone and dialed 911, ready to punch SEND if I needed to.

"I'll be back in ten minutes. He's just over at his place at Ninth Square."

"Sure, I'll meet you out front," I said, with more bravado than I felt.

I could see him hesitate, the gentleman in him wanting to protect me, but then he got into the SUV. I sprinted toward the steps and up, turning at the top to wave. He flickered the headlights in response, and I went into the building still clutching my phone.

I let the door slam shut behind me and walked quickly through the chilly, open space reserved for unloading. I took a right toward the hall that would take me through the back of the building into the front, where the newsroom was.

The light was dim here, and the presses were running. I could hear their rumble somewhere above me as I stepped up my pace. When I first started at the paper, I used to get a thrill when I stayed late and went upstairs to watch the presses, the newsprint threading through the ink-filled maze. You could see the bright red and black masthead as it ran quickly through the machine on the long sheets of paper.

Sometimes the paper ripped — we call it a web break — and they'd have to start over.

I stepped into a room that housed all the rolls of newsprint that were unloaded out back. They were about four feet high and about the same width across, covered in brown paper to keep them from getting dirty. There was a sort of amusement ride out here for them; the rolls were placed on top of little metal flatbeds on a track and moved slowly through the room. I didn't know how the rolls ended up at the press, since it was upstairs, and the track was downstairs. I made a mental note to find out, since somehow that seemed oddly important at the moment.

I followed one of the rolls on the track, knowing that the roll would eventually go its way and I would go mine toward the newsroom.

I rubbed at my ears — it was louder here, the press was right overhead — and they popped a little.

When I felt the hand grip my shoulder from behind, my heart jumped into my throat. "What the fuck?" I said loudly. I twisted around to see Sam O'Neill, a lopsided grin on his face.

"What's your hurry?" Sam's words reverberated in my ear. At the same time, his hand slid down my arm and wrenched the cell phone from my hand. It fell onto the concrete floor. His other hand had come up like a vise on my shoulder.

My eyes moved back to where I'd come in, willing Vinny to walk in right then, willing him to have second thoughts about going to help Rocco.

Sam shook his head. "He's gone. I watched him leave. Too bad he didn't come in here with you. I was hoping to take care of both of you."

I could hear my heart pounding above the presses. He wanted me to be afraid; I could see it in his eyes. I tried to shake off his hand, but he held me tight. I frowned. "Listen, Sam —" I started, and that's when I saw the gun that he'd taken out of his waistband.

"What's going on?" I asked. "Why are you doing this?"

"We're going to go for a little ride, you and me." Sam leaned even closer, and I felt his hot breath on my neck. It sent a little chill across my shoulders, and I shivered.

"What's going on?" I asked again.

He shook his head. "You can't fool me. I know you know. You even made Tom start asking me questions. I had to sing a pretty song for him to shut up. How the hell did you get off that boat, anyway?"

Sam started pulling me back the way I'd come in, the gun pointed at me the whole time. His hand was steady, his face stony.

"So you were in cahoots with Lourdes?" I asked.

"Don't pretend you didn't know."

"Okay, fine," I said. "So you and Lourdes were smuggling those people into New Haven through the port, finding them jobs, giving them fake green cards, and taking their money?"

He didn't say a word, so I figured I might as well go on.

"But what about that guy who washed up in the harbor? Did he get stung by that bee accidentally during the botched trial with the FBI? Was he one of yours?"

I must have guessed right, since I saw his eye twitch, but he didn't say anything.

"And what about Tony Rodriguez? Was he getting too close to your operation with his wife's bees? Is that why he was murdered?"

Sam stopped, and my knees buckled. My bag slipped off my shoulder and fell to the ground.

"I don't know who killed Tony, but it made everything easier," he said flatly, then began pulling me along again. I glanced back at my bag on the floor, but he didn't seem to notice.

I had another thought. "What about Rosario Ortiz? Was she part of the plan?"

His face closed down again and he yanked on my arm so hard I thought it would dislocate. I tried to keep up.

He seemed to respond when I was accusing him of things he didn't do, and he didn't say anything when he'd done them. So I deduced that he did, in fact, kill Rosario, or have her killed and stuffed into my car.

Which did not bode well for my own future.

"Lourdes should've finished you off in that car accident when she had the chance," Sam growled.

"Lourdes was driving that car that day?" I asked, surprised.

He narrowed his eyes at me. "It's her car," he said roughly, before adding, "You ask too many questions."

Which is exactly what Lourdes had said on the freighter, but look what happened to her.

"So who broke into my mother's house? Was Lourdes supposed to get the fax? Did I screw that up by showing up so you had to break in later?" I couldn't stop talking. I needed to keep asking questions or I knew I'd fall apart. "Why did you want the fax, anyway?"

He bit his lip. "We wanted to know who was helping her, who was talking."

"Was Rosario on that list?"

His eyelids flickered a little, and I knew I was on the right track.

"Did you kill Rosario just because of that, or because she was talking to me, too? She didn't tell me shit, you know that. So why did you have to kill her? Did you ambush her at the warehouse? Why did you put her in my car?"

He grinned, showing off a black tooth off to the side. I hadn't noticed that before. But then, I'd never been this physically close to him. "It was almost too easy."

I ignored the lurch in my stomach. "You know, it was Hector who went to my mother about the scam. Rosario was just a name on a list."

Sam frowned. "Hector?"

This was news to him. Which was probably why Hector was still walking around.

My brain scanned through everything that had happened today, and it landed on one thing. "What about the cameras at the port? Didn't you realize someone would see us on those monitors at the police station?"

Sam gave a low growl. "A couple years ago, three Turkish guys got off a ship over there and no one saw a fucking thing. They disappeared, and no one's seen them since. Let's just say I didn't have any real reason to think anyone would see you."

"But obviously someone did. What about Lourdes? Didn't she know about the monitors? Didn't you tell her?"

A hint of a smile tugged at his lips, and I saw the truth. He really didn't give a shit whether Lourdes was caught over there.

"Who would everyone believe?" he asked, confirming my thoughts. "Some crazy woman who's smuggling in illegals? Do you really think anyone would think I was involved in that? I was never there when they came off the ship."

"But you were running things, weren't you?" I asked. "You set her up, didn't you?

Was it your idea to send her out to my mother's house, and to Lin's house, calling her Lourdes rather than Lucille and trying to get information?"

"Lourdes is her name. Those people — they didn't need to know who she really was." He snickered. "She really fooled you that day, didn't she? She was one helluva actress."

I remembered how scared she'd looked in my mother's pantry, and I'd bought the whole thing. I wondered, though, about Marisol. This was my chance. "Did Marisol know what you and Lourdes were up to?"

Something crossed his face, a softness, and even though it was gone in a second, I could see that he truly cared about Marisol. "She didn't know. Lourdes worked out of that office at the church. Marisol had nothing to do with it. She took care of the house for them — her and her kid, Lourdes, and Hector. That was her job. That was it."

While he was talking, I saw the rolls of paper out of the corner of my eye — this room hadn't seemed so big before — and spotted one of them coming toward us at a snail's pace.

I swung around as much as I could, bringing Sam with me. I pointed to my bag. "I dropped it," I said, noting that we were standing directly on the track.

"Forget about it," he said, but at just that moment, I felt something hit me in the back of the calves, causing my knees to cave in, and I went down. I hadn't seen the empty flatbed coming toward me.

Sam got hit exactly the same way, and he let go of me in his surprise and went down, too. His arm flew up, the gun still in a firm grip, and I rolled away, off the track, in the opposite direction from the gun.

Sam wasn't so lucky. His foot got caught under the flatbed and he couldn't get it free. "Fuck, fuck, fuck!" he shouted.

I scrambled to my feet and dove behind the nearest roll of paper that wasn't moving just as the gunshot sounded above the rumble of the presses. I wondered if anyone would hear it. Maybe in the press room upstairs, if I was lucky. But it was louder up there; they all wore earplugs. Shit.

Another gunshot rang out — thank God these rolls were so thick — and I peered out from behind the roll to see that the next flatbed with paper on it had crashed into the one on top of Sam's foot, trapping him further because now he had the weight of all that paper pushing against his foot. I glanced over at the entrance to the loading dock, just about ten feet away, and back at

Sam's hand, which was still waving that goddamn gun around. He was sufficiently distracted that he probably wouldn't see me, but if he pulled the trigger again, there was no knowing just where the bullet would end up.

I had to take my chances and get the hell out of here.

I made a mad dash toward the loading dock and didn't hear any shots, only a couple more angry *fuck*s. I couldn't be sure he didn't see me at all.

Chapter 40

I ran through the cold loading dock again and pushed open the door, stepping outside. I wanted to see the Explorer — I hadn't been inside that long and I knew Vinny had been worried. But it wasn't there, just a few cars parked off to my left.

I needed to let someone inside know about Sam, but my phone was still on the floor in there.

I didn't have much time — I didn't want him to get away — so I ran around the building to the visitors' entrance, ignoring the fact that my feet were sinking slightly into the fresh pavement. I pushed open the door and saw that the security guard's booth was closed and locked. Shit. He was off on his rounds somewhere, and I didn't have access to unlock the door and get inside. My card key was in my bag near Sam.

I peered through the glass door, looking

through the waiting area and into the hallway ahead that led to the advertising department. No one would be there now.

"What are you doing?"

The loud, gruff voice came from behind me, and I swung around to see a heavyset man with a close-cropped Afro towering over me.

"Call the cops," I said. "There's a guy with a gun in the back of the building near the loading dock."

He looked at me dubiously. I guess I didn't really blame him. My hair was a mess, my face scratched up, my clothes dirty, and the big bandage on my hand made it look like I'd gotten into some sort of fight.

"I work here," I insisted. "Annie Seymour. Call the cops."

"Where's your ID?" He didn't give a shit who I was.

"It's in my bag near the loading dock near the guy with the gun." Jesus, I was sounding like a nut. I probably wouldn't believe me, either. "Just call the cops." How many times was I going to have to say that?

His eyes didn't leave me as he unlocked the door to his area, which revealed eight security monitors, on which you could see pretty much everything that was going on in the building. Except, of course, the room with the flatbeds and the rolls of paper.

The guard looked at me like I was some sort of sad excuse for a human being, that I could be so deluded as to think there was a man with a gun somewhere in the building while he was keeping watch.

I grabbed for the phone. "If you don't call them, I will," I said sternly.

He took the receiver and punched in 911. "There's a report of a man with a gun at the *New Haven Herald,*" he said, although I could tell he didn't believe me.

I needed to call Tom. I saw the button to unlock the door and, before the guard could do anything about it, I reached over, punched it, and ran out and through the door toward the newsroom.

I grabbed the first phone I saw and dialed Tom's cell number.

"Where are you?" he asked. He was pissed.

"Sam O'Neill. He's here. At the *Herald.* He has a gun. You have to get here, fast. I think he's still out there."

"Annie —"

"Now!" I shouted.

Mr. Security Guard was standing next to me, his hands on his hips, when I hung up the phone. I thought for a second he was going to question me again about who I was, but my face must have convinced him I was telling the truth. "Near the loading dock?" he asked.

I nodded and he ran back down the hall. I hoped Sam was still there; this security guard was pretty big, definitely bigger than Sam, and he could probably hold him until Tom got there.

I turned around and saw that I had attracted a crowd. Marty was frowning, the copy editors were all looking up from their desks, and the news editor was scratching his head. Dick was standing next to his desk, staring at me with a funny look on his face.

"Annie?" Marty asked. "What's going on?"

I quickly told him what had happened. And then I remembered Vinny. I reached for the phone again and dialed.

"I'm halfway back there," Vinny said. "Are you okay?"

I gave him the short version, sirens getting closer.

"I'll be right there," he said quickly.

I hung up and went toward the front of the building. Marty and the entire newsroom followed, sort of like those faux fire drills we had occasionally.

We got outside just as the cop cars pulled

into the parking lot, crashing through the tape that had been put up to keep anyone from driving on the new pavement.

Tom's Chevy Impala was the last to come in, and he stepped out of the car, spotting me.

"Where?" was all he asked.

I pointed. "Loading dock. The security guard went after him."

In seconds the cruisers sped stealthily around the building and out of sight.

"What's going on, Annie?" Dick was next to me, his notebook open.

I glared at him. "No notes, Dick. Not right now."

We waited a long time. At least it felt like a long time, but when Tom finally came back, uniforms behind him with Sam O'Neill in handcuffs, I looked at the clock on top of the building and saw that only about ten minutes had passed.

Dick turned to me again, but before he could ask anything, Tom's hand was under my arm, leading me to his car. He handed me my bag and my phone, and I took them without a word. When we got in the car, he turned to me.

"We're going to the station, and you're going to tell me everything that's happened. You can't leave anything out. I want to hear it all." His voice was steady, his face unreadable. A stranger listening to him would never know that we'd spent a year sleeping together and that he still — and I quote — couldn't forget me.

I nodded, and he started the car. Vinny was just turning into the parking lot as we were leaving.

Tom opened the window. "Station. Now."

Vinny looked at me, nodded, and I nodded back.

The car that held Sam O'Neill was behind us. We were a fucking caravan.

I replayed Sam's words back in my head so I could remember them accurately for Tom. But even with Sam's admissions and all the puzzle pieces now starting to fit firmly together, I was still left with a question. Who killed Tony Rodriguez?

CHAPTER 41

The sun streamed into my bedroom the next morning, and I rolled over to see an empty pillow next to me. I sighed, but then smelled coffee and I smiled, getting out of bed and throwing on my robe. I padded out into the living room to find Vinny sitting at my kitchen island with a cup of coffee and the paper. He looked up and grinned when he saw me, grabbing me and kissing me before I could say anything.

"Hey there," he said softly.

"Hey there, yourself," I said, going to the cupboard for a mug.

I'd spent two hours at the police station waiting for Tom as he did his thing with Sam. I spent another two answering Tom's questions; he'd talked to Vinny for another two. He kept us separate, probably to make sure our stories jibed. And then he told us to go home, but that he might have more questions in the morning.

We tumbled into bed about five a.m., which meant I'd slept about three hours.

Vinny pointed to the paper as I poured my coffee. "Dick's got a story."

I took the paper and scanned it, taking in Dick's words. He actually had two stories, the one from the port earlier and a very short story about the "incident" at the *Herald.* There was no mention that the acting police chief had been arrested; Tom probably wouldn't give anything to him on the record. My name was missing, as was Vinny's.

The first story told of "an abduction and subsequent shooting of Lourdes Gomez, who was behind a scheme to bring illegal workers into the city and then rip them off by promising green cards in exchange for two thousand dollars each." There was no mention of my mother or her possible lawsuit.

"Lots of fucking holes in it," I said, going back to my coffee. "Sounds like Lourdes was the one abducted."

Vinny grinned. "You could write it."

I shrugged. "Yeah, but I can't." I didn't want to know what was going to happen to my job. I was going to take my sweet time going in to the paper today, just to put it off.

"Don't worry," Vinny said, coming over to me, taking my cup, and putting it on the counter. We were well into the kiss when my cell phone rang. "Shit," he said.

I grinned, then flipped the phone's cover up.

"Miss Seymour?" It was a familiar voice. "It's Marisol. Marisol Gomez." Her voice was hurried, nervous. "I don't know who to talk to anymore now that Sam's . . ." She lingered on his name, then recovered. "I found out something. Something you need to know. Can you come to my house? I found out what she did and I got angry and called her to tell her I knew all about it. She said she's coming over. I'm afraid, and I don't know where Hector is."

She wouldn't tell me anything else, so I told her I'd be right over, hung up, and turned to Vinny.

"Something's up with Marisol," I said, quickly telling him about the cryptic conversation. "I'm worried about her. Maybe she's losing it, finding out her lover was in cahoots with her cousin and now is being held for all sorts of crimes."

We got dressed and headed to Fair Haven. When we turned off Grand onto Blatchley, I had an odd sense of déjà vu. I shook it off as we pulled into Marisol's driveway.

As we climbed the front steps, we heard voices inside and stopped.

"Why couldn't you leave us alone?" a female voice was asking loudly. The voice was familiar, and I nudged Vinny, pointing to the Pathfinder at the curb in front of the neighbor's house. Lin Rodriguez.

"I haven't called in months." We could hear tension and fear in Marisol's words. "I broke it off. I told you already. I was tired of waiting. I met someone else."

"He told me he was leaving me for you." Lin's voice was full of steel.

"I told him no. If you'd just waited, you would've known that."

Vinny motioned for me to follow him, and we tiptoed across the wraparound porch and past the window, flattening ourselves against the outside wall as we listened.

"Because of you, Tony's dead," Lin said.

"I'm not the one who pulled the trigger," Marisol said.

"Neither did I." Lin's voice was clear, steady.

"But you made it happen."

"I don't know why you keep saying that."

"If you didn't, then why are you here? Why are you going to kill me, too?"

Vinny glanced at me, a worried look on his face. He pulled his phone off his belt.

"Call nine-one-one," he mouthed as he handed it to me.

As I flipped up the phone, he stooped down and crawled under the window. I punched in 911, hoping the argument inside was distracting enough that they wouldn't notice we were out here.

Vinny stood upright when he reached the door and knocked twice, standing to the side of the door instead of right in front of it. "Marisol," he called. "Are you ready to go?" Like she was expecting him.

"Not just yet," she called back, playing along.

The dispatcher answered my call and I told her to send the cops here. I ended the call just as Vinny turned the knob and the door swung in. I stepped forward a little and saw through the window that Lin was holding a knife.

"Vinny, knife," I shouted as he went through the door.

Lin swung around, the knife gleaming in the light from the door, and she lunged toward Vinny, who, being a bit larger than she was, got out of the way and grabbed her hand, wrenching the knife from her grip. It clattered to the floor, and I stepped around them to Marisol.

"Are you okay?" I asked her.

She nodded.

"What did you mean that she's responsible for Tony's death?" I asked.

Marisol took a deep breath. "She hired Roberto to do it."

"She's a liar," Lin spat out.

"Then why were you holding a knife on her?" Vinny asked.

Lin shook her head.

"How do you know she hired him?" I asked Marisol.

"I went to see Roberto at the hospital. He's a good friend." She paused. "He woke up last night, out of the coma. I told them I was his sister so they would let me in. He told me she hired him, paid him ten thousand dollars." She stifled a sob. "He said with that kind of money, he could do anything."

A siren rang out in the distance.

Marisol didn't look as if she'd heard it. "Roberto met her" — she indicated Lin with a toss of her head — "through Lourdes, because Lourdes cleans her house. Lourdes knew what she wanted. She got them together." She hung her head.

"But why did he go back? Why did he shoot again after shooting Rodriguez?"

Marisol shook her head. "He wanted to marry me, make me respectable, give my son a father. He didn't like it that I was seeing Sam. He thought Sam was using me." She paused. "When he saw Sam with Tony, he thought he could get them both, you know, but he missed Sam the first time and that's why he went back."

"He has to talk to the police about this."

Marisol sighed. "He said he wanted to tell me first. He said I needed to know first."

I shook my head. "But why would Tony tell Lin he was leaving her for you when you said no? Didn't he know about you and Sam?"

She looked up at me, her eyes glistening with tears. "Sam said we should keep it quiet. He said he would tell Tony when the time was right."

"Why were you there that night?" I asked softly. "The night Tony was shot."

"Sam was with someone else. Maybe he really *was* using me."

Vinny still held Lin by the arm as the police cruiser came to a stop in front of the house. A few minutes later, Ronald Berger stepped through the open door. He was surprised to see me.

"Jesus, Annie, what are you into today?"

I shrugged and pointed at Lin. "She was holding a knife on Marisol here."

Berger looked at Lin. "Why?"

But she stayed mum, her face hard.

"Marisol says she hired out Tony's shooting."

Berger's face hardened. "What?"

I told him what Marisol had said.

Vinny let go of Lin's arm and Berger took it. "Lin, you have to come with us." He looked at Marisol. "And you, too."

Marisol nodded.

Berger looked at me and Vinny. "Hell, you, too. Jesus, you might as well join the force."

As we went outside, we could see that the skies had finally parted and there wasn't a cloud in sight. April had come full force overnight, and the air was warm. I could see the daffodils just starting to open up in the garden next door. Vinny took my hand as we went back to the car.

"I guess you and DeLucia are back together," Tom said after he shut off the tape recorder and put his pencil down. The sun blasted through the window behind him, and I had to squint. I wished I had my sunglasses.

"Yeah, I guess so," I said, although I wasn't completely sure. Okay, so we'd slept together, but that didn't necessarily mean too much. We hadn't talked about what had happened yesterday, all the shit before

Christmas, or made any plans. We were pretty much living in the present.

"Roberto admitted everything," he said.

"So what Marisol said was true."

"He's acting like a fucking martyr. But killing a cop and shooting at another one, well, he should've known better. He'll probably get the death penalty." He paused. "And Lin . . ." He didn't have to finish that thought.

Tom didn't mention that he'd gotten shot at, too, but he didn't have to.

"So after he abandoned the car at Sherman Avenue after shooting Tony, what did he do? How'd he find another car?"

Tom sighed. "He says he knew he hit Tony but missed Sam. When he left the car, he ran through the back lots to a friend's house and borrowed the other car." He paused a second. "He was high as a fucking kite."

"Why would Lin have Tony killed and not Marisol? Somehow it seems like that would make more sense," I said.

Tom shook his head. "She was angry. She and Tony couldn't have kids, and when she found out about Marisol's son and that Tony was paying support and had decided to leave her and be a father to the child she could never give him, it pushed her over the edge. This way she could be the grieving widow, get all the insurance, and keep her dignity. She's one tough broad."

I remembered the way she'd been on the freighter and I had to agree with him. It was too bad, though, that she didn't think she had any other choice. Because now she had nothing.

I picked at the corner of the bandage on my hand. "Who tried to kill her with her bees?"

Tom snorted. "Sam was there that day. That TV reporter, you know, the one with the big breasts?"

Cindy Purcell. I nodded.

"She saw him. She said he told her and her van to get lost, to leave Lin alone. So they left." He paused. "That bee operation was going to screw up what they were up to down there."

"I assume Roger Hartley has been charged, too."

"That security guard, Springer, too." Tom nodded, his eyes instinctively looking at my hands.

I smiled. "I'm not taking notes, Tom."

He smiled back.

Something had been tugging at me. "Why the hell was Lourdes cleaning houses if she was making money off the scam?"

Tom chuckled. "She'd been cleaning

houses for a long time before she started this up. But, lately, she was only cleaning your mother's house and Lin's. She talked her way into Lin's because she wanted to find out more about the bees, see if they'd screw things up. The FBI had been hanging around the port, and Hartley told her what was up. As for your mother, Lourdes had heard around — but not from Hector — that your mother was asking questions. She also heard that she was looking for help. It was a great way to get inside, so to speak."

"But didn't Hector know Lourdes was the elusive Lucille? Wouldn't he have told my mother?"

"Hector was afraid of Lourdes. He knew what she was up to, but he wanted all the evidence first before he spilled the beans. That day you cut yourself? Hector was staking out the warehouse for us. But he wasn't in on moving everything out. Sam tipped Lourdes on that."

"So who broke into my mother's house? That seems like a silly thing to do, just for a fax."

Tom sighed. "Lourdes wanted to know who was talking to your mother. Hector said she'd seen the fax, but you showed up before she could copy any names down. She saw you go in and look at it and put it in the basket, so she knew it was important. But she didn't want you thinking she had anything to do with it. If the fax disappeared after you saw it, who else would've taken it? Who else had a key to the house? So she had Hector break in. He admits it, but he also admits to telling your mother when he spoke to her next. Lourdes told him to take other stuff, make it really look like a burglary, but he couldn't do it."

I thought for a second. "Who put the bees in Vinny's SUV?"

Tom grinned. "Sam took one of the hives. He wanted to warn you both off. He should've known it would take more than a few bees to get you off the scent of a story."

"So Garrett Poore had nothing to do with any of this?"

Tom chuckled. "Besides being an asshole who hires illegals? No." He stood up. "I guess that's it."

I nodded, following him to the door, but he didn't open it. He turned to me, his face close, and I could see the bright blue of his eyes as he smiled.

"If it doesn't work out with DeLucia, well, you know . . ." His voice trailed off, and I felt his lips brush my cheek.

But when the door opened, he was all business, shaking my hand at the elevator and thanking me for coming in.

The elevator doors shut and I felt my stomach drop as I went down.

No one was waiting for me when I stepped out and through the glass doors into the lobby. I hadn't asked Tom where Vinny was, or if they were done with him yet.

My cell phone rang, and I pulled it out of my bag. Marty.

"Yeah, I'm on my way," I said. "But I may have to walk. I don't have wheels. So it'll take about half an hour."

"Sure." Marty paused. "Listen, Annie, I've worked it out with Charlie that you're going to stay on your beat. You and Tom aren't dating anymore, so it shouldn't be an issue, right?"

I felt my heart jump up into my throat. But in a good way. "Hell, no."

"Dick needs your help with this story. You can write some, but for obvious reasons, it'll have his byline on it. Okay?"

I didn't have a problem with that. I thought about Tom looking for my notebook. Old habits die hard, on both our parts.

As I ended the call, dropping my phone back in my bag, I pushed open the door and went outside.

Rocco DeLucia was leaning against the

side of his Beemer in front of the station.

"My brother's still in there," he said, indicating the building behind me, "but he said I should bring you over to get that piece-of-shit car you rented so you can go to work."

He opened the door, and I got into the car. I may have still had those damn stitches in my hand, and my body felt like a fucking truck ran over it, but I was in a BMW with heated seats.

Too bad it wasn't mine.

"Do you have enough material for your book now?" I asked as I settled in.

He nodded as he turned the ignition and the engine started to purr. "I might want to talk to you about how you got into journalism. I need some backstory for my reporter character."

A memory nudged me, and I took a deep breath. "Yeah, sure, I guess so." What did I have to lose?

We were quiet for a few minutes. As we reached State Street, Rocco glanced at me. "Vinny was saying that next weekend we should all go kayaking. You up for that?"

Okay, so maybe Vinny and I would never talk about what had happened four months ago. Maybe we wouldn't talk about what happened on that freighter or what happened afterward.

But who wanted to do all that navel-gazing shit?

We were making plans.

The employees of Thorndike Press hope you have enjoyed this Large Print book. All our Thorndike and Wheeler Large Print titles are designed for easy reading, and all our books are made to last. Other Thorndike Press Large Print books are available at your library, through selected bookstores, or directly from us.

For information about titles, please call:

(800) 223-1244

or visit our Web site at:

www.gale.com/thorndike
www.gale.com/wheeler

To share your comments, please write:

Publisher
Thorndike Press
295 Kennedy Memorial Drive
Waterville, ME 04901